Fae by the Bay

BARGAINS WITH BENEFITS

JILLIAN WITT

Cover Artwork by Flourishing Fables

Map by Holly Dunn

Editing by Your Editing Lounge

Copy Edit & Proofreading by Isla Elrick

Published by Myth and Magic Book Club

N
W
E
S
LAKE OF THE GODS
BURY
COMPASS LAKE
SANDRIN BAY
SANDRIN
MARCIL
LOCH

For everyone brave enough to break the mold

1

Luna

"In this case, the Benefit of Magic is simple—the grains and honey used in the spirit are tended by earth-wielding fae. Their talent with the soil adds extra flavor to the rich honey liqueur. Expect the Sweet Solstice Sip to be the *drink at upcoming solstice celebrations.*

Ingredients:
Two parts Suden honey liqueur
One part traditional amber ale"

ANY TRUE *BENEFITS of magic* were never simple, if they existed at all, but the phrase was an unfortunately catchy title for Sandrin's go-to recommendation column. I finished reading the article and skimmed the ingredients. Making this would be simple. I was pretty sure we had the spirit in the tavern already, which was good because this newest endorsement in *The Bayside Times* would surely be a hit—like all the others.

A cold breeze blew in, and I glanced up, setting aside the paper. More customers opened the tavern door and found seats. My smile was warm as I greeted them from my position behind the bar. With each guest, the knot of worry in my chest loosened. For the first time in what felt like years, the bar stools of Parkview Tavern were finally filling. There were still empty tables. That was fine because those seated chatted animatedly over warm dishes and stiff drinks while a few adventurous patrons mingled in between. This place had been near-empty for too long. My tense shoulders fell a few inches with my next deep breath. Maybe it wouldn't be anymore.

"No time for reading, Luna." Earl, one of my regulars, pointed to the paper. "You've got customers."

"I was studying." I pushed it toward him. "Everyone is going to want this new drink."

He laughed, skimming the column. "If you say so."

Our server, Evelyn, arrived with another order, and in the moments it took to pour two glasses of spirits, the door opened and closed again in the distance, bringing in more guests. I passed the drinks to Evelyn and shimmied with delight, garnering looks from a few patrons at the bar. They could laugh at me all they wanted. This was cause for celebration. It felt like only days ago that Seraphina had been considering closing.

Evelyn returned with another order in minutes. "The new couple that sat down, they want that fashionable drink. The one that guy wrote about in the thing."

"Ah-ha!" I beamed, shooting Earl a wink. Evelyn could recite the continent's history and knew the details of every fae court and their leaders, but she refused to bother cataloging social trends in that brilliant mind of hers. Even without proper nouns, I knew this was what I'd been preparing for. "It's from 'Benefits of Magic.' The drink is the Sweet Solstice Sip. I was just telling Earl what a hit it would be." I smirked at him again as I turned and began rummaging through the spirit bottles for the one I needed. "No one has ordered that spirit in ages, but I'm sure we have some."

"Yes, 'Benefits of Magic,' that's what they said. Thank you." Evelyn tucked a strand of black hair that fell loose from her braid behind her ear. I could tell her mind was already elsewhere as she leaned against the bar, scanning her tables for guests needing refills. "I'll be right back." She dashed off to a table that must have flagged her while I made her drinks.

Even if I disagreed with the column's title, I liked that the author didn't only recommend new things. They shined a light on hidden gems. This particular spirit had been available for years. The column had simply repackaged it, making it feel unique and exclusive by emphasizing the proprietor's magic. Then they had invited readers to enjoy one on the upcoming holiday, seamlessly connecting the drink with festivities all of Sandrin celebrated. Almost everything recommended in "The Benefits of Magic" was an instant hit.

The honey spirit was around here somewhere. I let my fingers glide along a few bottles, trying to remember what it looked like. The label was gold, and I thought it was clear glass? We had bottles of all shapes and sizes lining multiple shelves. Usually, I loved the chaos behind the bar, but at this particular moment, it proved inconvenient. Spinning another label toward me, I continued my search.

I glanced at the tavern owner, Seraphina. She hastily tied her blond hair back and rolled up her sleeves, exposing her white skin. Her fingers moved across bottles, and she counted under her breath, doing a rough inventory. The city's workday wasn't officially over, but the door opened again, and more customers entered. We would be packed in a few more hours if things kept up. Now that we had patrons, she was clearly nervous we wouldn't have enough supplies, but it was unclear where she thought she'd get more if we ran out; I let her obsess over it anyway.

In my opinion, it was better not to know. I'd improvise if necessary. The cook could do the same in the kitchen. Maybe that was how the Sweet Solstice Sip had been invented: necessity and ingenuity. Humming to myself as I lifted a few more bottles, reading the labels, I doubted it. The article noted the drink originated from one of the old fae establishments. They didn't cobble anything together. They thrived on tradition and planning.

Two more bottles turned, and I found the golden label I sought. Honey liqueur in hand, I grabbed a rocks glass and poured. Earl caught my attention while I did. "Any of these out-of-towners stop by that inn of yours this morning?"

My face fell briefly as I shook my head. "Not that I saw."

His returning smile was encouraging. He meant well.

When not working here, I was the groundskeeper of Cliff House Inn. Unfortunately, the inn hadn't been doing well in recent years due to the lack of travel on the continent. A mist plague had put many into an endless sleep and had only recently been lifted by the fae court leaders, the Compass Points. We were all still adjusting to the impact. Earl was right, though; I didn't recognize many faces in the tavern. If they were all visitors for the Long Night, they would need to stay somewhere.

"Maybe some will have inquired while I was here," I added cheerfully.

Most visitors took care of their accommodations once they arrived in the city. I shrugged. Maybe the other inns would fill, and they'd have nowhere to go but Cliff House.

It was six weeks until Long Night, the celebration of the winter solstice in Sandrin. The city by the bay was a crossroads on the continent. It might not be Compass Lake, where the fae courts were ruled, but it was an energetic mix of human and fae, history and innovation. The first set of visitors had arrived from the south today, and already, the city was more alive with the influx. More would come before solstice.

A few ideas of things I could do to direct visitors to Cliff House Inn popped into my head. Just as quickly, I dismissed them. The inn manager made it very clear that I was only the groundskeeper. He didn't want my help and had repeatedly told me so. In his view, I only lived in the cottage on the property and kept the grounds because my father owned the place.

Earl must have seen the worry in my expression. "I'll take one of those fancy drinks too Luna." He paused dramatically. "I want to be fashionable like the fae."

I laughed and nodded. Behind the bar, Seraphina bumped my hip affectionately as she finished counting the bottles. "I can't believe there are so many people." Another group entered the tavern as she whispered, "We might actually make it."

My smile widened. "I always knew you would." And I had. This place meant everything to Seraphina, like Cliff House Inn to me. Even when it had seemed bleak, she'd been determined to pull through.

"You certainly always had hope." She snapped a towel at me playfully.

When she turned, I pretended not to notice her wiping what I could only assume was a tear from her eye. Good. She deserved this. I hope she enjoyed it.

Evelyn returned with another order and gestured to a table in the back. "She asked for you specifically, Luna."

I glanced at the unfamiliar woman sitting there. She wore a navy-blue dress, and not a strand of hair was out of place in her dark brown bob. The fae were difficult to distinguish from humans. They generally looked the same, except that every fae was extraordinarily beautiful. Their only real tells were slow aging and some quirks of their magic. This woman was stunning. She had light brown skin and looked to be in her mid-twenties, although she carried herself with a superiority that made her seem older. It was that, and the conservative dress, that led me to believe she was fae, and if she wasn't part of one of the old fae families in Sandrin, she at least worked for one.

In Sandrin, there were fae, and there were old fae.

I didn't think the distinction existed elsewhere on the continent. The old fae in Sandrin were so named because the families had been here since the city's creation. They considered themselves founders of sorts. A made-up title, but one that held weight for some reason.

As much as I loved reading about fae trends in the paper, no one would mistake me for one of them. My dark brown hair was wild with waves and had uncommon white-blond streaks in the front. It was messily tied atop my head, ensuring it didn't get in my way while I worked. My strapless golden top exposed too much pale skin. The tavern was hot when it was filled, and I'd had a good feeling about today. I'd even worn my lucky bright blue skirt. It was a favorite because it matched my eyes. The silk material fell to the floor but was made of slitted layers of fabric that appeared to move with me. It was a purchase from the day I met Seraphina, the same day I arrived in the city.

I glanced at Seraphina. "You alright behind the bar for a minute?"

She nodded, a brief look of concern crossing her face as she surveyed the woman. I had no doubt she drew the same conclusion I did. There weren't many good reasons someone working for an old fae family would want to speak with me. "I'll be here if you need me."

Wiping my hands on a dry towel, I collected the woman's order and headed to the table. Her smile was too warm at my approach. Something twisted in my stomach with every step. I knew what she would say before I arrived, though I had no idea why she was here. The words I feared were out of her mouth before I set down the drink.

"Hello, Luna. I'm Nora, your father's assistant."

My stomach bottomed out.

I kept it together, apparently not needing to introduce myself since she knew me already. She seemed perplexed by my lack of response but recovered quickly. "He would like to speak with you."

I bit the inside of my red-painted lips, trying to guess why. My father and I hadn't spoken in years. The last time was when I'd moved to Sandrin after my mom's death. That was when he'd offered me the groundskeeper's cottage at Cliff House. My fingers twitched at my sides as I remembered the brevity of even that conversation. He'd spent mere moments with me before retreating to Pierce House and leaving me to my grief.

"Why?" I raised my hands to my hips.

She looked briefly taken aback at the bluntness of my question, but again, she recovered quickly. The old families of fae rarely asked what they wanted in the obvious way. It would likely have taken one of them an hour to arrive at the question I dropped in Nora's lap.

"He'd like to tell you that when he speaks with you." She took a sip of the drink I'd delivered.

"And when does Darius want this conversation to take place?" I asked sweetly, knowing I would not like the response by the way she scrunched her nose.

"As soon as possible." She cleared her throat. "This afternoon is preferable."

I glanced out the window. It was afternoon now, nearly evening. He meant for me to drop everything and come to him. My hands balled into fists at my sides. This was unreasonable. I took a step closer, dropping my voice while keeping a smile plastered on my face. "I'm not sure if you're new, Nora, but my father and I don't talk often, or at all. So, you'll have to forgive me, but I need more information if I'm to leave my boss in the lurch to meet with him." I hated to be rude even as I gestured to the filling tavern around us.

None of this was Nora's fault; she only did what she was told. She paused, considering. "It's my understanding, Miss Luna, that he, too, is your boss. This conversation is about your other employment."

I tipped my head back and stared at the ceiling. Darius did ask very little of me at the inn. He didn't exactly pay me, but he gave me a steep discount on the cottage rental. I would be hard-pressed to find a home that I loved as much anywhere else in Sandrin. Seraphina would understand, and if I went now, I could return before the evening meal rush.

"Alright." I gestured toward the door. "Let's get this over with."

2

Vincent

H*ave we lost all semblance of etiquette?* I took a seat in the gold velvet chair. The Bayside Times staff gathered on the top floor of the old three-story building in the city's center that served as our office. I cringed at Arnold's audacity—he'd dared to bring his sandwich to the team meeting. He took a bite as everyone took their seats, and a glob of... was that jam?...dropped on his wrinkled white shirt.

How was he our feature writer?

"Do you know what this is about?" Daisy took the seat next to me. The rest of the team filled the brown leather couch or the dark wood chairs handcrafted by a local fae artisan I'd recommended in my column.

"I'm sure she'll tell us momentarily." I folded my hands in my lap. My wind magic itched to swipe the crumbs from Arnold's shirt.

"Did you see how many people arrived today?" Daisy asked.

I glanced out the window where the sky had darkened,

though it was only late afternoon. The last of the sun's setting rays danced on the calm waters of Sandrin Bay. Crowds of people filled the streets, and we were still weeks from the Long Night celebration.

"I'm sure more will come," I said offhandedly. I wasn't dying to have Sandrin packed with tourists from remote villages on the continent, but I could admit it was nice that folk were no longer afraid to travel. Or that they *could* travel, for that matter. So many had recently been awakened from the mist plague. This year's solstice celebration was sure to be a grand one.

"I hope so," she said. Her black hair was pulled back, showing the early signs of aging on her brown skin. She was human and probably in her fifties, but I was sure there hadn't been a Long Night with this many visitors in her lifetime.

Our editor, Patricia, still hadn't started speaking. Daisy must have felt some pressing requirement to fill the silence. "They'll all want one of those...what did you call them? Sweet Solstice Sips?" Her voice turned playful.

I stretched my neck, never quite sure if she was speaking in jest. "Yes, well, they should go nicely with the festivities."

She hid a smile that leaned toward teasing. A muscle in my jaw twitched as I refrained from clenching my teeth. It would do no good for her to know it bothered me. Before I could find a suitable reply, Patricia spoke. "Thank you all for joining on such short notice. As you can see, tourists are pouring in." Our leader had white skin, short blond hair, and wore dark glasses. She was small in stature and had a no-nonsense attitude that I appreciated.

"We must tailor our content for the next few weeks to the visitors and the upcoming celebrations." She glanced at Arnold, who had moved on to dabbing at the red stain on his white shirt now that the sandwich was gone. Her mouth pressed into a thin line, but she continued. "Arnold, we'll need one feature per week on the visitors. Where they are from, why they traveled, what they hope to wish for on Long Night."

Arnold looked up, mouth slightly agape at being referred to while busy with his shirt. "Oh...yes, alright."

Patricia either didn't notice or ignored his hesitation. "We will also need features that dig into the city politics with so many tourists here. With recent changes in fae court leadership, we'd be remiss not to survey the people on their opinions. I hope you can help cover some of these topics, Daisy."

"Has there been any news on the magic school?" Daisy asked. "It'd be great to poll visitors on how they feel about it." Her gaze slid hesitantly toward me. "Since reactions in Sandrin have varied."

I sat up straighter, my wind and anger rising at the implication. The changes in fae leadership allowed half-fae or fae with mixed court lineage to be educated in their magic for the first time. Apparently, it was well known that some old fae families weren't thrilled with the change.

"No news on the school since it was announced." Patricia pushed her glasses up the bridge of her nose. "But great idea, Daisy. Add it to the list."

Unsurprisingly, Daisy brimmed with excitement. I wanted to roll my eyes. If anyone should be writing about the changes to the fae courts, it should be, well, a fae. The stories Patricia mentioned would be the perfect material for me to sink my teeth into as a more serious journalist.

Patricia looked my way next. "We'll also need to help the tourists make the most of their trip to Sandrin. The next few issues should have lists of 'Benefits of Magic' greatest hits." She counted off her requirements on her fingers. "They need to know where to eat, where to shop, where to stay, and where is best to make their wish on Long Night."

Of course they needed that, but I could write my weekly column and some bonus feature content for the celebration, especially if she wanted to highlight pieces previously reviewed. "Not a problem."

"We should do one new big recommendation as the city fills," she added.

I nodded and raised my quill hesitantly.

"Yes, Vincent," Patricia said as she leafed through a stack of papers in her hand.

"I thought I might be of assistance with the feature articles, given the overflow."

Patricia stopped sorting her notes and glanced at me over the cat-eye glasses that had fallen back down her nose. "With the success of your Sweet Solstice Sips, and was it that zesty tasting dressing before that...?" She let the sentence hang. It was clear she didn't even remember what had come before the dressing. She'd never give me better material if she didn't take me seriously. "Well, with all your column's success, we must put our best foot forward with recommendations for our visitors."

I opened my mouth to press the point further, but Nathaniel interrupted, asking about his series on traditional Long Night celebrations. This wasn't over. I'd approach Patricia after the meeting. This was the perfect opportunity to write something other than "Benefits of Magic." I need only find the right angle to convince her.

"Vincent." Daisy turned to me when Patricia finally adjourned the meeting. I tracked Patricia's retreat to her office, but Daisy pressed, "Do you have a moment?" Patricia sat down and started writing, so I nodded, deciding I had time before missing her for the day.

"Well, you see...my husband..." Her tone was softer all of a sudden, more hesitant. Something prickled at the back of my neck, and I knew what this was before she finished. It had become all too common since my column had gained success.

My nostrils flared. "You want me to recommend something?" This part of the job was wearing on me. Daisy and I weren't close, but I'd thought she had more professional integrity than to ask for a favor for her husband. What, did his business need a boost?

"My husband loves Parkview Tavern. Do you know it?" She rambled, not waiting for my acknowledgment before continuing. "It hasn't been doing well. I thought a feature in 'Benefits of Magic' could help boost visitors."

While it was slightly better that it wasn't his business, I still didn't appreciate the ask. Recommendations were not requested. They were earned. They were demanded by superior products and experiences, usually with a dash of magic somewhere in the mix. Occasionally, I'd feature an establishment or product with no magic whatsoever, but those columns never did as well. I never regretted those products I recommended, though. My toes wiggled in my well-worn walking boots. The bootmaker had been my last human feature and these were the most comfortable footwear I owned.

"I don't think so, Daisy. I don't take requests."

Her face pursed in consideration. I knew she would say something I didn't appreciate. "You might not take requests, Vincent"—she stood, wrapping her sweater more tightly around her chest—"but you should try to experience things outside of your fae bubble."

My brow pinched in confusion, then in rising anger. First the comment about the old fae's varied reaction to change, now this? This city had been my home since birth. I experienced all parts of it. How dare she. There was no fae bubble I hid in.

Movement in Patricia's office caught my attention. She stacked papers on her desk, placing some into her travel bag. I was about to miss her for the day. "Please excuse me." I gave Daisy a final glare. My conversation with Patricia was more pressing than a fruitless argument. With my head held high, I walked across the room to Patricia's office and knocked gently on the door.

"Oh, Vincent, do come in." She still sorted papers into piles on her desk.

"I was hoping we could speak more about the opportunities for feature pieces." My mouth felt dry all of a sudden. "I can help."

"Do you have a particular angle or topic you wish to cover?" While this was an innocent enough question, one any editor would want to know before assigning a story, it occurred to me that her hesitation might not be only because of my successful recommendation column. Daisy was human, and Arnold was Vesten, or fire fae, but I was the only one of old fae descent working at the paper. Unfortunately, as Daisy had alluded to, the old fae families were known to resist the court changes the hardest. Maybe Patricia didn't think me up to the task of writing pieces potentially misaligned with my family's perspective.

"I want to dig into something meaningful." I paused.

That wasn't good enough. The words she wanted to hear were on the tip of my tongue, but I couldn't force them out. I wasn't sure I was genuinely willing to do it. I may not get on with my parents, but that was a private matter, a family matter. It wasn't something I'd share with colleagues. I rubbed the back of my neck with indecision. This job was what I wanted for myself—outside of the Andiveron name. If I needed to say something...distasteful about old fae families, I could do so.

Probably.

Internally, my wind surged against the cage of my upbringing, which demanded I not publicly air family business, but Patricia was still waiting for a response. At least, it seemed she was taking my request seriously.

"Sandrin is my home. I want to show everything it offers. If you're asking, I'm not afraid to dig into the best and worst of the fae here."

Her smile flashed too eagerly. Then, a little too quickly, she pulled a file from the drawer on her left. Had it been waiting there for this conversation?

"It happens I have an unverified tip requiring investigation." She sniffed the air with distaste. "I'd ignore it, but...if we have someone able to verify it, it would be quite the story." She handed me the folder.

I restlessly tapped my foot on the floor as I flipped through it. I was positive I'd set myself up for this. There were financial records of Darius Pierce, head of another old fae family, though he was Norden, or water fae. They showed a significant transfer of funds from his estate to the human governor a few weeks ago.

"I'm sure Darius didn't share this willingly." I flipped to the next page. It was a scrap of paper. The tear was too deep to read everything, but the words *stop* and *school* were quite clear. Lastly, the folder held a memory stone. I picked it up slowly. It was a rare gift of some Suden, or earth fae, to see and manipulate memories. With more recent experiments in blood magic, memory stones had become fashionable. One could pick a memory and think it into the stone. Those who rubbed the stone could review its contents in the future. I'd written about them weeks ago.

"You'll want to watch that, but I can tell you it shows Darius meeting with Marion, the governor. They were having lunch at that restaurant outside the park. He handed her an envelope that corroborated the transaction detailed in those documents."

"Was the memory holder close enough to hear anything?" I understood why she thought this could be a big story if verified, but these collected scraps were weak.

She shook her head. "The tip, as you can guess, says Darius is bribing the governor to stop the development of the magic school."

Unfortunately, this would conveniently explain why we hadn't heard any news about the school since its announcement weeks ago. Still. "This is a serious accusation on no evidence." Rumors about the position of old fae families was one thing. Printing a story like this was another. The Norden Point would not take kindly to an old fae family trying to undermine her authority.

Patricia gave me a half smile. "The payment is clear."

I laughed. "Yes, but he could have been paying her for groceries for all we know."

She reached for the folder. "I'd never print it as it is, but you said you wanted to dig into something."

The folder didn't immediately release from my grip when she tugged. My fingers clamped around it, and I wasn't sure why. "Why me? I don't know Darius. He's Norden. I'm Osten. What makes you think I'm capable?"

"All of the old fae in this city know each other." She sighed. While true, the statement didn't consider the court prejudices the old fae still held. "Look, you were the one that asked for more. I have this. It needs work, but it could be a story worth telling. An old fae family fighting against the progress the Compass Points are pushing for. It's news."

"If it's real," I hedged.

She conceded. "If it's real. That's part of feature writing, Vincent. You can't simply pick the new *it* thing like you do with your recommendations. You attempt many wrong directions before finding the right angle for a story. The facts have to be there, but so does the why. Why should our readers care? What are we showing them about the continent? What can they do about it?"

Patricia was usually reserved, but there was a swell of emotion in her voice. This story meant something to her. Maybe she had friends or family who wished to attend the school. Could Darius have done something to put a halt to it? Why?

I didn't like that this tip assumed the worst, but I was also a realist. I could hear my parents' opinions in my head, and I hadn't even spoken to them about it. *"The half-fae will make a mockery of our magic. They don't know how to use it."*

The fact that no one had taught them how to use it like the rest of us would be irrelevant. My wind magic swelled within me.

I'd rather someone with good intentions investigate than someone who painted all old fae with the same aversion to change. I clenched and released my teeth in consideration. My fingers still gripped the folder.

"I'll look into it."

3

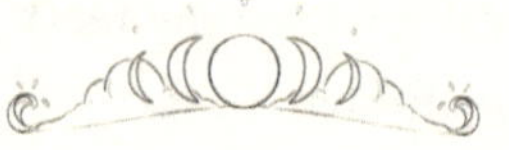

Luna

With a quick explanation and a promise to fill Seraphina in upon my return, I left with Nora. I'd do almost anything for Cliff House Inn. It was my favorite place in the city—even if that was at odds with my relationship with its owner. The inn didn't feel like part of the city, with the forest covering most of the coastal property—where water met woods in a mighty display.

As we exited the busy tavern, I remembered why I loved it nearly as much. Parkview Tavern was precisely in the center of the city. If Sandrin was split into four quadrants, one for each of the fae courts, Central Circle was neutral ground. It was hubris, of course, that the city districts were named after the fae courts. In all likelihood, it was only because the courts represented cardinal directions as much as they did elements. Norden was the northern district for the water fae, Suden southern for the earth, Vesten was western for the fire, and Osten was eastern for the wind. The city was more human than fae, and humans lived throughout all four districts and Central Circle, but that wasn't how the fae saw the continent.

Maybe it was a *benefit of magic* that they named everything. I chuckled at my own joke as we walked in silence.

A bubbling river ran through the park, ending in a moat-like circle surrounding the tavern. One had to cross a small footbridge to reach the tavern entrance. After that, a slice of greenery stretched before succumbing to the city's more traditional sights and sounds.

I wasn't surprised to see a coach waiting beyond the park. The city was large but walkable for those with a bit of time. Darius seemed like the type with a tight schedule. Why take an afternoon stroll when a coach or horse could get you there more efficiently?

Nora gestured to the open door. "Shall we?"

It was too late to turn back now. I clambered inside, and Nora slid in elegantly behind me. Without a word, we began to move. She glanced at me again, and her eyes widened as if only now noticing my strapless top. "Shall I halt the carriage? Did you have another top you needed to grab? It can be quite chilly by the water." She wasn't actually worried about the temperature. Her concern would be my appearance when I entered Pierce House.

I shook my head. "This is all I have."

"No matter." She rummaged in a box under the seat. "I have a few options."

A few options? My mouth hung open, and I wasn't sure if I should laugh or be offended. Had she come all this way expecting me not to have the proper attire? I now respected this female in a way I hadn't previously. My father didn't have the forethought to worry about my clothing choices. Nora must have come up with this task all on her own. I wondered how long she'd studied me before approaching.

She held up a new black dress with short sleeves. So much

for her excuse that it was chilly by the water. Sandrin's temperature never changed. It was moderate year-round, so sweaters weren't strictly necessary, even approaching the winter solstice. I shook my head at the dress. Undeterred, she pulled out another option: a mostly inoffensive crème-colored sweater. I could easily wear it over my current outfit, which was likely easiest. Glancing at the other items in her box, I decided not to continue the gamble. "That's fine," I said, and she handed me the top.

I pulled it over my head, letting it cover my exposed shoulders. Nora seemed satisfied with her work as she assessed my new look. The carriage rumbled west toward the coastline, and the multi-story stone buildings of Central Circle gave way to smaller, more charming homes outside the window. "Shouldn't we head north? This is hardly the most direct path to Pierce House."

Nora shook her head, something like pity in her gaze. Pierce House was recognizable enough on the bay. I knew where it was, but I'd never been invited there. Maybe she knew I was no authority on direct routes. I folded my arms over my chest. Heading west wouldn't get us there. We were headed toward...

"We're going to Cliff House Inn," she said.

I schooled my features, masking the disappointment I didn't fully understand. Of course we were. As a half-fae, I'd never been welcome in Pierce House. The inn was where Darius had met me last time, too. I wasn't sure why I'd thought that would change now. I gestured down to the sweater. "Then why did I have to put this on?"

She smiled gently and shook her head while assessing the rest of my outfit. At least the side-eye she gave the skirt was amusing. Her lips pursed, likely concluding there was nothing to be done about it. "It's just good manners to wear appropriate attire to meetings."

I exhaled a long breath, leaned back against the seat, and

returned my gaze to the window. The park stretched from Central Circle out to the coast. The pockets of forest made places like Parkview Tavern or Cliff House Inn feel like the wilderness, yet the convenience of the city was only a short walk away.

Some wondered why the tavern was in the park at all. I'd heard complaints that it ruined the serenity of the space. Seraphina said it provided a different kind of peace. If the fae considered themselves the unofficial city leaders, Parkview Tavern was one place fae of all courts, and no courts, like myself, were always welcome. I'd wanted to be in the center of Sandrin society for longer than I could remember. It might have had something to do with being half-fae and, up until recently, having to pretend I wasn't. The city had been through a lot of changes, but that was all in the past—or it was trying to be. I guess it wasn't in the past at Pierce House yet.

The coach rolled to a stop outside the inn and I stared up at it as I exited. I decided something about it changed, knowing Darius was inside, but it was still picturesque. A charming ten-bedroom building, white with dark brown accents that made it pop against the green of the surrounding forest. The trees did nothing to disrupt the inn's seaside view. From the library porch, you could sit and listen to the waves crashing against the cliffs for hours. The consistent roll of the water was the sound of home to me. My cottage was barely visible through the thick trees, but I knew it was there—another small comfort.

Nora coughed politely. "We should continue, Miss Luna."

I nodded and followed. Not much made me nervous. I firmly believed things were meant to be, and whatever happened needed to happen to shape me into the person I was to become, but my heart beat faster as Nora led me through the front doors. I'd like to think the city taught me how to deal with all manner of people, those who liked me and those who believed me not worth their time. The one person I never learned how to deal with was my father.

Now, here he was, on my turf, sitting behind a large wooden desk in the manager's office. His dark brown hair matched mine in color, except for my blond streaks, as did his blue eyes. My nostrils flared at the reminder.

"Miss Luna Pierce to see you," Nora said unnecessarily before closing the office door behind her.

I felt ten years old again.

The first time I'd seen Darius, Mom and I lived just south of the city. The village had been mostly human, since that's what Mom was and what she'd claimed I was, too, for the first ten years of my life.

"It's good to see you, Luna." His voice was warm, like a blanket you wanted to wrap yourself in on a cold night. All it did was put me on edge, since comfort had been the furthest thing from my experience with Darius.

When he'd come to see me as a child, it had been only to test my magic. Upon realizing I had none, he'd left. I could count the number of times I'd seen him after on one hand.

Half-fae were unpredictable like that. Some had all the magic of the fae court. Some had magic under specific circumstances. Others were almost human in how ordinary they were. I was the latter. The only thing I was all but guaranteed to be granted from Darius's fae lineage was the slowing of age.

"Hi, Darius." I held up the only shield I could—his name. I didn't know him well enough to call him anything else. He might have flinched as I said it but recovered too quickly for me to determine if it was real or imagined.

"Thanks for coming on such short notice. Please take a seat." He gestured to the chair in front of the desk.

I glanced around the office as I sat, wondering if he really thought I had a choice. "I do need to get back. The tavern is busy tonight."

"Yes." He cleared his throat, sitting up straight and putting forth what I could only imagine was his business tone. "Unfortunately, we have yet to see the same influx at Cliff House." He gestured to the all-but-empty building outside the door. I was sure Byrd, the manager, was out there somewhere.

"What is this about?" He'd been as direct as he was capable, mentioning Cliff House so quickly, but my heart kicked in anticipation—and not the good kind.

"Well"—he ran his hand through his hair, pushing it back from his face—"Byrd resigned today."

Good riddance. Byrd had been the manager since before I'd taken residence on the property. He always looked at me like I was filth on the bottom of his boot.

"With a hundred new people pouring into the city, not one came to Cliff House. That proved too much for him."

I wasn't exactly surprised, even though it sounded shortsighted. Just because none of the first visitors came to Cliff House didn't mean others wouldn't. Byrd had never seemed interested in driving guests to the inn. He thought they should come because it was an old fae property. I didn't speak, wondering where Darius was going with this.

He cleared his throat again when I asked no follow-up questions. Was he nervous? I didn't know Darius well enough to judge. "The inn hasn't had visitors in months, as you know."

I was pretty sure it had been longer than months, but I wasn't about to correct him. This conversation was already not what I'd expected.

"I don't have time to find a replacement. Nor does anyone want such short-term employment."

"Short term?" I asked.

"Yes, well." He hesitated again. This time, I was sure it was nerves, but I didn't know why. "I'm selling the inn after solstice."

Anger surged hot within me, and I stood, leaning forward

and placing my hands on the desk. "You can't." Mom had always told me I was terrible at hiding my emotions—another reason I made a terrible fae. Mine were currently written all over my face, but I didn't care. This place was my home. He couldn't sell it. I couldn't believe he was even considering it. Realizing too late that my outburst wouldn't help with someone like him, I pulled back, retaking my seat.

His lip appeared to twitch. "I wondered if you wanted to run it until Long Night."

It felt like there was a low buzzing in my ears that must have blocked what he was saying. I couldn't have heard him correctly. When I decided maybe I had, because those familiar blue eyes were staring almost earnestly at me, I was speechless for possibly the first time in my life.

"What?" It was the only word my mouth could form. My fingers gripped the armrests on the chair as I leaned forward again, inwardly cursing my inability to hide my emotions. "You want me to run Cliff House?"

He nodded. "I know you have other responsibilities, but my other option is to close the inn now and put it up for sale."

I was surprised that he knew I worked at the tavern. Part of me had assumed tracking me down was another task delegated to Nora, not one he had any interest in. The word yes was fully formed and ready to leap from my lips, but I needed to think about this rationally. Learning from my last two overly animated displays of emotion, I considered the offer. He was planning to sell the inn. I didn't want that. A different plan formed in my mind.

"I have a better offer for you."

He tilted his head but gestured for me to continue.

"I'll run the inn, but I'll do it my way between now and solstice." I sat up straight and rolled my shoulders back. Darius had no idea how many suggestions I'd given Byrd about the inn that had gone ignored. Over the years, I'd put a lot of thought into how I'd run this place differently to grow the business. That knowledge could be put to use. "I want your word." I gestured toward the empty inn outside the office door. "If I can fill it by Long Night, you won't sell it. I can keep running it." I bit my lip. Like he said, he could easily close and sell it now. I wasn't sure why he'd offered me until Long Night in the first place, but I wanted this place too much to press. I'd never asked him for anything, and I had to say I didn't care for this feeling—waiting for his decision.

He leaned forward almost immediately at my words. Whether he was pleased by my response or eager to fold his arms atop the desk, I couldn't be sure.

I held my breath. My gaze fixed on the barely there lines by his eyes crinkling as if he were smiling. He wasn't. "You sure you're up for the challenge?" He tapped his fingers on the desk. "You do know it's been more than a few months since the inn has had a guest, right? I was being generous." His gaze held mine like he was searching for something he wasn't sure was there.

My metaphorical hackles rose at the condescension. "I'm aware. I'm a little surprised you are." Inwardly, I winced. Insulting him wouldn't help.

He huffed a laugh and stood, walking toward a bookshelf against the wall. His finger ran across the wood, and he glanced at the captured dust on the pad. "This place could benefit from a little—" He cut himself off, meeting my gaze.

But I had no doubt what he'd been about to say.

This place could benefit from a little magic. No doubt his water magic could clean this place in minutes. I shrank in my seat as he reminded me how much I didn't fit in here—with him. It didn't matter. Elbow grease could clean the same as magic, even if it took longer. "Do we have a deal?" I pressed.

He turned and stuck out his hand for me to shake. "Fine." I stood to meet him, sliding my hand into his. "You have until Long Night to change my mind."

4

Vincent

I continued reviewing the memory stone and other items in the folder until I was the last person left in the office. My meeting with Patricia confused me. This was the kind of story I wanted, and I wasn't afraid of the work, but something felt off. I rubbed my forehead as if to squeeze out the thoughts I couldn't entirely organize. She had been too ready for me with this particular assignment. I didn't like it. The tip felt flimsy, and this fae's reputation was on the line. I didn't care if he wasn't of my court. The Compass Points would not look kindly on anyone, especially an old fae, working against their new policies.

Where had the tip come from that Patricia wanted to dig into it?

Putting the folder into my bag, I left the building. I couldn't press her further because I wanted this. No matter how unorthodox it seemed, I wanted the chance to write a feature, and this was what she'd given me. Maybe this was how they all started. Between Patricia handing me this uniquely old fae story and Daisy's earlier comment, I wondered if everyone only saw me as old fae.

You should try to experience things outside of your fae bubble. The words still irked me. What was the tavern her husband liked? Parkview? I glanced behind me into the trees—the warm glow of the single building in the middle of the natural setting called to me. I was sure I'd been there before. I didn't have a fae bubble, but I could prove her even more wrong by going to check it out now. If it didn't live up to my standards, that was that.

I could begin my investigation tomorrow. Tonight, I would experience the city with the tourists—those who didn't know my family name or my column. I'd surround myself with a few strangers at Parkview Tavern. My feet carried me across the street and into the park before I could change my mind.

As I pulled open the door, I hated to admit the energy inside was immediately contagious. Patrons filled the wooden chairs and stools; their animated chatter was comforting as it bounced from the dark brown rafters. I took the only seat as it opened at the bar. It was hard to believe Daisy said this place wasn't doing well. The tavern was packed, and though I was still unsure that warranted a recommendation, this was precisely what I needed.

Abruptly, a woman with hair dark as night and silver strands the color of moonlight framing her face stormed behind the bar. She tugged an apron from the hook and tied the strings around her waist tighter than seemed necessary. Her gaze raked over those of us seated before her, and her eyes locked with mine when she spotted the empty place where my drink should be.

She leaned forward. "What'll it be?" Her voice was bright and welcoming, even with the anger she had recently displayed. My brow arched in silent question. "Do you want a drink?" she pressed at my silence.

She gave me another once over, her eyes lingering on my dark brown jacket. Her gaze was penetrating, not at all the lost-among-the-crowd atmosphere I sought. Something flared hot inside me at her perusal all the same. My wind surged, a gale waiting to break free. *Relax*. I took a deep breath. Her nostrils flared. She was definitely judging me. I needed an answer to her question.

"Sweet Solstice Sip." Was ordering the drink I'd put on the map a tad indulgent? Probably. I shrugged. I'd been so intent on stretching myself with my new assignment that I needed to remind myself I'd done alright so far.

"Sure." She turned her back to me and reached for the ingredients. My lip curved into a satisfied smile, noticing they were already at hand. The new column was doing well already.

"Busy day?" an older man beside me asked, pulling my attention from the perplexing bartender.

I nodded noncommittally. Enjoying being around people and actually chatting with a stranger were different. I wasn't prepared for the latter.

"Lots of people here today," he said. "You looking for someone special?"

My gaze tracked the bartender's movements at his words. I wasn't sure why. Dating was not my strong suit. I knew I was good-looking—I was fae. That was never my problem. Too many women I'd been interested in only cared about the Andiveron family name, though. Now, with my column taking off, most were only interested in getting a product or business recommended. I tapped my fingers on the bar top. There was no way I would tell a stranger any of this. I gave him a tight-lipped smile.

"You visiting for Long Night?" he asked, unbothered by my

silence. He scratched his head in thought, giving me a look like he was trying to place me.

"No, just trying out a new tavern."

Recognition flashed in his features, though I couldn't imagine why. He smiled and lifted his glass. "Way better than those stodgy fae establishments, am I right?"

I pursed my lips, looking around. *Get out of your fae bubble.* Daisy's words replayed in my mind. This place had an energy, to be sure, but I wondered if that only had to do with the visitors for Long Night. The tavern itself lacked charm. It had no distinguishing features. Dark wood lined the walls and the bar. The chairs and tables were old and scratched. Even the lighting seemed lacking, although the moonlight streaming through the windows helped. This was probably a part of the park where tree cover didn't block it.

"It could benefit from a little magic." I let that confident smile I'd been taught from birth cross my face. The phrase was an old fae one. That's why I used it for my column, but this man wouldn't know that. *Get out of your fae bubble.* Daisy's words echoed again.

Well, I was here, and I was unimpressed.

The man looked like he'd say more, but the bartender returned, drink in hand. My gaze tracked the liquid sloshing in the glass, then slid to the bartender. The fury she'd first displayed was back, and I had to say it made her fiercely beautiful. I was too distracted appreciating the sharp lines of her anger that I didn't even register as my Solstice Sip splashed onto my face. I blinked, ignoring the alcohol dripping down my chin as the scent of moonflower filled my nose. That was not part of the drink. It only bloomed under the full moon and in the presence of Norden magic. I scanned the counter behind the bar for the flower but found none.

The scent drew me forward like a moth to flame. Then, the man next to me was on me with a napkin, dabbing my face.

Honey spirit and ale were all over my jacket. My gaze flicked to the bartender. The glass in her hand was empty, her brow pinched, and her gaze narrow.

Wait, was her anger for me? Did she throw my drink at me? She did not look apologetic.

A gust of my wind magic slipped its leash and swirled, further tousling my hair and immediately drying my face. The bartender's bright blue eyes widened, almost like she was laughing at me, and my cheeks flushed as I reined in my wind.

Another woman rushed toward me with a towel. She glared between us, throwing the towel at me before turning to the bartender. "Outside. Now." She pointed toward the back.

I held the cloth uselessly in my hand. I didn't need it to dry off anymore; my magic had seen to that. Instead, I found myself standing and following the bartender through the employee entrance. The door dropped us at the back of the building, and she was already striding toward the moat surrounding the tavern, shucking her boots off as she went.

"Hang on a second," I chased after her.

She didn't slow. I jogged to keep up, only halting when we reached the moat's edge, and she hopped down into the water. She bunched her skirt in her hand, holding the layered pieces above her knees to stop them from getting soaked. Ignoring me, she stared at the moon, taking deep, defiant breaths.

I didn't know what to say. She still hadn't acknowledged me. "Excuse me," I said, unsure how this would play out.

"I'm sorry," she whispered.

Had I heard that right? Was that an apology? She hadn't turned to meet my gaze.

"I didn't mean to—" She continued to stare at the moon like she was demanding an answer to some unspoken question. "Well, I don't know what happened, but I didn't mean for it to."

"You threw a drink at me," I said flatly.

She turned to face me and shrugged like she wasn't sure

that was accurate. I didn't know why she'd deny it. It had been clear she was angry. I'd thought her displeasure was for whatever had brought her into the tavern in a huff, but the way her brow still pinched at me, I wondered if it was personal. What had I done?

"Did I do something to offend you?"

She sighed. "It wasn't actually about you, but I supposed your words about this place struck a nerve."

I felt like an ass, instantly deflating as I realized how pompous my comment had sounded. "I didn't mean to insult this place." I'd let Daisy's words get in my head, willing to say anything to prove them wrong.

Her gaze was perplexed like she was trying to read something written in another language. "You're old fae, aren't you?"

I straightened. "I'm not sure why that is relevant."

She pushed back the sleeves of the crème sweater she wore. The style was familiar but didn't mix with the rest of her outfit. I'd guess it was from the boutique where my sister worked—an establishment I'd recommended a few months ago. It was the only recommendation I'd made that I regretted. Seeing the top on the bartender, I regretted it further. The sweater was all wrong on her. It seemed too timid, too reserved for someone whose eyes still raged like a summer storm.

"Were you angry at someone who was old fae?" I crouched closer to the water against my better judgment.

She pursed her lips before letting out a heavy sigh. "It doesn't matter. I apologize for ruining your jacket." She looked...well, not peaceful but perfect, standing there in the water. The bartender was a tempest at sea and I watched from the safety of shore. With her chin still lifted high, she was crashing waves and swirling clouds at the cyclone's center. I couldn't look away. My wind was a gale force inside me, straining to get out. I wanted to let it. The water rippled around her, and I thought for a second I had. The pattern on the water was too precise to be from her jump into it.

"Why are you standing in the moat?" I asked.

The smell of moonflower struck me again, and I realized what it was as the small waves circled her—her magic. She must be Norden, water fae.

She laughed, and the sound was lyrical. I was drawn forward, wanting to hear more. "I find it calming, and I've had a bit of a day."

"What caused your day?"

It was an impertinent question. This female—this fae—was a stranger. She didn't seem to like me. Maybe I'd earned some of it, but certainly not all of it. Either way, there was no reason for her to answer. Still, I wanted to know, and she didn't seem the type to let propriety hold her back. Her bright red lips, messily knotted hair, and even the high slits of her bright blue skirt were choices a little bold for most fae in Sandrin. I held back a smile, deciding that was precisely why she'd chosen them. She seemed so sure of her place in that moment. My wind surged with longing, like a squall in my chest.

It must be nice. I might be old fae, but I no longer knew where I fit in this city.

"My father." Her gaze was downcast, and the word, the change in her demeanor, struck like an unexpected cut. She was showing me too much.

"He's who I'm angry with." She held my gaze as if forcing me to hear her words. Little did she know there was no chance I could look away.

Her mouth opened like she was about to say more, but then someone called from the backdoor, "Luna Pierce, are you done wallowing? Or do I have to run this place myself?"

She gave me a fleeting smile and stepped from the water. "I've got to get back. I'm sorry again I spilled on you."

I was still unsure why we were calling it a spill. She'd

thrown the drink at me. Before I could say so, my wind surged toward her feet without invitation, sweeping around them and drying them off.

"I'm so sorry," I said, mortified.

Apparently, it was a night of apologies. My cheeks heated again as I stepped toward her, my hand reaching out to fix something that couldn't be undone. I could only hope my flush didn't show in the dark. It had been a long time since I'd lost control so blatantly.

"For an old fae, your wind is kind of alright." Jamming her foot back into her boot, she glanced up at me. Daring me to argue.

We were too close. I'd invaded her space, but she hadn't retreated. She stood there, a smirk tugging at her lip due to my obvious discomfort.

Though it wasn't all discomfort, was it?

She was breathtaking. Our faces were so close I could see flecks of dark blue in her irises. They looked like crashing waves. I glared at her, unamused by her words but intensely distracted by our proximity, even as I fought to stop my lip from lifting into a matching smirk.

She broke the moment, winking, then running to the door and disappearing into the tavern.

My heart beat rapidly as I watched her go. She was the sea retreating from the shore it bore down on, and I feared she took a piece of me with her when she left. I shook my head free of the haze. One thing finally stuck out. Her name—Luna Pierce. There was only one Pierce family in Sandrin. An old fae she'd admitted to being mad at.

Maybe I'd started my investigation earlier than intended.

I think I just met Darius's daughter.

5

Luna

"Did you really throw a drink at him?" Seraphina asked.

Blond strands flew from her messy ponytail, and her sharp features were made all the more so by the ferocity of her question. I knew I was in trouble when her hands went to her hips as she waited for me at the back door. I glanced over my shoulder at the retreating figure. No surprise he didn't come back inside after whatever that was. I winced as I thought about it.

"I don't remember deciding to throw it at him." I shrugged. "I'm so sorry. I don't know what happened." Honestly, I didn't. One minute, the drink had been in my hand, ready to deliver, and the next, the glass was empty. Most unexpectedly, I'd felt completely calm about it. Like I'd unlocked some inner peace for the evening. It didn't make sense. I could swear I didn't flick my wrist to toss it at him.

But the empty glass in my hand had been pretty damning.

Even more so was the drink dripping down his perfectly carved features.

Seraphina waved dismissively. "Earl said he pulled some fae snobbery about the tavern. I can only imagine you were on edge after talking to Darius."

In this case, I was lucky that one of my best friends was also my boss. "He said this place could benefit from some magic." My skin prickled as I repeated the words. That eerie calm resurfaced. "It enraged me after Darius all but said the same about the inn." That was true, but I still swore my wrist didn't move. I didn't toss the drink at the fae.

"It's fine. Get back out there. We're busy, remember?" Things must be alright if she could tease me. I turned, and she pushed me down the hall. "Try not to throw any more drinks at handsome fae."

I glared at her over my shoulder and headed toward the bar, grumbling. Of course he was handsome. One glance at him told me the male was pureblood fae through and through, and old fae at that. His strong jawline and high cheekbones were framed by expertly tousled dark brown hair. My fingers had itched to run through it before he opened his mouth. *That* had ruined the view a bit.

What had happened with his wind, though? Old fae especially weren't usually so quick to show their element. They had magic because they were fae, but it was more of a power symbol than a practical thing. His wind had swept in twice, and if the shock on his face was any indication, it wasn't a common occurrence. I hadn't lied to him outside, though. His wind was alright. It was...considerate that it dried my feet before I shoved on my boots. I even thought I had seen that consideration, if a little hesitant, in his deep brown eyes when he asked me about my day.

Odd for an old fae to show any consideration for someone like me when his jacket cost more than my entire wardrobe. I winced, remembering the stains from the alcohol. His coat would have been Nora-approved, no mid-carriage ride change necessary for him. I glanced down at my sweater. Nora had insisted I return with it—*for next time*. The evening had cooled, so I'd kept it, but it felt all wrong. I rolled my shoulders, trying to get comfortable. Finally, I gave up, lifting it over my head, and hanging it on a hook. Maybe the fae's words offended me because I still felt like one of them. This sweater made me feel like I was trying to fit in —trying to be something I was perfectly fine not being.

At least, that's what I told myself.

Darius offering me the position at the inn wasn't acceptance. I knew that, but I still found it confusing. He had never shown outright malice like Byrd. Darius's crime was one of apathy, and maybe it still was. Perhaps this was only a temporary crossing of paths.

Another quiet part of me said that even if he hadn't seemed invested in the inn's fate, he had at least offered me the position. That was something. I was determined to save it. When I did, this crossing of paths would be more than temporary. We'd have to address our relationship at some point. Although that was not something to look forward to. If anyone deserved a drink thrown at him, it was Darius.

I silently cursed myself for my lack of control and slipped behind the bar. Seraphina followed, and I could feel her worried glance. Upon my return, Evelyn was at the counter with orders before I could fully organize my thoughts, and I was swept back into the buzz of the tavern with little time to think about my father or the handsome fae.

Earl flagged me down to order another. His wave was more energetic than usual.

"What can I get you?" I asked. His wife had joined him—a woman with black hair and a generous smile.

"Did you figure out who he was?" Earl asked, leaning forward conspiratorially.

I shook my head. "Who?"

"The 'Benefits of Magic' fae!" Earl squeaked. His wife touched his elbow, trying to calm him down. He turned to her. "You don't get it, Daisy. Luna might have thrown a drink at him, but she's his biggest fan."

I waved him off. "Just because I read everything he's ever written doesn't mean I'm his biggest fan." Then my mind caught up with his words. "Wait, what?"

My mouth opened, but nothing came out. I was speechless for the second time tonight. I needed to wish things to return to normal for Long Night. This was getting out of hand. "That was not the recommendation columnist," I whined, placing my forearms dramatically on the bar and letting my head hang between them.

"Afraid so," Earl said.

Seraphina sidled up next to me, gently patting my back. "Everything alright over here?"

"The fae from earlier," I said. "The pretty one with the bad attitude that I allegedly threw a drink at—"

"Not a lot of wiggle room on the drink, dear. We all saw it," Earl cut in.

"Whatever." I waved dismissively. "He writes the 'Benefits of Magic' column." I lifted my head, meeting Seraphina's gaze before turning toward the back door. "I will now throw myself in the moat and die of embarrassment."

Seraphina snorted. "Well, at least you're feeling better if you're back to dramatics."

I shot her a glare before turning to Earl. "How do you know it was him? No one knows who he is—I didn't even know he was a he." Then it clicked. I turned to Daisy. "Oh, right. You work at the paper, too, don't you? Sorry, Earl has mentioned that."

She nodded, smiling warmly. "I can't believe you like his column."

I tilted my head at her in question.

"It tends to be...very fae," she said carefully.

"Ah." Earl must have told her I was half-fae. "I think that's the interesting part." I pointed at my boots. "He has good recommendations even outside of snobby fae standards. These boots were in the column a few months ago. They're human-made and amazing for walking around the city."

Daisy raised a brow. "I can't say I've read all his stuff, but he doesn't act like he cares for anything he considers below fae standards."

I could admit I got that impression, too. Maybe I read his column all wrong. Maybe the human recommendations were charity pieces. His magic had seemed...different, but that didn't mean anything! This was why you should never meet your heroes.

Before I could spiral too far, Seraphina cut in. "You should ask him to recommend the inn."

My head snapped to her. "What?"

Seraphina wiped the counter. "Even I know 'The Benefits of Magic' is huge. He could help you," she said, her voice low. "With the inn."

When I'd returned from Cliff House, Seraphina and I had only chatted briefly, and despite being concerned about Darius's offer and motives, she hadn't questioned my decision to accept it. The beauty of working for my friend was that she knew what the opportunity to save Cliff House meant to me and wouldn't dream of standing in my way. I'd still help here when I could. Leaving her high and dry was the last thing I wanted.

"I know you have your own list of things to do to drive customers to the inn. You've been dreaming of running that place as long as I've known you." She probably knew my list as well as I did at this point. I glanced at the barstools, where, when things were slow like usual, we'd sit and talk about our dreams and goals. She tracked my glance and must have understood its meaning. "I wouldn't be your friend if I didn't mention that having Cliff House featured in the column would be a huge help. It might be worth swallowing your pride and asking."

I sucked in a breath. She was right, and I hadn't even reached that conclusion yet. "It's not about pride," I said, only half sure of my comment. "He thinks I hate him and all old fae." I'd tried to explain. I couldn't tell if he'd heard me; he'd looked so...distracted.

Daisy lifted her drink. "Don't worry, he wouldn't have helped you anyway." Her voice turned prim, like she was trying to mock his. "He doesn't take suggestions for recommendations."

That did not surprise me.

"What's his name?" I asked.

Daisy bit her lip like she wasn't sure she should tell me. Like she didn't want to support my madness. Earl elbowed her, and she sighed. "Vincent. His name is Vincent Andiveron."

"You didn't see him back there with Luna," Seraphina said as if to make Daisy feel better about sharing. "He couldn't keep his eyes off her, even when she jumped in the moat like a lunatic."

Instead of letting Daisy defend her position, I cut back in. "You were watching?" I asked, mock-offended.

Jumping in the water was what I did when I needed grounding. It had been that way since I was a child.

Seraphina shrugged. "I wanted to make sure everything was alright." She narrowed her eyes at me. "You did throw a drink at him."

I opened my mouth to argue, then gave up. No one believed me.

"Then I heard you mention Darius," she said quietly. "I can't remember the last time you told anyone about him. Let alone another old fae."

I stared at her. Her words had been intentional. In the strictest sense of the word, I was old fae, too, even if everything about me rebelled from the label. "Low blow," I said.

Her lip twitched. "You needed to hear it."

Earl and Daisy pretended to sip their drinks while Seraphina shook out all my dirty laundry.

"I wasn't sure where all of that was heading." She gestured wildly. "You know what they say about love and loathing. Someone needed to keep an eye on you until you both decided if you'd end up fighting or fuc—"

Earl snorted before Seraphina finished her tirade, giving up any pretense that he and Daisy weren't listening. My cheeks heated. We might have had a moment there at the end, but we were nowhere near *that*.

"I don't know if I would have bet on that," Daisy hedged. "He's quite reserved at work."

Seraphina laughed. "Luna had him wrapped around her finger."

Her defense of my supposed charms was priceless, even as Daisy extolled the fae's stuffy nature. I no longer listened to them, wondering what to do with the information that our rude customer was the city's taste-maker and possibly the solution to my problem. Vincent Andiveron might not take suggestions for his column, but I only had six weeks to fill the inn. Cliff House wasn't miraculously going to end up with guests, no matter how many people came to the city for solstice festivities. I'd been clear—full occupancy. I needed every room spoken for. Seraphina was right. I did have a list of ideas to implement. Being the manager was all I had wanted since I'd moved to the city. The property felt like home, and I wanted others to experience the same thing I did. I couldn't let this opportunity slip away.

At least eight out of ten recommendations in his column ended up as hits. The less successful ones were the human ones, like my boots. But, as Seraphina had harshly reminded me, I was as much old fae as I was human. Maybe I could lean into my old fae side for an article. I might not have magic, but the typical old fae never showed theirs off anyway.

My gaze strayed to the hook with the sweater Nora had given me. My skin prickled at the idea of putting it back on, but I steeled my resolve. I couldn't ignore a lead on that kind of publicity. I'd do whatever was necessary, regardless of Vincent's recommendation policies or what he thought of me.

Cliff House Inn was too important.

6

Vincent

I didn't sleep, too wound up and too sure that I wouldn't like the answers I found when searching for information about the bartender.

Her name was Luna Pierce.

That couldn't be a coincidence.

I might not be well acquainted with all the old fae families of Sandrin, but I generally knew who they were and the family members. Darius Pierce did not have children. He didn't have a partner. It was only him and his mother currently residing in Pierce House. His father was in the north somewhere on some family business. The name Luna Pierce was unfamiliar, but I was determined to find out who she was.

Something like a strong gust blowing over rough water circled in my chest, as if my wind was determined to remind me of her beauty. The fact that she was beautiful was now irrelevant. My magic disagreed, as it usually did, but with her, its outbursts were...more. I was used to my wind partnering with me in more tasks than another old fae might care for, but usually, I could control when that happened. It had slipped its leash twice with her last night. I might have found her attractive, even by fae standards, but if she was my ticket to gathering intel on Darius Pierce, that had to be my priority.

My wind surged as if to question why she would help me. I hadn't sorted out all the details yet, but I would start with figuring out who she was to him. While that happened, thoughts of her beauty needed to be off the table.

That's how I ended up in the Central Circle at the records office when they opened the following morning. Other than Compass Lake, this was the only place I could think to investigate the members of each fae court and their relations. The austere building was white stone, like many of those in Sandrin, and three stories, like the newspaper office. The third floor was the governor's office, while the first two held records of all humans and fae in the city. Its real draw was the fae court records. I needed access to the Norden Court list. From there, I could look up the Pierce family and place the mysterious Luna.

I only needed access to the records. They weren't strictly private. Court affiliation was technically optional, although anyone who understood the fae would find that statement laughable. Either way, the humans considered it public information, and the fae, well, we expected anyone who mattered to know already.

This meant the records were open to anyone with a valid inquiry. I wasn't sure my reason was valid, per se, but I was confident I could come up with an acceptable query.

"May I help you?" the woman behind the desk in the large entrance hall asked as I approached. My fabricated story spilled from my lips before I could think twice.

"I met someone last night and only caught her surname. I know she's of the Norden Court, though. I hoped to review the court records and find her name."

Her heavy dose of side-eye said my story was weak, but the rules were in my favor. She waved her hand, and another man strode forward from the back of the room. "Take Mister..." She paused, waiting for my name.

"Andiveron," I offered.

"Take Mr. Andiveron to the fae court records room. Make sure he signs in."

I couldn't believe it was that easy. The associate walked me up a flight of stairs into a large room filled with thick wooden tables and shelves of books. He pointed toward four giant tomes in the center. I didn't need further explanation to understand there was one book for each fae court.

"Sign here." He held out a much smaller book at the room's entrance.

I did. Since they'd granted me access, there was no reason not to follow the rules.

"I'll sit here." He pointed to the chair. "Only those four books are public. Everything else in the room requires a better reason than *I met someone*."

At least I knew where we stood. The rule was fine with me. I had no interest in the other documents. My focus was solely on the woman I'd met last night and her relation to Darius Pierce.

My wind slid along my arm as if to ask *Is that really your* only *interest in her?*

Of course it was. I flipped through the pages. She may have complimented my wind, but she'd still thrown a drink in my face. My only interest in her was for my feature story. I needed a source. It was too good an opportunity to pass if she was related to Darius Pierce.

The book was organized by surname. It looked like the newest court members were at the bottom of the page by the dates. Alphabetical order was at least attempted for the surnames. But with the recent influx of half-fae and mixed-fae joining courts, some order had been lost. *Better late than never*, I thought. My wind flipped the page in agreement.

The Pierce page was easy to find, the family having been included since the beginning of the courts. Laid out like a family tree, the document listed parents and children back to the creation of the fae. As I scanned the page, my gaze snagged on Darius's name. He didn't appear to have siblings or children. He was lowest on the Pierce family page and he had to be at least a hundred. His parents were listed above him, and their siblings were in the same row. I doubted she was older than Darius and there was no way she was more than two generations of fae back.

Her temper had flared multiple times in our short acquaintance. The emotions streaking plainly across her face told me she couldn't be older than me. A consistent calm, often considered devoid of emotion, was a trait of older fae. One my parents often reminded me that I, or more aptly my wind, was lacking. Luna hadn't seemed shy with her words, and her face was even more expressive. My lip curved as I remembered the smirk she'd given me when offering the backhanded compliment about my wind. It swirled inside me like it remembered, too. I shook away the memory to focus. There was no Luna Pierce on this page.

Where was she? The other woman had called her Luna Pierce. I know I'd heard it. Luna's water magic hadn't been ostentatious, but it had been obvious once I saw it for what it was. She had to be in this court record.

"Excuse me," I called to the gentlemen waiting by the door. "Any reason why someone wouldn't be on the family page in this document?"

The man tilted his head like he considered this a trick question. "If they weren't part of the Norden Court?"

I sighed. "Besides that. I know she was of the Norden Court. As I said, I have her surname."

"Maybe she didn't want to be associated with the family in question."

I blinked, staring dumbly. "Is that...allowed?"

"Of course," he replied. "That list is a voluntary declaration of court association. It's not a detailed family record."

Not having realized this, I considered updating my own Osten record. *This is not the time,* I thought, even as my wind swirled with excitement, flipping the cover of the Osten Court book. I shook my head, focusing on the Norden book. "Where would those names go? The ones not associated with a specific family."

He pointed to the book. "Flip to the end. They're usually listed there."

I thanked him as my wind flipped the pages, ready to work backward. The entry I was looking for was there at the bottom —Luna Pierce was the most recent addition to the Norden Court.

My fingers grazed the page, circling her name. Luna was young, but she obviously wasn't a recent birth. For an adult fae, there was only one reason to add yourself to the court listing now.

If you hadn't been previously allowed.

Luna Pierce was half-fae.

Things started falling into place with that revelation. She'd been upset with her father last night. A father who, according to her surname and where she listed herself in this book, she didn't claim as her own. Her father was either Darius or Darius's father, Klein.

My wind blew in short, pointed blasts against my temple as if tapping to say *You can't use this.* Something in my chest constricted as I realized what this meant. It was more than names on paper. Luna, the bright and confident fae I'd met last night. The one I was almost jealous of because it seemed she knew her place in this city. Half her family had ignored her, likely up until very recently.

Did she have any human family, or was she essentially an orphan? Even as I thought it, I knew my wind, acting as my conscience, was right. I couldn't ask her to investigate a family that had disowned her. Rationally, she wouldn't even have access to the information I needed.

They didn't disown her, did they? She said her father was the one she was angry at.

I couldn't decide whose side my conscience was on, but it had a point. How bad of terms could they be on if she'd seen him yesterday?

Of course, her overreaction to my words, and me in general —even if I'd been a *little* rude—didn't speak of a happy encounter.

I was more confused than ever as I left the records room and headed into the stairwell. The attendant didn't bother to see me out. I weighed my options as I walked. Luna was my only lead. I had to try, right? What kind of journalist would I be if I gave up without asking? I'd be honest with her. She could say no if she didn't want to participate.

My mental spiral was interrupted by another set of voices in the stairwell above me.

"You've made your position clear," a stern feminine voice echoed more loudly than I was sure she intended.

"Not clear enough if you've still taken no action," replied a deeper, more masculine voice. I froze. That voice was familiar, like I'd heard it before. I couldn't be sure if my imagination was playing tricks on me or if I was indeed this lucky, but it sounded like the voice I'd listened to repeatedly in the memory stone from Patricia. I would bet anything that Darius Pierce was speaking a floor above me.

"I will take action in my own time," the feminine voice said. "I don't appreciate your persistence."

The human governor's voice had been harder to hear in the memory stone, but the floor above *was* her office. I needed to hear more.

"That only means you have someone on the opposite side being as persistent as me. And you're still not sure which of us to listen to."

I ducked and took silent steps up the staircase to the landing. They shouldn't be able to see me from this angle. I only needed to peer around the short wall to glimpse them. Without much thought, I risked it, popping my head around the corner. The man's back was to me, his arm resting along the railing, only the back of his head visible as he stared at the woman. I was sure it was Darius, though. The woman was a little to the left in the stairwell, her pinched expression clearly visible, though thankfully it was locked on Darius, not scanning the stairwell for eavesdroppers. I recognized her face immediately from a recent speech I'd attended.

"I am taking the time to research the impacts on this city, as is my duty. A magic school is no small matter," Marion Smith, the human governor, said.

I sucked in a breath, unable to believe the conversation I'd stumbled onto.

"I agree." His voice grew louder, and I knew he'd changed the direction of his face. I chanced another glance. This time, I could see his profile as he looked over the railing. It was absolutely Darius Pierce, and he looked as frustrated as the governor.

"Glad to hear it. Now, please leave. I have your contributions. You will hear when I've made a decision."

He laughed. "And I thought it was the fae who were supposed to be controlling."

"You've been doing it longer, but that doesn't mean you own the skill. Not everything is about you."

Darius pressed his lips into a thin line and turned to leave. I needed to get out of there. I stayed low and returned to the second-floor door, opening it loudly as if I were only now entering the stairwell. I began the descent as if I had nothing to hide and hadn't been listening to their private conversation. Darius didn't catch up to me as I left. I slipped my hands into my pockets, tucking in to the flow of people on the street, and headed for the paper office.

This matter was more confusing than I'd anticipated. I hadn't heard anything that asserted guilt, but I couldn't deny that the conversation echoed Patricia's tip. My thoughts returned to Luna. If she was half-fae, this whole thing impacted her more than I'd initially realized. She'd gone through the work of adding herself to the Norden Court records, which meant, on some level, she wanted to be acknowledged for her magic. She wouldn't have grown up with the resources a school like the one proposed could provide. If anything, she deserved an opinion on her family's alleged involvement.

I had a list of excuses to justify what I'd already decided.

My wind ruffled my hair as if to point out *You just want to see her again.* Maybe it was the way her hair caught the moonlight. Maybe it was because no one had made me feel like an ass like that in a long time. All I knew was that I couldn't stop thinking about her, and it wasn't only because of her surname.

7

Luna

The groundskeeper's cottage was perfect for me. The bedroom was separate, but everything else was encompassed in a single room. Plants of all kinds hung in baskets from the rafters, and a fire crackled in the stove. When I was a girl, Mom would bring us here for vacation. I hadn't thought it strange then that we didn't stay at the big house. Instead, I'd imagined we were so special we couldn't stay in the inn with everyone else—we required our own space. Or maybe Darius hadn't wanted to give away one of the paid rooms to his ex and disavowed daughter.

I sighed and put more wood in the stove before setting a pot of water for tea atop it. The cupboards were full of mismatched dishware, and I pulled a bright red mug from the front of the stack. I needed a plan before approaching Vincent at the newspaper office. I may have decided to do it—to set aside my pride and approach the old fae for a favor—but my whole plan for the inn wouldn't revolve around a single shot at getting attention in the popular column. Cataloging and cleaning the inn, then executing my ideas about gaining new customers, suddenly seemed daunting. I'd had suggestions for years, but finally, no one stood in my way to implement them.

Darius hadn't even asked to see a plan. He told me I had a modest budget and could do what I wanted. It might be modest in his mind, but when I looked at the number, it was...large. Large enough that if I did the cleaning myself, I could invest the rest in my improvement ideas. I'd need to go through each room today and determine what I could clean versus what might require professional assistance. I had my notebook open on the table while the water boiled. Sea air gave the place a fresh scent I couldn't get enough of, but it did mean I left a window cracked all the time, no matter how cold it got.

I wrapped a knitted blanket around my shoulders and watched the pot for bubbles. A cool breeze slipped in through the cracked window, and I wrapped the blanket closer. The pattern was obnoxious, even to me—each square a different color, making it one of my loudest items—and I loved bright colors. When we stayed here in my youth, Mom always had activities for us. One year, we started this blanket. Mom was a seamstress, so we made each square from materials she had left over from other projects. She brought as many as she could reasonably travel with on our visits, and the tradition was born. We'd only half finished by the time she passed, but I let the spirit of the idea live on. The new seamstress in our village would sell me her scraps at a discount, and I added them to the pattern. A few years after Mom was gone, I'd ended up with this finished piece, and I thought Mom would have liked how it turned out.

The bubble of boiling water pulled my attention back toward the stovetop. The special moonflower tea blend I kept hidden was already on the counter. Byrd didn't believe that the flowers bloomed on the property, so he didn't miss them, but I also wasn't one to draw attention to the fact that I harvested them for tea. The scent was immediately calming to my busy mind. With a final deep breath, I had nothing else to stop me from making my list.

As long as everything was on the list, it could be done. It didn't matter how many items there were, they only needed to be prioritized. I moved to the couch, letting the comfort of the blanket fall from my shoulders as I leaned forward to write.

Taking stock of the inn seemed as good a place as any to start. If the office looked dirty to Darius, I couldn't imagine how the guest rooms looked. Byrd didn't like me in the inn, so I hadn't been through the rooms in years.

I wrote *clean and inventory bedrooms* on the list.

The library would need attention. I hadn't checked it yesterday, too distracted by my conversation with Darius. It was a beautiful room leading to the back porch overlooking the sea. I'd always felt it was underutilized. Now that I was in charge, I needed to determine what that meant. My instinct had always been to make it a breakfast area. The inn didn't serve meals. Byrd had said there were plenty of restaurants in Sandrin. This was true, but what about those earlier risers who wanted something comforting before heading out on their adventure for the day? The other major inns all served breakfast. It seemed a simple addition. I need only decide what to serve.

I added *explore breakfast options* to the list.

Of everything on the property, I was most proud of the grounds. They were the one thing I was allowed to maintain in my own way. I'd ensured healthy flowerbeds around the inn and had maintained a usable path from the cliff down to the seaside beachfront. It was over a hundred steps. Visiting when I was younger, I'd realized not many guests knew about it and even fewer used it, but the water was a feature of Cliff House. I loved going down there to listen to the sea crash against the rocks. It was peaceful. I knew I wasn't the only one who would love it once I got guests here.

So much relied on bringing awareness to new customers.

I moved to another part of my list. There were a couple of paths to get the word out. "Benefits of Magic" was one option—it might be a long shot, but I would try. Maybe Vincent would like this place. He seemed to enjoy things and places that weren't new but could be represented in a new light. That was his angle with the Sweet Solstice Sip, the last clothing boutique, and even a furniture maker. My cheeks flushed as I remembered Earl's words from last night. Maybe I *was* his biggest fan.

Wind whipped through the window crack, bringing the scent of sea and storm. At least Vincent's magic would like it here, if I could get him to the property. I certainly hadn't made the best first impression yesterday, but worrying about his reaction wouldn't help. Seraphina had also said I could put signs in the tavern. I'd check with a few other taverns near the inroads to the city to see if they would allow the same. If I couldn't make a big splash with a feature like "Benefits of Magic," it was best to catch the visitors as they arrived.

My list looked as complete as it could for now. I'd expand on it when I determined what needed to be done in the guest rooms and the library. I took my teacup and pulled the blanket around my shoulders again as I trekked through the woods to the inn.

THE ROOMS WERE WORSE than I'd thought. Byrd really must have given up, and I wondered why Darius hadn't tried to sell the inn sooner, even though my heart wrenched at the thought. I'd been through almost all the rooms, and while nothing was wrong with them other than the dust and dinge of disuse, they weren't welcoming. I hoped a good clean would help as I twisted the knob of the final door. It was my last to review. I stumbled into the door, realizing it hadn't opened. Tilting my head, confused, I tried again. The handle turned, but the door didn't budge. I gave it a little shake. The door seemed to mock me with its stillness. I got down on my knees to peer in the keyhole. It didn't appear locked, but it was undoubtedly not opening.

I jiggled the handle once more, and nothing happened. With my hands on my hips, I glared at the unmoving door. I'd need to return to this one. I noted its stubbornness on the list next to the room needing a small leak repaired. I moved downstairs to the main floor, and a knock stopped me in my tracks as I passed the front door.

It couldn't be that easy, right? I hadn't changed anything. This couldn't possibly be a customer. I hurried toward the entry. Whoever they were, I didn't want them to think we were closed.

Upon opening the door, the last person I expected to see stood before me: Vincent Andiveron.

My heartbeat raced as I took in all the features Seraphina and I had labeled a paltry *handsome* last night. He was a work of art, as stunning as the view from the back porch over the sea. His wind must have knocked on the door for him because he was a few steps back, leaning against the porch rail. Even in the casual pose, he was taller than me. I hadn't noticed yesterday. Likely because I'd jumped into the water. We were on even ground now, and I still tilted my head slightly to take him in. He wasn't big and bulky, but he looked strong, lithe, and even graceful as he appeared to await my assessment. His thick brown hair had that just-tousled look that I was confident his wind helped with.

Since meeting him, his dark brown eyes had swept into my mind more than once. Today, they didn't hold the warmth I remembered. I tracked their focus...reminding me that I still wore my mismatched knit blanket around my shoulders. He stared at it as if it offended him. It likely did.

This was fine.

Of course, his deep brown jacket from last night had been freshly cleaned. I held in an eye roll. This was off to a great start. "Hello, Vincent. Nice to see you again."

His gaze pulled away from my offending garment to meet my eyes before he pushed from the porch rail, his spine straightening like he'd been slapped. A muscle ticked in his jaw, and all I could think was that my blanket wasn't *that* bad. Rationally, I knew the change couldn't be from my clothing, no matter how off-putting, but I had no idea what I'd done. How dare I...greet him?

Silence wasn't my strong suit. So, I did the only thing I could—I invited him in. He still hadn't said anything, just stared at me icily. Words flooded from my lips to fill the gaping space between us. "I was heading to the library. Would you care to join me?"

If possible, this was going worse than last night, when a drink had ended up dripping down his face. He would never agree to feature the inn in his column at this rate.

Yet, to my utter bewilderment, he nodded at my invitation and entered. I guessed that made sense. He had come here, after all, no matter what had changed in the last few seconds. My mind reeled as it caught up with the scene. Had I even told him my name yesterday? How had he known where to find me? I'd been so focused on the fact that I'd found out who he was—and what I needed to ask him—it hadn't occurred to me that he might also be looking for me. Gooseflesh covered my arms and neck, less comforting than when his wind had wrapped around my legs the other night.

I gestured for him to head down the hallway into the library. This was an inn; anyone was welcome. His audible gasp as the view from the library windows became apparent was my first sense of comfort. If he could appreciate the beauty of this place, I could deal with whatever he was here for. My hand swept to the plush leather chairs, offering him a seat. Although they had seen better days, I still deemed them acceptable for a cozy library.

"Would you like some tea?" I asked hesitantly.

He looked unsure but nodded. "Thank you." His gaze still showed no warmth, but the tick of his jaw was gone. I took that as a good sign. "I was hoping to talk to you."

"And I was hoping to talk to you," I replied. His shoulders stiffened again, and his brow furrowed as his gaze narrowed with suspicion. Apparently, that was the wrong thing to say. "Let me get the tea. I'll be back momentarily."

There was a small kitchen between the library and the main office. It didn't have much, but it was easy enough to find some tea. I could almost imagine baking here. Nothing too extravagant. A few loaves of bread, muffins, maybe pastries. It would be tight, but it could work. I loved baking. Perhaps I could do it and wouldn't need to hire someone. The ideas wouldn't stop coming now that they'd started. Guests first, I reminded myself. The water boiled as I considered my current guest. What could he possibly want? The answer wasn't going to appear in this kitchen.

I collected two mugs, poured the water, and rolled my shoulders back as I summoned all the confidence I had with my return to the library.

Vincent sat quietly where I'd left him, his gaze fixed out the window, on the sea.

"So, what did you want to talk about?" I asked as he took the offered mug.

It seemed he was doing everything he could to avoid making eye contact with me. I couldn't help but remember Seraphina's words from last night. *He couldn't keep his eyes off her.* Well, he certainly could now. It was unclear if that was a point for me or not.

"This view is breathtaking," he said as he thanked me again for the drink.

"It's one of my favorite places on the property."

"One of?" A touch of warmth flooded back into his gaze with the question, like maybe he couldn't help himself, but I was reminded how quickly his mood seemed to change.

"I don't think you came by to hear the list of my favorite locations at Cliff House. How did you know where to find me?"

He shrugged. "Your boss mentioned your name last night when she called you. It didn't take much searching after that."

I took the seat across from him in another plush chair. "And you're a reporter. You couldn't help but investigate."

He flinched again at that.

"So..." I prompted. He had found me first. I couldn't help thinking it would be better if he said whatever he came for before I asked for my favor.

Indecision was plain on his pale face. And maybe regret? He wrapped his long fingers around his mug. "You go first."

"Well." That was easier said than done. "I know we didn't get off to the best start, but I wanted to ask you a favor."

He seemed to steel himself for whatever came next, but the thin line of his mouth and the returning tick in his jaw said he was preparing himself for something truly awful. Maybe this was a bad idea.

You sure you're up for the challenge? Darius's words echoed in my mind.

I had to try.

"Well," I started again. Setting down my mug on the end table, I lifted my hands. "I can see you appreciate the beauty of this place. I need your help to save it."

Vincent looked around the room, his gaze cautious. "Save it? What's wrong with it?"

"It has no guests," I clarified.

His eyes narrowed. "I need more information. I thought you worked at the tavern."

I forced a smile. This was going better than I'd hoped. "I work at the tavern, but I've also been groundskeeper here since moving to the city. I was recently promoted to manager. As you can see"—I waved my hands around us—"it's quite empty. Even with the influx of travelers to Sandrin, no one has come to inquire about vacancy."

His head snapped up. "No one?"

I shook my head. He was trying hard not to look interested. His gaze roamed the room again, carefully avoiding mine. It landed on the water outside the window. "I can't believe that, with this view."

"I didn't want to believe it either, but it's true. The manager quit. He couldn't take the failure." I wasn't sure how to proceed. Yesterday, as part of my apology, I'd told him it was my father I was angry at, not him, but it seemed too much to explain our history and what saving this inn would mean to me.

Vincent seemed to put some pieces together as his careful gaze slowly met mine. The warmth was back. "This is your father's property," he said cautiously.

"Yes."

He appeared to understand what that meant. He couldn't know the details, but he apparently remembered the strain I'd mentioned between Darius and me. More than that, he wasn't shutting me down. I swallowed thickly and reminded myself of my promise to be honest with him if I asked for this favor. "He knows I've been interested in running it for years." I forced the words out. "If I can get it filled by Long Night, he'll keep me as manager. If not, he'll close and sell it."

Vincent's gaze was calculating. He smiled in a way that didn't quite reach his eyes as he spoke. Like what he was about to say was a joke at his expense, and he wanted to beat me to the punchline. "You know who I am," he offered. "And you want me to recommend this place."

I considered Daisy's words from last night—that he didn't take suggestions. It couldn't be this easy, could it? Daisy knew him. She wouldn't have tried to scare me away. His face was masked of any emotion. He appeared carved from stone, for all I could read. Maybe more telling, his wind hadn't appeared since he'd entered the inn. "Yes..." I said slowly, drawing it out.

The sharp lines of his face were momentarily drenched with disappointment. Then, his expression quickly morphed back to calculating. At least he hadn't already declined. I readied to fill the growing silence, but he spoke again.

"I need something from you, too. Maybe we can strike a bargain."

In my nerves surrounding my request, I'd forgotten he wanted to discuss a topic of his own. Now, he made it clear he wanted something of me as I did him. Given my request, I couldn't exactly be upset about that. My heartbeat spiked as he let the silence hang between us. His appraising gaze had words tumbling from my lips. "What do you need from me?"

My mind roamed through the possibilities and came up with none. He knew nothing about me. What skills would I have that he required?

Then I remembered how he'd found me. Seraphina had called my name. Warning bells started ringing in my mind. He was old fae. He knew my name. The only piece of information important to him would be...my surname.

My fears were confirmed when he finally said, "I need your help on an article investigating your father."

8

Vincent

Her already pale face went white as a sheet at the mention of her father. Something uncomfortable churned in my stomach at the sight. *She wanted to use me first*, I reminded myself. My wind raged at the assertion, but it didn't have a leg to stand on. She'd known my name when I showed up today, and had planned to ask me a favor. I'd thought she was different, but I'd been wrong. She was like the rest, only interested in my ability to recommend.

It bothered me more than I cared to dwell on.

I shoved down the useless emotions that bubbled in my throat. *She'll get her recommendation—it's what she wanted. This way, at least, we're both getting something out of it.* I swallowed another sip of now lukewarm tea. Maybe if I told myself this enough times, I'd feel better about it.

"What's the story?" Her voice was flat, lifeless. Whatever part of her had graced me with welcoming chatter and made me tea in an attempt to salvage our disastrous first meeting was gone. Part of me wanted it back.

Pushing my hand through my hair, I leaned forward. Asking for more information suggested she was considering my bargain, no matter how much pain was on her face.

You put it there. My wind surged violently in my chest, yet it didn't try to break free. It seemed to sense things weren't quite settled here. *No, Darius put it there,* I reminded myself. This was part of why we'd come. If she looked this hurt at the mention of her father, she deserved to know what I knew. She deserved to determine for herself whether he was involved.

"You know about the proposal for a magic school in Sandrin?" I asked. "Not limited to only those traditionally educated by the fae courts?"

She nodded, pulling that ridiculous shawl tighter around her shoulder. "A magic school for humans, half-fae, and those of multiple courts."

"The Bayside Times received an unsubstantiated tip that your father was bribing the governor to stop its progress."

I didn't think it was possible, but her face went whiter.

Before I knew it, my tea was on the end table, my forearms propped on my legs as I leaned farther forward, interlacing my fingers to stop myself from reaching for her. "I have to stress that the tip is unverified." I didn't need to mention what I'd overheard in the stairwell yet.

"Then why are you investigating it?"

There were a lot of things I could say. I didn't want someone with prejudices doing it. It was my job. I shook my head, letting my hair fall over my face. If we were doing this, I was going to be honest. Our bargain would benefit both parties, and I would ensure she knew that. I lifted my head, meeting her earnest gaze. "I've been trying to write something other than 'Benefits of Magic' for over a year. This is my chance—the story I was given." I swallowed. It was odd to admit such a private desire to a stranger. I knew I'd done the right thing when my wind quieted with the admission.

She looked...understanding.

Too much raw truth hung between us. I strived to wipe some of it away, like it was a stain that needed cleaning. "I was the only one on the paper who won't assume he's guilty from the beginning." Admittedly, the stairwell conversation had tipped my opinion a bit, but still, I'd do a proper investigation.

"Because you're old fae?" she asked.

"Yes." I cleared my throat. "Others on the paper don't have the best opinions of the old fae families in Sandrin. I recognize some of it is deserved, but it's not universal that all old fae oppose change."

She tilted her head. "So, you're different? You're not like them?"

I wasn't entirely sure if she meant I wasn't like other old fae or like others on the paper. My wind swirled as I considered her question. I wished I knew the answer to either. As far as old fae went, my parents and I saw things very differently. So much so that I'd moved out of our family home last year. Leaving was a big deal for a fae, especially since I was my father's heir. Few were aware—my parents had kept it quiet to save the public embarrassment. I didn't care so long as I was free of them. Moving out and working at the paper hadn't magically granted me clarity about all things fae and human, though. I still didn't know where I fit.

"I'm not sure." I shook my head. My honesty about such personal topics was uncharacteristic. Usually, I'd avoid them, but something about her drew me in and churned at my insides until verbal vomit spewed forth. Even with the offensively bright patterns of the mismatched blanket wrapped around her, she was enchanting.

No, I couldn't think that way. Maybe we'd had a moment last night before she'd been called away, a shared smirk and understanding of my magic. It surged inside me at the thought, but I tamped it down. Whatever might have been, I'd most certainly ruined it with my request to investigate her father. I gritted my teeth, unsure if that bothered me.

She ruined it first, though. All she wanted was my recommendation. I'd lost count of the number of times I had thought people liked me only to realize they wanted something from me instead. Our bargain would be transactional, nothing more. I'd cling to that.

"What would my help investigating him entail?" she asked.

"I'd need to get into Pierce House, probably look in his office."

She stared blankly.

"Even if you can't access his financial records, I only need time there alone. I know what to look for." I'd been raised to run my family's estate. I was sure Darius's records were similar.

Her bright blue eyes blinked faster, almost like she was holding back tears. Wind ruffled my hair and hers. It was the first time it had made itself known in our conversation. I tilted my head as I considered why. Then Luna's hair swirled, and a smile broke the sadness that had crept across her features. Her hand raised as if...

"Are you trying to pet my wind?" I asked, dumbfounded.

She glared at me, pulling that hideous shawl closer. "Maybe. It was being good." Her words were defensive, but she was smiling. "When do you need to know?" she asked, changing subjects.

"Know what?"

"Know about the bargain?"

My brow furrowed. "What is there to know? Either we do it or we don't."

She ran a hand through her hair, pushing the out-of-place blond streaks back. "I don't know if I can get you into Pierce House." She folded her arms across her chest.

The picture of her name on a separate page in the court record flashed in my mind. I knew there was strife between father and daughter, but maybe I'd miscalculated how much.

She shook her head again. "I've never been to the family home. I don't know if I can get you in. And even if I could, I don't know where anything is. If that's what you need in this bargain, I can't help you."

I am an asshole of the highest order. Wind rushed through me in agreement, like the bottom was dropping out of my seat. Words flew from my mouth without thought. "If you're willing to try then I am." I held up my arms, gesturing to the inn. "You'll have to talk to him about this place, won't you? We can work on your piece and only publish it when both sides of the bargain are met."

She studied me, and her bright blue gaze was penetrating in a way I didn't care for. I broke from it only to be captivated by her mouth as she sucked the inside of her lip in consideration.

"What's the full bargain?" She folded her fingers in her lap. "What would I get out of helping you?"

I bristled at how directly she spoke of the exchange, but that was the point—this was transactional. Of course we needed to outline the terms of whatever bargain we struck. I looked around the room and at her. "You want fae to come to this place?"

"I want anyone to come. I want to spread the word to all potential guests," she said. "You may write your column for the fae, but I assure you, *everyone* in Sandrin follows your recommendation."

My cheeks heated at the compliment. At least, I thought it was a compliment. "Yes, well." I looked around the room again. The inn needed cleaning, but it had charm. I could sell this place. It didn't even bother me that I was bargaining away a recommendation. Cliff House Inn was the kind of hidden gem I'd select for my column. The problem was that my recommendations were usually half about the product and half about the proprietor. Readers loved to connect with the person behind the product. They loved a good story. My gaze landed on the ostentatiously patterned blanket she still wore as a shawl. "We might need to update your style to help you better sell your old fae heritage."

She flinched like I'd slapped her. That was the first time it occurred to me that she might not consider herself old fae. It wasn't that far-fetched of a conclusion if she'd never been to Pierce House and didn't claim the family page in the court record. I kept misstepping with that. She held more confidence than anyone I knew, old fae or otherwise. The idea that she might not see herself that way kept slipping through my fingers.

"I—" I wasn't sure what to say, but she cut me off.

"No, don't hold back now. You said what you meant." She stood, letting the shawl fall from her shoulders as she moved toward the windows. The dress she wore underneath was also colorful, if not as bad as the wrap. "I won't insult your investigative skills. I'm sure you've done your homework. It's why you thought I'd agree to investigate my father in the first place. I'm half-fae. I don't count myself as one of them, but if you think to sell the inn I'll have to sell myself as such...fine."

I wasn't sure how to recover from that. My fingers twitched on the armrest as I tried to consider my following words better. "I don't know if you've read many of my recommendations, but I've done a few that weren't fae-focused. They didn't catch on the same. The products weren't as successful." I glanced at my favorite boots, remembering my disappointment when that article had run. "I'm only suggesting what gives you the best chance at success."

She didn't turn around, still looking at the sea. "I'll try whatever it takes to save this place. We can do it your way, so long as it works."

I stood. "We have a deal, then?"

Finally, she turned to face me. Her previously inviting expression was gone, making me feel unwelcome here. Maybe she was better at being old fae than she realized. "So, you'll prepare me for the attention of the fae. When you think I'm ready—before Long Night—you'll feature me and the inn in your column?"

"When you're ready, and you get me access to Pierce House." Something like a cold wind rushed up my spine, a prickling sensation I wasn't entirely comfortable with. It wasn't the playful comfort of my wind. It was just foreboding.

"Agreed." She held out her hand.

I wondered briefly if we needed to clarify that any romantic inclination sparked last night would need to be put on hold during this business arrangement. My cheeks flushed at my stupidity. She only wanted a recommendation. The sharp lines of her previously open face told me that romance was far from her mind.

Fine. I slipped my hand into hers. Wind wrapped around them and then spiraled up my arm. I could only assume it did the same to her, as she shivered and glanced longingly at the shawl still piled on the chair.

We were doing this. "Agreed."

9

Luna

Days later, I still stewed from the bargain struck with Vincent. *We might need to update your style to help you sell your old fae heritage better.* His words pulled at the seams of defensive stitches I had in place for whenever the old fae were mentioned. Convincing myself I didn't need them was one thing. Being told I needed to become one of them to save my inn was another. Hearing it from someone who was using me to get close to my father, a male he knew I didn't get along with, was icing on the cake.

I shook my head, working my frustration out on kneading bread dough. The counter was a mess, and I added to it, sprinkling a little more flour on the surface. As my palms pushed into the dough, I tried to push in my anxiety about this bargain. When I folded it to continue the process, I imagined I was covering up my worries and hiding them away. The bargain was my only choice. I needed Vincent's help, and this was his condition.

Hiding my nerves in bread-making didn't seem to work, though. I gave the dough a stern glare like it had let me down, even as I continued to knead. My fingers slid into the mixture. It surrounded and stuck to them—still not ready. I needed to speed up. This wasn't the only item on my list today.

No matter how disappointed I was, I could admit I needed Vincent's help. I'd spent the last few days studying the other inns in Sandrin and their offerings. While I believed Cliff House had a chance, I would be up against some strong opponents. Winchester Inn was by far the most popular. It was directly on the path where the eastern road poured into Sandrin. The inn itself wasn't much to look at. It was clean and had no particular style, but nothing could top its location. Convenience to travelers couldn't be understated.

On the way into the city from the south, there was another popular inn, Earthbend. It was run by a Suden couple and tended to cater to friends and family visiting the military base on the city's southern tip.

These two were my main competitors. Others scattered the city streets, but they were extra rooms above taverns or boarding houses, offering less comfort than a traditional inn. I would focus on giving visitors a reason to bypass these two easily accessible inns and come to Cliff House. One good thing was that both were almost full. Soon, visitors wouldn't have a choice but to keep searching. I wasn't too proud to work with that, either.

I pulled my hand back from the dough to test its tack again. Seeing it was still sticky, I kept kneading.

I tried to remember my childhood visits to Cliff House. Though we'd stayed in the cottage, we'd often encountered guests on the beach. The inn had always been full. I tried to remember some of them—what had drawn them to the inn, their stories. Most recollections of guests were too fuzzy; I'd been pretty young. I shied away from some of our clearer memories, like our last visit. Our haste to leave after Darius's impromptu arrival had put a damper on the event in my mind. He never visited us when we were at Cliff House. It seemed he and Mom had some understanding. He must have at least known to stay away the weeks we were there. It was further proof he'd rather have nothing to do with me, as if I needed any.

I kneaded faster as the memory snuck in.

Mom had woken me up for a moonlit swim. She knew I loved the full moon—said I'd been born under one. "We need to celebrate you." She pointed to the sky through the window.

Caught up in her enthusiasm, I was too young to care whether this was a good or bad idea. I dressed for swimming and followed her by lantern light down the wooden staircase to the beach. The lantern didn't help much. The moon's light was so bright, it was all I could see. Mom laughed loudly, splashing into the water. She was giddy, free in a way I rarely saw her. Worry usually hung heavy on her brow. I didn't know the context, but I knew enough to understand that the weight was lifted while we were here.

"Come in, the water is nice!" she called.

I didn't hesitate, throwing myself into the softly crashing waves of the sea. We played for what felt like hours beneath the moon. If only the memory ended there, I could have filed it away as a happy one, but as we lost track of time, the tides changed. The current strengthened, and before I knew what was happening, my next dive into the waves had me pulled away by a strong current.

I thrashed to the surface, gasping for air. Another wave crashed, pushing me back under. Up and down had no meaning. Water surrounded me, beating me back. I surfaced again, unable to open my eyes—to find Mom—before I was pulled back under.

Her screams reached my ears, though.

I was sure it had only been seconds, but it felt like so much longer. Mom couldn't get to me, to the cove around the cliff where the current dragged. I was sure she tried her best, sure she tried everything she could to get to me, but it wasn't enough.

I should have drowned.

The next thing I knew, I was sinking. No more breaking through the surf, no more moments of breath. My body fell like a stone beneath the waves. I rolled myself into a compact ball and lay against the sea floor. Water surrounded me, but I was sure it also poured from my eyes.

And then I could breathe.

I'd never understand what happened or how he was there, but the next thing I knew, Darius was pulling me from a whirlpool in the sea. I was in its eye, curled like a cat on the seabed. The water that previously tried to drown me was pushed back on all sides, giving me access to fresh air. I didn't know how long I'd lain there before he found me. The scent of moonflower and juniper surrounded me—an unfortunately comforting scent for his magic. He pulled me from the center of the storm, dried me, wrapped me in warmth, and told me everything would be alright.

I remembered waking up in a room at the inn later with Mom tucked next to me. We'd stormed out shortly after.

It was hard to admit, even to myself, but I'd clung to Darius like a life raft in a storm. In that moment, he had been one. His magic had dried me as he carried me from the beach. It had flooded me with a familiarity I'd been too young to know was false.

I pulled my hand from the dough again, testing it. That round of kneading had done the trick. The memory had swept me away, and the bread benefited. Many would consider the experience of near-drowning traumatic on its own, but for me, it was the experience of Darius saving me that stuck.

The look of concern on his face as he pulled me from the sea was haunting. I would have sworn he cared. And if he cared that much, why did he ignore me for the rest of my life? How could someone turn their emotions on and off like that?

It was all too similar to what Vincent had done when he'd arrived at the inn to strike our bargain. Maybe that was a trait of the old fae. Another reason I'd never count myself as one of them. My thoughts were interrupted by a knock on the cottage door.

"Come in," I called, picking the remaining dough from my hand. I moved to rinse them under hot water as my friends entered. Seraphina had a mop in one hand and a bucket filled with bottles of cleaning liquids in the other. Evelyn had a broom, a feather duster, and many rags tucked into an overly large belt.

"What are you two..." I trailed off, realizing why they were here.

"We're here to help clean. I assume you haven't heard from the fae yet?" Seraphina said.

I'd seen them shortly after my bargain with Vincent, giving them most of the details and listing everything I had to do. "Not yet. He said he needed to create a plan."

Seraphina pressed her lips together in a thin line, telling me all I needed to know about her opinion of Vincent. "Did he at least take your input?"

"Yes. Though I told him I wanted no part in his plan to make me seem old fae. I did share the information I had about the other inns in the city."

She looked like she'd say more when Evelyn cut in. "I think we should start in the library." Her hair was pulled back in a smooth, low ponytail, and she had a look of determination that I didn't understand.

"Is something not going well with your research project?" I asked. She worked part-time at the tavern and spent the rest of her time in the Vesten Library. Though she was half-Vesten, her scholarly achievements were unmatched and had earned her the position.

"You could say that," she said, not making eye contact. "I'd like to clean, though. I think that will help."

I smiled, very in tune with that feeling.

"Looks like Luna was already working through something with her bread dough here," Seraphina said. "We didn't mean to interrupt. I knew you needed help, and this was our only free afternoon."

"You're never interrupting." I waved her worry off. "This has to rise, and if you're offering to help clean, I am accepting. Let's get started."

Evelyn's suggestion won, and we started in the library. This would ease us into the cleaning process. It was by far the best-kept room, probably because before Byrd had banned me from the inn, it was where I'd sneak in to read with the view of the sea. By nature of having been used the most, it looked less sad.

"This is truly a stunning view." Evelyn removed books to dust the shelves. She held them reverently, then placed each back where she found it. "I can't believe people aren't flocking to stay here."

"It never made sense." Seraphina swept the floor. "This is by far the best view in town, and back in its heyday, it also had the most charming rooms for the best rate. I can't figure out what happened."

"The rooms are decidedly less charming now," I warned. "Byrd stopped any general upkeep. There was a leak in the northernmost room."

Seraphina scratched the back of her neck as she glanced at

her supplies. "We didn't bring anything for patching or repair, but I'm sure we can get that taken care of in the next week."

This was part of why I loved Seraphina. She always knew what to do. When I met her my first day in Sandrin, she'd walked right up to me and said that I looked like I could use a friend, and she happened to be in the market for one. We hadn't looked back since.

It shouldn't have surprised me they showed up ready to help with the more mundane aspects of this challenge. Their presence soothed my nerves in a way neither baking nor list-making did. I was happy with our progress on the first floor, but not even my friend could prevent my heartbeat ratcheting when I realized it was time to head upstairs.

"I'm warning you two, it's bad."

Evelyn shook the mop at me like it was a weapon. "We're ready."

We turned left and marched with determination to the end of the hall. As soon as I saw the door, I remembered it was locked. It had slipped my mind with Vincent and our bargain. "Actually,"—I pointed across the hall—"let's start over here."

"What's wrong with that one?" Evelyn asked.

"It's locked." I hesitated. "I couldn't open it last time. I tried everything."

Evelyn's head tilted. She loved a mystery. I should have known this would be right up her alley. "Locked how?" She stepped closer to the door. "Can I touch it?"

"I did." I shrugged. "It didn't hurt me, but it also didn't open."

"So, I take it you don't mean locked and missing the key." Seraphina rested her hand on her hip.

I gave her what I hoped was an apologetic smile and shook my head. "The actual door lock isn't secured. I peeked through the keyhole."

"Lovely." Seraphina's voice dripped with sarcasm. "You have a mysteriously locked door."

Evelyn ignored Seraphina's sass. She wrapped her fingers around the handle and twisted. Nothing happened. She tried again and pushed a little harder against the door with each new attempt. I saw the exact moment this became more interesting to her than cleaning.

Seraphina and I shared a glance. "I think we should leave her to it."

Knowing she was correct, I laughed and followed her into the bedroom across the hall to clean.

"This is...worse than I thought." She pulled back the drapes to let in the light. I didn't know why they had ever been closed. The sea view should be the first thing to greet guests upon entering this room.

"I know. I meant to come over here yesterday to get started, but I went to the other big inns in town instead."

"You wanted to do your own research, not trust the old fae's?" She elbowed me as she dusted the flat surfaces.

"It's not about him," I said a little too quickly.

She gave me a knowing smile. "I'm sorry that went so sideways on you. It was better to find out what he wanted from you early, though, wasn't it?"

I wasn't sure. I kept telling myself the same thing, but Seraphina's comment from the night we met kept playing on repeat. I had told him about Darius—with little to no provocation. It had been so long since I'd connected with someone so quickly, even given the unfortunate circumstances of our meeting. I couldn't help but think it was a missed opportunity. I shrugged. We'd both shown where our priorities lay, I guessed.

"It is what it is. If he recommends the inn, it can only help."

"What about helping him with Darius? Have you thought about how you'll do that?"

"I have. I just really don't want to do it, but if it's to save this place"—I glanced around the room—"I will."

Seraphina nodded. She knew what the inn meant to me. "What's your plan?"

"I'll try to find something juicy about the inn to report. I realized I've never...asked to talk to him...asked for an invite to Pierce House." Seraphina's brow furrowed as I continued. "He's never invited me, but I don't know. I was thinking that would be a place to start." I shrugged again.

"Do you think it will be that simple?"

"I don't think asking Darius for something is simple," I said defensively.

Seraphina raised her hands in surrender. "Fine. Remember we're both here when you need us."

"Luna!" Evelyn called from the hallway.

Letting the conversation drop, we returned to the locked bedroom door. Evelyn's smooth black ponytail was mussed, and I couldn't imagine what she'd gotten into in the minutes we'd left her alone out here. Glancing down, I saw a burn mark on the wood door and ashes smeared across her skirt.

My hands were on my hips before I could stop the motion. "What did you do?" I asked, half worried but mostly holding back a laugh.

"This door is magically sealed," she announced.

It was my turn to tilt my head in question. "What? That can't be right."

"It is. I tested it. And I know I haven't spoken much about my research, but..." She took a deep breath. "I'm one of the foremost experts in blood magic, especially when it's connected to fae elemental magic. This door connects both, like a spell, to the inn. I'm sure of it."

Horrifying news poured from her lips, but I wouldn't skip the information she'd let slip. "You're one of the foremost experts on blood magic?"

Seraphina's mouth was open at those words as well. "Why are you working at my tavern?"

"That wasn't the actual point of my sentence," Evelyn replied.

"It's pretty damn relevant," Seraphina said.

I laughed. "We will be talking and celebrating that part more later, but what does this mean, exactly?" I was still reeling from Evelyn's revelation. She was usually so reserved about her work. All half-fae were different, so I didn't pry. I had no magic, but Evelyn had some. She could wield fire, evidenced by the burn marks on the floor, but she couldn't shift, which was a second part of Vesten fae magic. I'd assumed she hadn't spoken of her studies because it involved shifting or some magic she wasn't comfortable with. Now, I wondered if she didn't want to intimidate us. We would be fixing that.

"It means that blood magic was enacted on this inn." She put her hands on her hips, matching my pose. "And the fact that this door is locked shows it's active."

"Is there a way to figure out what the magic is?" Seraphina asked.

"I haven't been able to yet. I need to do some research." Evelyn tucked a strand of hair falling from her ponytail behind her ear. "I'm sorry. I should go start now." She then turned and headed down the hall.

While it wasn't unusual for Evelyn to slip away for research at a moment's notice, something about this had my hair standing on end. There was something she wasn't saying. It took time for my brain and mouth to connect. I had so many questions.

"Evelyn," I called as she walked down the hall toward the staircase. I jogged to catch up to her. "Do you think it's...bad magic?"

I was unfamiliar with this kind of magic. The fae courts each represented an element, but humans could do all manner of interesting things using blood magic. Recent reports from the Compass Points indicated that even more could be accomplished when the fae elements mingled with blood magic. I guess it shouldn't surprise me that someone was studying the connection between the two.

"I don't think it's good." Evelyn's gaze shifted toward the door again.

Seraphina came to my side. Her hand was on my shoulder, and her gaze lingered between me and Evelyn. "Evelyn won't say so because she's a researcher, and her hypothesis is not substantiated enough even to guess, but I'm not." She gave me a look that said *don't shoot the messenger*. "I'd wager she believes unlocking that door is the key to guests returning to the inn."

Evelyn glared at Seraphina but didn't refute the statement. "I need to go."

I nodded, and she scurried down the stairs. I could only assume she was headed for the Vesten Library.

A magically sealed room, somehow preventing guests from staying at the inn? What had I gotten myself into? Maybe my bargain with Vincent wouldn't matter after all.

10

Vincent

It was as if she existed to vex me.

Luna floated down the street toward me. She may have rid herself of the offending shawl, but her outfit was no less vibrant. The cropped black sweater might have been fine, but she wore it with the brightest skirt I'd ever seen. Pinks and purples swirled through the layers. It was the exact opposite of everything behind me in the store's window front display. My brow furrowed as I wondered how intentionally she'd selected this outfit.

Our objective at Fae Fashions today was to purchase her a few pieces that would make her seem more old fae. It appeared we had a lot of work to do. Her dark hair fell in untamed waves, and those pieces of silver hair drew me to her bright blue eyes. I didn't have to search to see a spark of challenge there.

This was going to be a problem.

"Hey, Vincent." I was sure she was mocking me as her gaze roamed the store window, her lips curving into a smile.

"Thanks for meeting me," I said curtly. My mind was spinning on where to go from here. Should I even take her into the store?

She smiled in a way that said we both knew why she was here. After all, we'd struck a bargain, and this was part one in accomplishing it.

"Vincent, are you coming in?" a voice called over my shoulder. Any chance we had of escaping was gone with my sister's question.

"We'll be in momentarily, Skye."

I turned my icy glare back on Luna. If we were going in, I wouldn't let her have this battle with my sister.

"You agreed to this, remember?"

Luna's gaze met mine, and any warmth was gone. "I'm here to save my inn, Vincent. We already discussed this. I'll do what you think is best."

My gaze narrowed on her skirt. She followed it, and her fingers smoothed over the bright fabric. I saw the moment she realized what I was upset about. Her cheeks pinked in a way that had nothing to do with the brisk breeze. My wind surged, wanting to rush to her and shelter her from whatever she felt.

"I see." She swallowed, glancing again between her skirt and the window. "I'm more than willing to do whatever you think is best. I know it doesn't look like I'm trying to fit in, but I didn't consider it before leaving the cottage."

Asshole. Table for one. For the first time, I wished I was Suden fae to burrow into the earth and never be found. My wind surged in agreement.

Of *course* she wasn't mocking me. She had just been confidently herself upon her arrival. As I watched her hands nervously tangle in the skirt, I knew I'd taken that from her, and hated myself a little for it. My wind's silence on the matter was confirmation enough.

"Right," I said, with no recovery whatsoever, "let's get this over with."

She nodded and followed me into the shop. Thankfully, we were the only ones at the boutique and had free reign. Skye smiled at us from behind the counter. She stepped forward, offering her hand to Luna.

"I'm Skye, Vincent's sister. It's wonderful to meet you."

I winced from my position behind Skye. Luna's gaze shifted briefly to mine as she greeted my sister warmly.

"Vincent says you were looking for more traditional old fae outfits." She gave Luna a brief once over, somehow doing so without judgment. "Are you alright if we tone this down a bit?" Skye bit her lip as she glanced around the store.

I tried to see it through Luna's eyes. The colors were all muted in comparison: browns, whites, grays, and navy blues.

Luna smiled. "I'll be happy with whatever you suggest."

Though I hadn't thought it fit her style, I'd selected this place because of the sweater she'd worn when I met her. "You had a piece from here, didn't you?"

Her head tilted, and then her lip curled into a smirk. It didn't quite fit her face. "That wasn't mine," she said. "Just something I was required to wear to meet with Darius."

A tempest swirled in my chest as understanding dawned. Her own father had toned her down to meet with him. This was a mistake. I shook my head, wondering if I should call the whole thing off. The article could focus on the land—on the cliffs and the sea—I could leave her out of it. Once people got to the inn, they'd fall in love with it.

You're selling her as old fae to get them there.

"It's fine." She waved her hand. "That sweater was nice. Let's see what else Skye can find."

"You only need a few," I hedged. "We need you to be seen in a few fae establishments over the coming weeks. You'll only need to blend for those events."

Skye gave me a questioning look. I'd told her I was bringing a friend who wanted some new clothes. I hadn't thought she'd approve of my current deal with Luna. She'd told me in no uncertain terms how she felt about the other time I'd bargained with my column.

Even though she'd benefited from my last bargain, whether she liked it or not.

Skye and Luna walked around the boutique. Skye suggested the most unique styles within the more neutral colors. An off-the-shoulder sweater, a cropped sweater with a draped neck, and my favorite, a long cardigan-like jacket. I may have bargained to get Skye this job, but she was good at it. She watched Luna's reaction to everything she suggested and adapted her recommendations based on what she saw. My prior bargain with the column may have wounded my pride, but I was glad, at least, Skye got this from it.

The pair moved to the dressing rooms in the back while I took a seat on one of the chairs I assumed was precisely for my use. Well, maybe not precisely. Partners, lovers, and friends probably waited in these chairs. Not whatever I was. I stewed over that, wondering if Luna and I would ever stop assuming the worst of each other and regain that small slice of intimacy we'd found the night we met.

Unlikely.

I was too far from them to hear their conversation. There was more giggling than I'd anticipated. Luna did have that way about her. Friendly. Adored anywhere she went. It had appeared that way at the tavern. The older gentleman next to me at the bar and the owner had seemed protective of her. I bet she was the type who always saw the best in people, too. I bristled. Except with me, of course. My wind spun like a top, tilting this way and that as if to say *You didn't deserve it.*

Sinking farther in the chair, I folded my arms across my

chest. I was glad Skye was welcomed into Luna's warmth, at least.

Lost in thought, I didn't hear anyone approach. "Vincent, I didn't know you'd be here." The voice was one I, unfortunately, knew too well. My wind was immediately on edge, slicing through me, wrestling to break free. It would not be a playful wind if it slipped its leash.

"Kristin." I stood to greet her. Although she may have played me in our last interaction, there was no need to let her know.

She breezed toward me with no hesitation. Her long blond hair fell straight down her back, and her outfit, a sophisticated black dress, had her looking like old fae—even though she wasn't. Was this really what I wanted Luna to be like? The thought caught me off guard as Kristin's hands rested gently on my chest with an ownership I didn't care for. She placed featherlight kisses on both of my cheeks. I wanted to step back, to push her away, to do anything so we didn't appear quite as familiar, but doing so would only prove she'd affected me.

"You should have told me you were coming in."

I'd selected this time precisely because Skye had said Kristin wouldn't be here. I wondered what had gone wrong.

"What brings you in? Finally here to invite me on one of your secret recommendation tours?" She smiled. "Or maybe to your family's solstice party?"

I let my wind cool me from the inside, positive a blush touched my cheeks. This was the problem with Kristin. While many had taught me they only valued me for the recommendations, few had reached shamelessly for my column and my family name. That honor belonged to Kristin only—and I'd been the last to see it.

It had been an...unfortunate lesson to learn.

She'd asked me something. What was it? Oh, inviting herself to both an Andiveron family event and my work. I shook my head, feeling foolish that there had been a time where I would have offered her both. Finding the words for this situation was proving more challenging than I thought.

"Vincent, I think we're about—" Skye cut off when she noticed Kristin with her hands still resting on my chest.

"Skye, I was telling your brother how naughty he was for not mentioning he'd be here. I hope you were unaware as well."

The look Skye gave me was apologetic. Kristin must not have been expected. I took a step back, freeing myself from Kristin's touch. Only then did I realize Luna was standing with Skye, a pile of clothing draped over her arm and a curious look on her face. How much had she heard?

"It was a happy surprise when Vincent and Luna arrived." Skye turned fully, taking the heap of clothes from Luna's arms. Whatever passed between the two was a mystery to me, but when Skye stepped out of the way with the clothing in her arms, Luna was the picture of old fae, and she smiled...at me.

This was the first time Kristin took notice of Luna. Her brow arched in question as Luna, in a black skirt and matching sweater that separated at the back, sauntered toward me. She held my gaze, something earnest in those bright blue eyes. Like she was asking for permission? I had no idea what she wanted, but I must have responded appropriately because she slid into place between Kristin and me. She looped her arm around me, pulling my hand across to her back.

My hand met exposed skin. The back of her sweater parted in a daring display. She might be all old fae fashion from the front, but she'd found a way to remain Luna with the outfit. Wild wind whipped in my chest. I didn't stop it as it blew the hair from her shoulders in an embarrassingly possessive display.

Her brightly painted lips curved into a radiant smile, and she snuggled closer to my chest. Unsure what was happening, I did what came naturally: I let my fingers slide across her lower back, curl around her waist, and pull her close. Then I leaned in, taking in her scent. There was no moonflower and juniper this time; she smelled like a fresh breeze by the sea.

"Vincent..." Kristin's tone was unamused. "You haven't introduced your friend."

"Oh," I said with genuine surprise, having completely forgotten Kristin was there. "This is Luna—" I cut myself off, unsure if Luna wanted to share her surname. It would come out eventually with the article; there was no way to make the declaration we wanted without making the family connection, but that didn't mean she had to do it today.

"I'm Luna Pierce." She held her hand out to Kristin.

Kristin's jaw flexed at the surname. She knew the old fae families better than most. I could only assume she spent her free time searching for an heir to one that she could sink her claws into. It had worked with me for a while.

When Kristin said nothing, only briefly clutching her hand in a semblance of greeting, Luna glanced back at me. "We should go, Vincent."

"Did you get everything you need?"

She shared a look with Skye. "These will work."

"Wonderful." I clapped my hands together, pretending this had gone according to plan. "I have another stop in mind, and it seems you're already dressed for the occasion."

Kristin gave a terse nod and slipped away from us without another word. Skye handed me the stack of clothing, and her arm slipped into Luna's, their heads bent together to whisper as they walked to the storefront. I was loathe to remove my hand from Luna's back, but clearly, some bond had formed between the women that took precedence over my odd mix of confusion and desire.

"These were perfect, Skye. Thank you," Luna said.

Skye waved her off. "I told you it was about blending, not

changing. We still found a way to be you." She giggled as she added, "Vincent seemed to appreciate it."

Luna flushed, and something swelled in my chest at the sight.

"Thanks for your help back there," Skye whispered.

It took me a minute to understand Luna's dismissive wave. She glanced at me, not quite pity in her gaze, as she replied. "We've all been there. Unfortunately, not everyone is who they seem to be in this city."

My eyes widened, and Luna smirked. "Just because I give people the benefit of the doubt"—she paused, giving me a once over—"usually, doesn't mean I can't tell when someone is abusing it."

She and Skye hugged goodbye, and I stood stupefied as Luna strode down the sidewalk, slipping on a new knee-length jacket as she went. My wind raced to catch up, and her lip tilted in amusement when it reached her. "Come on, Vincent, we've got work to do."

"I don't know what you've gotten yourself into, Vincent, but I am quite sure you're not ready for it," Skye said. "I like her, though." She gave me a soft shove that sent me stumbling out of the shop to meet the fate I'd bargained for.

11

Luna

Wind whipped around my hair as I worked to calm down before Vincent caught up. "What was that?" I mumbled to myself. Vincent's wind swirled in... pleasure, if I didn't know any better. That wasn't helping.

Skye had been so charming. She'd helped me find things that met Vincent's requirements for the fae, but didn't completely dismiss my style.

Then she'd barged into the area where I was changing, her face pale. "She wasn't supposed to be here," she had said in quick, whispered tones. "You have to help him, Luna."

I might not have known what that entailed, but I'd heard the desperation in her voice. When she'd asked me to pretend that Vincent was mine, I'd done so without much thought.

It was all I was thinking about now.

His hand had wrapped possessively around the bare skin at my waist, and the way he had pulled me close and...smelled me...it should have been odd, not hot.

I shook my head again, attempting to free my thoughts as Vincent approached.

"I'm sure I should simply thank you, but I'm also horrified to know what Skye said to you about Kristin," he said quietly.

Of course he was.

"She didn't tell me anything, Vincent. All she said was that Kristin wasn't supposed to be there, and she shoved me out to play your lover."

Our gazes locked even as we kept walking. Something charged swept between us before my glance returned to the path. "Where are we going?" I changed the subject.

"You don't want to know who she was? Why did you do that? You were willing to help with no information?"

"I guess we're not dropping this," I said under my breath.

Wind pushed my hair back playfully as we walked. "I'm confused, Luna. That wasn't exactly part of our bargain."

"Not everything has to be part of our bargain," I said with exasperation. "Sometimes when someone asks for help, you just...help them." I shrugged.

I could feel him sneaking another glance at me, though I didn't meet it. Was accepting help with no strings attached so foreign to him? Maybe it was if I'd overheard that female correctly. She'd been demanding a lot from him, all for the cost of her company. The juice didn't seem worth the squeeze to me, but they clearly had history. So, it had been worth it at some point to Vincent. I couldn't imagine someone demanding so much from me. She'd seemed to target the power of his recommendations and what I could only assume was the power of his family name. Her goal had been clear, and it couldn't feel great to be so blatantly...used.

My cheeks flushed. Hadn't I wanted to blatantly use Vincent for his recommendation? *That's different. We aren't together.* I wasn't sure if that made it better.

"Have you tried the Sweet Solstice Sip?" he asked, changing

the subject and ushering me to the entrance of a grand tavern. We hadn't walked far, but we'd crossed Central Circle and entered the Suden District.

I nodded, unwilling to cop to the fact that I'd read all of his articles and tried most of the items he recommended.

"Today, we're reviewing my recent successes to help us plan how to attack your problem." He spread his arms wide as we walked into the tavern. It was much nicer than Parkview. Thick gold fabric covered the bar stools and chairs. The wood of the bar and tables was a warm brown hue. The walls were covered in vines on the inside. The owners' Suden nature must have been at play; it was stunning. I didn't know where to look until I felt Vincent's hand lightly on my back again, directing me toward the bar.

"This is the tavern that started the craze," he said. It was shortly after midday, in the middle of a work week, and there were nearly no empty seats. My eyes widened.

"That piece came out a week ago and it's this busy?"

He nodded. "I think this was one of my best ideas, although I didn't come up with it alone."

Two stools opened. The man behind the bar smiled as we sat down. "Hey, Vincent."

"Hello, Markus," Vincent replied. "May I introduce Luna?"

He smiled at me in welcome. "Two Solstice Sips?"

"Sounds great," I said.

"Coming right up." Markus turned to prepare the drinks.

"Markus came up with the mix; he was convinced the honey spirit should be used for a solstice celebratory drink," Vincent said. I knew what he'd say next because I'd read his article, but I wasn't sure I wanted him to know that. I let him continue. "He was convinced honey should be the new flavor of the season. Cinnamon and vanilla were out. Honey was in. It wasn't a bad choice, but I had no idea what he'd mix it with."

Markus returned, handing us the drinks. "So, I made Mr.

Tastemaker sit here at this bar and try each of my concoctions until I found one that worked."

Vincent held up his drink in cheers. "And you found it."

"You helped," Markus replied before drifting away to another customer.

"Is that how all of your recommendations work? Is it collaborative like that?" I asked.

He shook his head. "No, Markus was unique. I'd recommended something of his brother's before. He told me he didn't need my recommendation so much as my taste to tell me what worked, but I loved it so much I gave him both."

I considered that, taking a sip of the drink. So many people seemed only to know him or need him for his ability to recommend. I wondered how many people he had who didn't care about his column. At least not for themselves. Even Skye had said that his column had helped her get her job. However, I was sure that wasn't the whole story, and her adoration for her brother was obvious.

It must be tiring, though.

"Hope that wasn't too far of a walk." He interrupted my thoughts. His gaze was fixed on my boots.

"Why don't you ask what you want to ask?" I said, taking another sip of the drink. Eyeing my boots the way he was, I knew what he wanted to know, and I wouldn't make this easy for him.

He coughed. "When did you..." He cleared his throat and started again. "Do you find..."

"Oh my goodness, Vincent. This is uncomfortable to listen to." I leaned forward and gently pushed his shoulder. He grabbed my hand with his free one, holding it there.

"Then put me out of my misery and tell me if you bought the boots based on my column." His smile was hesitant. It was mesmerizing. I thought it was the first real smile I'd seen on him. He was beautiful without it, but when genuine mirth was present, it was like staring directly at the sun. I had to look away.

"I read the column and bought them after." I sat up straight. His smile widened, and I snuck another glance at it. "I don't know why these didn't sell as well. They're the best walking boots I've ever owned."

He took a sip of his drink, likely to hide his perfectly white teeth. "Agreed," he said. "The lesson I learned from that piece was that the story's angle matters. It was one of my earlier pieces, and I focused solely on the cobbler's qualifications and the boots' features. While the features certainly benefited the readers, like being comfortable walking boots, they didn't offer more than that."

"The rest of your pieces offer some kind of feeling of belonging to the reader," I said, tilting my head in thought.

He scratched the back of his neck. "I hadn't thought of it that way, but yes." With a sudden intensity, he narrowed his gaze on me. "Who was responsible for having the Solstice Sip on the menu at Parkview Tavern?"

"Now you're fishing."

He beamed. "It was you." He leaned forward, his windswept hair falling charmingly over his face. "How many of them have you read?"

I put my hand on his shoulder, partially to stop his progress and partially to make sure I didn't do something embarrassing like run my fingers through his thick hair to push it from his face. They itched to do so, and I'd have no reasonable way to explain the action. "A few."

"I'm not sure I've ever met a fan before." He beamed.

"That Kristin sure seemed like a fan," I said offhandedly.

He leaned back, sitting up straight, and I knew immediately I'd said the wrong thing. "Not quite," he said.

I hadn't expected him to acknowledge the comment.

"She was more interested in wielding recommendations

than actually reading any of them or trying any of the items out."

"I see."

"I figured it out eventually." He took a long pull of the Solstice Sip. "It just took a little longer than I'd have liked."

"I can imagine that was disappointing to realize," I said carefully.

He shot me a smirk. "Quite. At least I used it to get Skye a job. She wants to design clothing and open her own boutique, but she couldn't gain an apprenticeship without experience."

"And you got her the experience."

"Well, she's getting the experience herself, but I may have pushed her foot through the door with Kristin."

"So, this isn't your first time bargaining with your column?"

He ran his hand through his hair, pushing back the strands I'd been eyeing. "Unfortunately, no. Although it's the first time I've done it so blatantly. With Kristin, I...wanted to get something from her when I realized she was using me." He cleared his throat seemingly unnecessarily as if to distract from how honest that was. "I always stand behind the products or services I recommend, though. That can't be faked."

"And you think the inn is worth standing behind?" I asked. This felt too raw. I needed to remind us both that our interaction was transactional. This was a bargain from which we were both benefiting.

"Yes," he said without hesitation. "The property is beautiful. I still need to explore it further, but it's exactly the kind of place I'd want to recommend. It's kind of like this drink." He lifted his glass. "We used a spirit that was already available, but we put a new spin on it."

"I understand what you're doing, Vincent. This is what I asked of you. You don't need to worry about whether I can handle your plan. No matter the spin you want to put on me or the inn, I'll be fine with it. I want my inn to succeed, and I've read enough of your pieces to know you can help."

"How many pieces, exactly?" he asked, and that wicked smile was back. One that I was sure had charmed many females into his bed.

I laughed a little stiltedly. Anything not to focus on him directly. "You can hardly expect me to admit to being your column's number one fan."

Our gazes locked. A moment of intensity flared between us. It reminded me of the night we met, the intimacy we'd had before I got called back inside. What could have happened if Seraphina hadn't interrupted us? I found myself wanting to know.

The moment was interrupted by Markus returning. "Another round?" he asked, leaning against the bar.

My drink was nearing empty, but I needed to return to the inn. I had more work to do cleaning and refreshing it. "I'm good." I glanced at Vincent.

"Me, too." Vincent offered Markus coin for the drink.

Markus waved him off, focusing on me as he leaned against the bar. "So, how do you know our friend Vincent?"

I wasn't entirely sure how to respond to that.

Vincent jumped in. "I'm helping her with her inn."

Markus gave him a *sure you are* look, and I tried to hide my smile. He returned his focus to me in an intense evaluation. "Which inn?"

"Cliff House."

His eyes widened. "Oh, that one is stunning. The cliffs out there are beautiful. We hike out that way every weekend."

"I completely agree." Although I laughed a little at his reference to the cliffs instead of the sea—it showed his Suden nature, to be sure—I also bristled, realizing my draw to the water showed my Norden nature, even if I didn't truly have one.

We quickly slipped into an easy conversation about the

hiking trails in the area. Markus glanced at Vincent once or twice. He appeared to be actively listening but not participating.

"Vincent." Markus called for his attention. He seemed lost in thought. "Vincent."

"What? Yes, sorry."

"Luna and I were saying you should check out the hiking trails."

He nodded, but I wasn't sure he understood what Markus was saying. I wondered where his thoughts had been.

"Maybe the angle here can be more than an inn. It's a quiet respite from the busy city life," I said.

Vincent's eyes finally brightened in recognition. He glanced out the window. "Maybe it's time you gave me a tour of the property."

12

Luna

Why was I suddenly nervous as we walked toward the inn? The tavern Vincent had taken me to was on the southwest side of the Suden District, meaning it was a short journey to the inn. My palms grew sweatier with each step. This was silly—Vincent had already seen it. We'd sat in the library and struck our bargain. *But that was before I got to know him.* I shook myself free of my thoughts. I still didn't know him. Just because I now knew he had an ex who used him for his position and a sister he'd do anything for didn't mean I knew him. This was a bargain, nothing more. *Why did drinks feel more like a date, then?* The sound of waves crashing and the refreshing scent of the sea hit my nose before I could wrestle with that unwelcome question.

I led us to the familiar stairs to the inn's private beach.

"Didn't Markus say we should start from the north side? That's where the hiking trails drop off, right?"

He was correct, and I guessed that should be part of the

tour. Especially if he thought the story might have a hiking or city escape angle. "Yeah, sure, those stairs are this way."

We crossed through the forest on Cliff House property, staying close to the edge so Vincent could enjoy the view.

"It's a wonder this is here at all," he said. "I can't believe more people don't know about it. Markus is right. It feels like such an escape from the city, and it's less than an hour's walk for most."

I liked that he liked it here.

So few people took the time to appreciate it. I know Darius didn't.

We fell into a comfortable silence again as he took in the sights. I wondered where his thoughts had taken him as we approached the second staircase. Something prickled along my spine as I led him down the stairs just north of the property. Too late, I realized why I never came over here—realized why my instinct was to go to the inn's private beach instead. This was the cove where the current had hauled me to as a child, the night I should have drowned. I was swept under again as we descended, the memories resurfacing as they had only a few days ago.

Water. Darkness. Waves. Moonlight.

Attempting to avoid those thoughts while we walked, I did what I did best—rambled.

"My mom and I came to the inn on vacation when I was young. Does your family have any favorite vacation spots?" I kept a wary eye on the sea, like it would splash forward and drag me under at any moment. No. The water didn't scare me—I loved it. In any other circumstance, I'd dive right in. Something about this beach, though, and the memory of Darius reaching for me left me cold. I wrapped my arms around myself, rubbing them over my jacket, searching for warmth.

Vincent's gaze heated my skin. I gave it even odds of whether he found the question impertinent or whether he saw too much in my words. Thankfully, he decided to answer. "We didn't travel much as children. My parents claimed we had too much responsibility in the city."

"Oh, right, old fae family. I knew that." I ran my hand through my hair absentmindedly. Darius always seemed to be in town. Not that I knew the details of his comings and goings. It was reasonably public knowledge that his father worked on something in the north, but no one ever spoke of Darius or his mother going to visit. I thought that was odd for an old fae family. Usually, they all lived together on the family estate. The one I had yet to visit, but needed an invite to for my bargain with Vincent.

"Luna?" Vincent tapped my shoulder hesitantly as we walked along the beach. I must have missed a question...or the end of his explanation. I'd missed it all.

I shook my head. "Sorry, what did you say?"

"I was just..." He waved his hand dismissively. "Nothing. I was answering your question."

Now I was being rude. That couldn't stand. It wasn't his fault I was worried about the terms of our arrangement. "No, I apologize. I'm listening now. Please, continue."

"I was thinking about what you said at the tavern—about my articles."

Heat touched my cheeks, finally ridding me of the bone-chilling cold brought by the memories of this beach. Although, it only reminded me of my earlier stupidity: confessing how much I'd read his column. He continued, not noticing, or pretending not to notice, my embarrassment.

"The column is most successful when what I recommend is also a product or experience that I can welcome the reader into. You and Markus might be onto something with the 'in-the-city' escape. So many get too tied up in the hustle and bustle and forget that this is here." He spread his arms, gesturing to the cliffs and the sea. "Maybe part of the key to saving the inn is reminding them."

It sounded nice, but I wasn't sure how we would accomplish that. "It's still an inn," I pointed out. "My primary customers are not those who live in Sandrin but those visiting."

"Agreed. I think there is value in ensuring the locals think it's the best place in town to stay, though. As many visitors are here now for friends and family as they are for trade."

This was true. I'd checked the stats myself in the governor's office as part of my research. The most recent *Bayside Times* had also included many interviews and polls about visitors and what brought them here.

"We should turn around," I said, considering how to combine the two ideas.

"Does this beach wrap around the cliff?" he asked.

I looked up. "No, it doesn't. The first staircase I took us to leads to a beach on the other side." I patted the rugged stone, trying not to look at the water. "This beach ends here."

A playful smile curved his lip as he asked, "Can you get us around the cliff from down here?"

I turned and stared at him, my hands falling to my hips. "Excuse me?" My tone was frigid. Did he think this was funny? I felt my gaze narrow and my brow pinch in frustration. I thought we'd moved past fae snobbery.

His face paled immediately like he knew he had made a mistake, but it appeared he genuinely didn't know what it was. His hands were raised in defense. "Luna, I'm sorry. I don't know what I said, but I assure you I didn't intend any harm with it."

I let out a breath. He wasn't being cruel. He didn't know. Every half-fae had a different hold on their magic. I wasn't even sure how many he'd met. I studied his reaction as I spoke the words—the words that meant I had little value, especially to those of old fae families. "I don't have magic."

His brow furrowed slightly, but he was quick to smooth it

out. "My apologies, Luna. I never would have asked if I'd known."

I dipped my chin. "It's fine. We should turn around."

His wind surrounded me before I finished the sentence. It blew through my hair, and I could feel it circling my body beneath my jacket, slipping against the exposed skin of my back. I shivered, giving him a look.

He flushed as he pulled it back. "I must apologize again," he started. Then, with another heavy dose of hesitation, he said, "I could get us across, if you'd like."

His wind seemed so different from him. Reasonably, though, I knew it was him, and the fact that it was so eager to be near me was a little intoxicating.

I ignored his question and replied, "I think your wind likes me."

He sighed, rubbing his hand across his forehead. "You have no idea," I thought I heard him mumble under his breath. He turned, taking my segue as refusal, and walked back along the beach where we'd been.

"I thought you were going to get us across," I called. This was such a bad idea, but he'd looked so hesitant in his offer, and I liked the way his wind made me feel. He didn't seem like he got a lot of opportunities to use it for fun. Ferrying us over the sea was practical, but it was also unnecessary, and I felt a deep desire to encourage any unnecessary usage of his magic.

He paused his steps, turning to evaluate my sincerity.

"That sounds frivolous enough for me to approve," I said, pulling out my brightest smile. Now that I'd decided to do it, I couldn't wait to feel his wind lifting me and gliding me around the rock face jutting into the sea. It would require me to be airborne for more than a few moments. I knew he was old fae, and I knew his wind was strong from how it whipped around me when freed, but was he capable of this?

He tilted his head like he wasn't sure he'd heard me right

and returned to my side where the beach ended. "You think gliding around the cliff on the wind is wasteful?"

"That's not what I said, Vincent. I said it was frivolous. Fun. Something you should lean into while you can. From how your wind slips free, I don't imagine it gets many chances to...play."

His lip tilted into a half smile. It was adorable, and I needed to think about anything other than how charming he looked. His wind-tousled hair was next on the list of things for me not to focus on. "Where do you want me?" I asked.

"I should go around the corner first to see where I'm taking you." His brow furrowed like he was now unsure of the offer.

I wanted to giggle as we approached the jagged edge of the cliff face where the beach abruptly ended. His features flipped between determination and indecision with each step. Finally, Vincent gave me another crooked smile and did the last thing I expected. He took a running jump, his long brown coat billowing behind him as he fell onto a gust of wind that sailed him around the edge toward Cliff House beach.

My smile vanished when I realized I was alone. I hadn't considered it when he'd offered to go first. My gaze was drawn to the precise location a few feet into the water where Darius had pulled me from the waves.

I needed to get out of here.

With nothing left to distract me, my body shook with nerves as memories of that night poured in. Water swept me away from Mom. The current pulled me under and pushed me down to the bottom of the sea. Darius's strong arms, solid and warm, lifted me from the eye of the storm to safety. I'd been ashamed of how I clung to him, even as a child. When I thought about it now, all I could imagine was what a fool he must have thought me—half water fae, about to drown.

"Ready?" Vincent's voice was soft on the wind, his words slipping straight to my ear like a lover whispering at my shoulder. I shivered. The image of him standing so close broke through the haze of memories. I'd never felt wind magic do this. It was like he was right beside me. I nodded reflexively as I collected myself. Too late, I realized he probably couldn't see that.

I pushed more energy into my voice than I felt. "Ready!" I called.

"Run and jump. I'll catch you." His low voice was at my ear again, sending a confusing sensation down my spine. I needed to relax.

Run and jump? I should have known it would require something. It suddenly occurred to me precisely how much trust I was putting in Vincent Andiveron and his magic. My gaze raked the water. The cove was calm. This wasn't the unexpected change of tides from memory. At worst, I'd get a little wet, but a part of me wanted to believe that Vincent wouldn't let me fall.

At the thought, his wind was there, swirling and seducing. Tempting me to jump. Briefly, I wondered how long it'd be before I learned a hard lesson about the nature of fae. For now, I ignored the deluge of uncertainty.

I ran and jumped.

13

Vincent

D*id she truly agree to this?* I paced Cliff House Inn's private beach. My wind wrapped around her before I heard her response. Was she hesitating? I paused. Maybe I should call it off. I shook my head and continued pacing. My wind was too eager to prove it could do this. I wouldn't call it off unless she explicitly asked. Never mind that I wasn't sure I'd ever done anything like this with my wind. For whatever reason, that wasn't my worry. I was confident I was capable.

Then I heard it. Her words weren't a whisper on the wind but a shock to my senses.

"Ready!"

My instructions were simple, and she no longer seemed hesitant. I felt her shape on my magic despite her being out of sight. She did it. She threw herself out over the water, expecting me to catch her.

And I did.

My wind, purred in satisfaction. I whisked her around the

cliff's edge and brought her careening onto the beach. I aimed for the spot beside me, but I should have known that, with her, my wind had other ideas. With a final gust, I slid her to her feet. If I didn't know any better, I'd say a final bluster sent her tumbling toward me.

I caught her shoulders, and slid my hands down her arms to brace her. "Sorry about that."

She glanced up at me through long lashes, a little unsteady on her feet. A few lashes stuck together, and her eyes looked a little wet. I couldn't be sure if it was from the sea mist or if she'd been...crying before she'd jumped. Given her reaction to the other side of the cove, I assumed the latter and knew she wouldn't thank me for noticing. She thought she'd hidden it behind impertinent questions about my family, but I could tell something about the beach bothered her. That space meant something to her, and I didn't think it was something good. I was also sure she had no interest in sharing it with me.

Her lips parted slightly as our gazes locked. Propriety dictated we put distance between ourselves, but she didn't move. Wind circled us as if locking us in place, and I was overcome with a desire to bend and close the gap.

I clenched my jaw at the last second. *Get your head on straight.* I knew I needed to, but I was loathe to move before she did. A shy smile curved her lips as she finally pushed back, freeing herself from my grasp. My hands fell gently to my sides. The wind around us silenced.

"We've got to stop meeting like this," she said.

Is she nervous?

I thought we weren't supposed to discuss the night we met. Our proximity and our brief flirtation. Those things were gone now that we'd made a bargain fueled by ambition, forcing us both into uncomfortable situations. My wind surged as if to ask whose rule that was. I needed to stop talking to my wind. It seemed solely focused on crossing lines with Luna, which I was sure would only complicate matters.

"I don't mind it." The words were out before my mind and mouth connected. I wanted to smack myself. I wasn't even sure she reciprocated the interest I was desperately pretending I didn't have.

She held my gaze, and I almost believed her body swayed forward, returning to my space. That same open intensity from the night we met was apparent in the bright blue of her eyes. I didn't breathe as I stared into them. This move was her own. My wind was locked up tight.

"We should head up and finish the tour." Something halted her forward progress.

I let out a breath. "Of course." I turned, wondering if I'd imagined the moment.

She spoke from behind me, her voice was a little shaky as she slipped back into the original intent behind this trip—a tour. "The stairs are over there." She glanced around. "This is the private beach for the guests' use. It's only accessible from the inn property."

"It only adds to the feeling of being away from everything," I said as we started up the steps. "A person could forget the city, or their responsibilities." I swallowed thickly, needing to be careful because my words were truer than I cared to admit. Mooning over Luna Pierce was not part of the plan. Breaking the story about her father's bribery was. She was using me for a review, and I would get a source for my article about her father for my effort. As we ascended the staircase, Luna continued listing facts about the inn and the property, unaffected by any imagined moment on the beach. Today wasn't feeling like a bargain, but that was why we were here. I'd do well to remember that.

~

APPROACHING the inn this way brought forth another awe-inspiring view. I had begun to understand Luna's attachment to this place when she took me to its library. Even more so when we walked the edge between the cliff and the forested land. She'd even shared that this place had some connection to her mother, though I wasn't quite sure what that entailed. Seeing the charming building grow from the center of the wooded property, with a view of cliffs and sea, was...perfection. I wanted to get lost here, no matter how much I'd recently attempted to remind myself of my responsibilities.

It was a large building, even with all its character. I guessed it had ten or more guest rooms, which Luna confirmed as she spoke.

"Do you live in the inn?" I asked.

She paused, glancing farther into the woods. "The groundskeeper's cottage is in there." She pointed to a dense copse of trees, too thick to reveal a building. "It's small but perfect for me."

I had no doubt it was. I felt much the same way about my apartment. It was smaller and less grand than Andiveron House, to be sure, but it was mine, and it felt like home in a way the family house never had.

"Beautiful," I said as we walked toward the porch overlooking the cliff. My wind thrummed, and I was unsure if I'd been referring to her or the property. She moved with a natural grace. It was similar to when she'd stood ankle-deep in the water surrounding Parkview Tavern the night we met. *I needed to stop thinking about that.* But in the same breath, I couldn't believe this place might cease to exist for her if we failed.

It won't be my fault if she doesn't get me access to Darius. After only a few hours here, I was confident that I could sell this place in the column. If she lost the inn, it wouldn't be because I'd failed to hold up my end of the bargain.

"It is." She opened the door and waited for me to catch up.

"Come on, I know you already saw the library, but let me show you the rest."

As I approached, she reached for my hand, beaming when she tugged me into the inn.

Forgetting the warning I'd given myself only moments ago, I let her take it and held on tight, letting her drag me through the porch and library.

"There is a small kitchen, the manager's office, and this is reception," she said, leading me through the first floor. She dropped my hand as we turned, and she tilted her head back to look up the steps toward the guest rooms. Whatever rush of emotion had overtaken her was gone, and we regained the distance between us.

"Did the inn ever serve food?" I asked, thinking about the kitchen and the space for tables in the library.

She shook her head, not looking at me as she did. "It was never Byrd's preference—the old manager."

I couldn't believe Darius had had her live as groundskeeper on the property and only gave her the chance to manage it as he considered closing it. Something itched at my neck as I thought about her part of our bargain.

"The kitchen area is too small for a full meal," she continued, not noticing my discomfort. "The other day after our... conversation, I baked some bread in here. I wanted to prove it was possible. But light snacks is all the kitchen is good for."

"It's still something," I said. "And it could be a nice touch for trying to recruit weekend hikers to stop by for the view and something sweet to eat."

She seemed to ignore my comment, her gaze focused up the stairwell. "All the guest rooms are on the second floor."

"Why do you sound hesitant about that?"

She started up the steps. I thought maybe she'd ignored my question when she spoke again. "My friends and I spent last week cleaning. We did a little shopping to freshen up some fabrics, colors, and decor to make it more cohesive. It didn't need much," she rambled, and I wasn't sure I believed her.

She opened the door to the first room. It had the same energy that the library did. Plush fabrics and light, airy colors that mixed the idea of the seaside with cozy comfort. It felt like her—her style. It was a bit loud for my taste but wholly her and very welcoming for guests.

"We even patched a hole over in that room." She pointed to the right, and while impressed, I was desperate to know what she was *not* telling me. Lying about or obfuscating information clearly wasn't her strong suit—she seemed too genuine for that, even if she had done a more than decent job of convincing Kristin we were lovers. Images I had no business remembering flooded my mind.

"The only thing left is the room at the end of this hall."

Everything came to a halt as I processed her words. "What's wrong with it?"

She hesitated, like her honesty had gone a step further than she'd intended. This—whatever this was—had her nervous. "Well, it won't open."

"Won't open?"

"Yes, it has some kind of magical seal on it."

I tilted my head. Magic wasn't my specialty. I could barely control my wind, let alone the magic necessary to lock a door. My wind flexed as if insulted. It must be blood magic. I had no idea how that worked. However, I did know a magically locked room was bad for business.

"What are we doing about it?" I asked cautiously.

She smiled, and I realized my phrasing. The magically locked door wasn't my problem. I would tell people about the inn. If she had a room she couldn't get into, that wasn't something I had to solve. My wind swirled slowly with curiosity, though.

"Evelyn, my friend, she's a server at Parkview Tavern," Luna started rambling. "Well, she also works on research projects at the Vesten Library. She's looking into it."

We continued walking down the hall and arrived in front of said door.

"Do you mind if I try?" I asked, though I had no idea why. Blood magic was beyond me. I was confident there was nothing I could do. My wind pushed on the bounds I tried to hold all the same.

She gestured toward the door. "Please."

I twisted the handle and pushed. Nothing happened, but that was to be expected per Luna's explanation. I knelt and looked in the keyhole. My wind was off and sweeping through the small space before I could think twice. It was always a unique experience to have my wind somewhere I couldn't see. It didn't have eyes of its own, but like when Luna had jumped into my wind at the beach, I could feel the shape of things.

My wind swirled around each item, cataloging what was there. I tried to arrange them in my mind. A picture came together and seemed the same as the other rooms she'd shown me. A bed on the left, a wardrobe against the farmost wall, a writing desk and chair, and a moonflower lying across the desk, fully in bloom.

Wait.

My wind returned with a sudden gust smelling of moonflower. I'd smelled it with Luna the night we met. As the name suggested, those flowers only bloomed under the full moon's light and in the presence of Norden magic.

"Luna," I said hesitantly, wanting to confirm an assumption, "do you have moonflowers on the property?" I turned my head to look up at her over my shoulder. She stood closer than I realized, trying to peek through the hole over me.

"What are you doing?" she squeaked instead of answering my question.

I laughed, having not explained myself. "Oh, sorry, my wind, it's cataloging the room to see what's inside."

She put her hand over her mouth in surprise. "You can do that?"

I nodded, my chest puffing out without my consent at the awe in her voice. "Most of it seems similar to the other rooms. The only thing that feels out of place is a bloomed moonflower."

"We do have them on the property," she whispered. Her eyes darted back and forth in the hall like she was expecting someone to overhear our conversation. Like what she'd say next would be some big secret.

"Luna, the inn is yours, at least for the next six weeks." Something in the way she'd spoken about the previous manager in the kitchen gave me an inkling of why she whispered. *What was his name?* "Byrd can't yell at you for stealing the flowers," I said with a smile. "You can come clean with me."

She chuckled, probably realizing how silly she'd been. "I guess you're right." She rolled her shoulders back, straightening, as I stood from my place on the floor. "We do have them, but I don't think Byrd knew about them. I use them for my tea mix."

"Well," I said, finding her response too curious by half, "I guess we'll have to figure out why one is held in bloom within this locked room at some point. Add that to the list."

Luna's smile was bright, and I realized I'd inserted myself into this new problem to solve. *What am I doing?*

"I already have it on mine, but I'll add your new detail." She clapped her hands. "I think that's it for the tour. Did you say you wanted to go to one more of the places you recommended to get more ideas?"

My cheeks flushed. "I did, but the last place is Timeless Classics. And even if I put it on the map, I couldn't get same-day reservations."

She laughed. "Don't they know who you are?"

I ignored her jab. "I *was* able to get a reservation for two days from now. Evening meal. Does that work?"

"I still need time to work on my end of the bargain anyway."

My shoulders raised inadvertently, but she'd already turned and walked away. I tapped my chin and gave the door a final glance before following.

She harvested moonflower. They only bloomed in the presence of Norden magic. My own suspicions were forming, the same that had led me to assume she had water magic the night we met. Yet she'd made it clear she had no magic and no interest in discussing it, so I'd keep them to myself.

14

Luna

A few days later, Vincent sent me a note on the wind saying he'd pick me up at my cottage, and that we could walk together to the restaurant. Part of me thought that sounded lovely. Another part, the part that still hadn't even begun to fulfill my side of our bargain, thought it sounded too much like a date. I replied, saying I'd be at Parkview Tavern and we could meet there if he wanted. Evelyn would have an update on the room research. I wanted to resolve that before I requested an invite to Pierce House. If there was magic driving people away from Cliff House, it wasn't worth the article or the family drama.

I pulled out a navy dress Skye had selected. It was plain. Not every item she'd found had something unique and tailored to my taste. This was truly old fae, but it was the best choice for tonight since we would dine at the most fae establishment in the city. I chose matching slippers instead of my favorite boots and set off.

Theoretically, I knew why Vincent and I were having this meal. The restaurant was one of the few *places* Vincent had recommended. The other columns we'd discussed, the boots and the Solstice Sip, featured a product as the recommendation. For the inn, it would be a location and experience similar to that of Timeless Classics. It made sense to check it out even if our every interaction left me confused.

It had felt so natural to have him at the inn. His wind had enjoyed it, too. It had been apparent he appreciated the view. I'd gotten carried away on our tour, forgetting he was only there because of a bargain. I needed to remind myself that he thought Darius was involved in bribing the governor to prevent the magic school's construction. While that revelation was incredibly disappointing, it wasn't as if Darius had ever given me a reason to expect more. I think I still had. No matter how much I fought it, he was my father. How could he be so against someone like me being educated in magic? I didn't want to think about it as I opened the door and entered Parkview Tavern.

The city had only continued to fill, even if none of those visitors had made it to Cliff House Inn. I was glad Seraphina and the tavern were benefiting. Making my way to the bar, I passed table after table of patrons. Warm food, lively discussions, and full drink glasses filled every table. I searched for Evelyn and found her at the bar, picking up orders.

"Hey," she said as I approached. "I meant to come by today but lost track of time in the library." That seemed all too easy for Evelyn to do.

I waved my hand as if to wipe away her worry. "No problem. Stopping by here helped me out tonight."

Seraphina leaned over the bar. "Why is that?" Her gaze turned mischievous as she took in my appearance. "You look all dressed up."

I coughed, sure my cheeks were also heating. "I'm meeting Vincent."

"Surely, you didn't wear that outfit to eat here?"

Evelyn smiled at Seraphina's teasing.

"He's taking me to Timeless Classics," I said quietly.

"Well, now," Seraphina straightened. "That's something."

I rushed to explain. "It's the only other experience he's recommended instead of product. He thought it would be good to do some research."

"I'm sure he did." Seraphina laughed before giving me a searching look. "Do you know what you're doing?"

She'd been worried about me since initially hearing me mention Darius to him. So what if I didn't talk about Darius often? He had been very relevant to why I'd been so angry with Vincent the night we met. At least, that's what I told myself.

I nodded, then glanced at Evelyn. "I wanted to know if you found anything on the door. I'm sure Vincent will ask me about Darius soon..."

"And you don't want to bother with that if we haven't solved this magically locked door bit," Evelyn finished for me.

"Right."

She bit her lip. "I have an idea. I can't do it tomorrow—I'm needed at the library. Day after?"

"Thank you, Evelyn. That sounds perfect."

Seraphina's gaze drifted over my shoulder to the door. I felt his wind slip around my shoulders before I saw him.

Vincent had arrived.

Seraphina held my gaze again before he got close enough to hear. "Be careful, Luna."

I pressed my lips into a thin smile, hoping I would be but fearing my heart had plans of its own.

SERAPHINA'S LINGERING worry fresh in my mind made me even more on edge as we walked to the restaurant. The darkened streets didn't help my nerves, this close to solstice meant the sun had already set.

"Everything alright?" Vincent asked, pulling open the door to Timeless Classics.

"All good," I said, a little self-conscious, feeling eyes on me as we entered. Could they tell I wasn't comfortable in this dress? Did they know it wasn't *me*? A part of me felt they must be able to, no matter how well it matched the expected appearance of those dining here. "I think it's these slippers. The flimsy fabric is much less comfortable for walking than my boots."

His smile didn't meet his eyes, like maybe he knew that wasn't the real problem—but he didn't press.

Candles lit the entry, and every table in the small restaurant somehow appeared private. Any hope I'd had that the early meal wouldn't signal a quiet romantic evening was lost when I saw the room. This place screamed romance with every detail. The proprietor had grown walls of plants to set between the tables, which meant the room was a maze, but the servers seemed to know precisely where they were going. Candles hung from chandeliers on the ceiling and were set on every table. The warm glow created a mood I was having a hard time ignoring.

I glanced at Vincent, but his stony exterior gave nothing away. This was probably a standard evening meal for him. He probably wasn't thinking of romance at all.

We were greeted quickly and with perfect manners, the host telling us our table would be ready momentarily. It was no surprise they knew Vincent here. Not only had he put the restaurant on the map, but this had been one of his first recommendations to take off with the fae. It was now almost exclusively reserved by fae families, which was interesting considering they comprised less than half of the city's population. We'd talked about that sense of belonging that his articles created. Whether he intended it or not, something about his writing, or the quiet places to hide in plain sight had appealed deeply to the fae of Sandrin.

Seraphina had tried to get reservations a few months ago to celebrate the new Norden Point and our place in fae society, since half-fae were now openly accepted in fae courts. The bookings had been filled for the rest of the year.

"Mr. Andiveron. This way." The host no more than glanced at me. Clearly, he knew who to cater to. "We have your table ready." He led us through the maze of greenery with practiced ease. "Your server will be by shortly. Do you require anything else?"

Vincent shook his head and pulled out my chair. Surprised, I sat, and my fingers fidgeted under the table. This was too much. I didn't need to be here to know this would never be Cliff House. If we had to make such a formal and exclusive experience for Cliff House to survive, it wouldn't.

"Luna." Vincent glanced at me, setting aside the written menu they'd left on the table. Something about his voice pulled me back from the edge of panic. "You're quiet tonight."

I nodded. There was no denying that. He probably found it strange, given my ability to ramble. I took a deep breath. This was part of what I'd signed up for. He wanted us to go through his successes together to decide what to do about Cliff House. If this was his process, I wouldn't complain about it. I simply needed to ground myself, and thinking about the exclusive fae nature of this establishment wasn't helping. My fingers stretched like they were reaching for some dough to knead. I had nothing. Like when I met with Darius, I had to wield what was available. I needed to remind myself why I was here.

"We've spent a lot of time on the inn," I said. "We should talk about your side of the deal."

He straightened in his chair. I hadn't realized how relaxed

he'd seemed until I broached the subject of our bargain. Doubt coated my tongue, weighing down any following words, but I couldn't regret bringing this up. This room was too intimate. After the other day together, I'd realized he was nothing like he initially seemed. He looked too good. My palms were sweating. I couldn't remember the last time I'd been on a date like this.

This isn't a date.

"What do you want to discuss?" he asked.

I focused on the conversation. This would put the necessary distance back between us. "Tell me why you think Darius is guilty."

"I am not sure he is." He cleared his throat. "That's why we must investigate."

"But someone thinks he is. Otherwise, we wouldn't be here." I lifted my hand to gesture to the room around us.

Vincent frowned at the comment. "My boss has a tip that shows a rather large transfer of money from his accounts to the governor's. Some rough notes indicate a school was in the discussion." He paused, fixing me with a glare I wasn't sure I'd earned. "I also overheard him talking with her in the records office stairwell last week. He was pressuring her for information about the school's development. Asking why nothing had been announced yet."

I leaned away, letting my back hit the rest of the chair. "When *exactly* did you hear that?" Last week, we'd made the deal, and he'd said nothing about having overheard his own evidence, only that he had a tip. *You didn't ask,* the quiet voice in my head called out.

He pressed his lips into a thin line. "The same day I came to the inn."

"Why didn't you tell me? You made it sound like you didn't believe the tip, but you had your own proof?"

He slumped forward in his chair, resting his head in his

hand, his elbow on the table. The posture looked so utterly out of place in this fancy establishment.

My anger receded—a little.

"I still don't think it's proof," he said with some exasperation. "He asked why nothing about the school had been announced. He indicated they had an agreement. Nothing he said directly ties him to trying to prevent the school from being built."

I folded my arms over my chest. "It doesn't look good."

Vincent lifted his head, rolling his shoulders back to slip into his usual confidence like he'd suddenly realized he'd let too much show. I couldn't help but wonder how much he kept bottled up beneath his exterior of propriety.

"I know your father is a sensitive subject," he hedged.

"Please, don't stop now," I said more sarcastically than intended. "I was the one who brought the topic up."

"Do you think he'd do something like this? Is he so against..." His sentence trailed off, and he held my gaze, something like sadness lined his face.

Is he so against you? That was what Vincent had been about to say. I shook off the hurt. At the end of the day, I didn't know much about Darius. I probably needed to admit that to Vincent.

"As I've said, my relationship with Darius is near non-existent. I'm still working on how precisely I'll fulfill my end of our bargain, so I'm not sure I know him well enough to judge." I sighed. "I know he came to the village where I was raised, when I was old enough to test for magic. He didn't return when he found I had none."

Vincent's hand stretched and flexed into a fist on the tabletop. I wondered if he was upset, or if he was wishing he had a quill to take notes. Maybe this was an eyewitness interview for his future piece.

He leaned forward as if he'd say something private, but we

were already as secluded as we could be. I didn't think I could handle whatever would be next to slip from his lips. I thanked the gods for perfect timing as the server approached our table.

"Wonderful to see you, Mr. Andiveron," she said, before smiling courteously at me. "The chef has requested to give you his newest creations. If you're not opposed." The server's gaze remained on Vincent, clearly communicating that it was his decision. My heart flipped when his gaze met mine.

"Luna?" he asked. "Do you want to select our own meals? Or take the chef's recommendations?"

I was already running on fumes. We hadn't been here long, and I was emotionally and mentally drained. Deciding what to order at this restaurant that already made me feel uncomfortable was one decision too many. "I'm happy to take the recommendations."

Vincent nodded to the waitress as if my answer was ours—together.

Bringing us right back into dating territory.

"Vincent," I said, "don't you think..."

He canted his head, preparing for my question, and a strand of his thick, dark brown hair fell over his eye. I don't know what happened. I couldn't explain my actions, especially when I was about to ask him about this whole evening and our last day together feeling very much date-like instead of bargain-like. Still, my fingers had other ideas. They crossed the table and pushed the unruly strand back into place. His wind wrapped around my finger, and he leaned into the touch, tilting his head ever so slightly into my palm.

I was in so much trouble.

Snatching my hand back when I finally regained control of my limbs, I stuttered an apology. "I'm so sorry. That hair consistently misbehaves."

His smile was shy, like he wasn't sure what to think of the

encounter, even as his wind blustered with something I could only call pride.

"I didn't mind," he said quietly. "I apologize if it has offended your sensibilities, having to be seen with me in such a state."

His tone had turned wry. I was sure he was teasing me—another switch I didn't know what to make of.

"It's quite alright," I said, using my primmest voice. It didn't suit me, but I appreciated how Vincent's lip tilted as I attempted it anyway. "I shall take care of it in the future so it doesn't embarrass us both."

Any walls I'd tried to build had been smashed to bits with one brush of my fingers. He wasn't helping me maintain distance, either. No, he was inviting me in, his brown eyes dancing with mirth.

"Make sure you do," he said, and we fell into a conspiratorial quiet as our first course was delivered.

I was in so, so much trouble.

15

Vincent

I was feeling too comfortable. This meal with Luna was too easy to fall into. I could almost imagine we were on a first date, following our cute meeting in the moat outside Parkview Tavern.

Almost.

She spoke of her job at the tavern, of her friends and their favorite regulars. The owner, Seraphina, had all but required her to try to save the inn, even if it put her in a tough spot with their customers. I couldn't think of anyone who would put my needs above their own in such a way. Skye, I guess, but I wasn't sure my sister counted.

I learned Luna baked regularly. She had an addiction to bread and dough that had to be fed every day. It didn't make sense to me, but her passion for it made me wish I had something to add to the conversation. I told her my favorite way to start the day was a walk in the park. Her head tilted slightly when I said as much, but she didn't press on the fact that the park wasn't exactly close enough to Andiveron House for an easy morning stroll.

It was too easy to be myself with her.

I shared how, for the weeks approaching Long Night, I loved going back to the park in the evenings to watch the stars, waiting for the last full moon of the year. She liked that, her smile lighting up her face. I'd known she would. She said she watched the sky regularly from the inn's private beach.

She was trying to distance us this evening, first by having us meet at the tavern and then with our discussion of the bargain. I knew her decision was wise, but I found myself wishing to ignore it. I'd been content when we seemingly broke past the guard posts she'd put in place.

I could tell she was about to ask me something I wouldn't like. We'd covered as many surface-level topics as possible, and it was companionable, but I could admit I also wanted to know more about her.

"What do you do for Long Night? Does your family or another wind fae family host a party?"

There it was. We were back, circling topics I'd rather not.

"My parents host a party." It was hardly a secret. The secret was that I hadn't attended in years. Everyone still thought I did, but it was easy enough with the crowd of old fae there to assume they missed me. "I think there is one prominent family for each court in the city that hosts something. Those at Compass Lake might be breaking down barriers between the courts, but I believe they are still very much intact here."

She nodded. It couldn't surprise her, given how her father still treated her. I tracked her tongue as it licked her lips. A nervous habit, I thought. She wanted to ask me something else.

I set down my fork and gestured for her to go ahead. "Ask." I took a sip of my drink and wondered what it would be.

Her lip quirked up into a smirk. "Why aren't you...more like that?"

I choked on the wine, covering my mouth quickly to hide the unseemly noise before other guests noticed. Too late—a few heads had turned at my outburst. "What a nice question, Luna. So, you're saying I'm not a pretentious ass too stuck in my ways to notice the world around me is changing? That maybe people shouldn't be valued based solely on their magic and court affiliations?"

Her cheeks flushed, but she didn't recant. "Yes, that's my question."

I laughed again, though, as I did, the hairs on the back of my neck stood on end, and I had the distinct feeling we were being watched. Her candor was intoxicating, and I decided I didn't care who witnessed as I gulped it down. I'd regret that later, but for now, I responded. "I think I had good examples—"

The rest of my sentence was cut off as the last people I expected stood beside the table.

"Vincent, we didn't realize you were here," my mother said.

In all their finery, my parents looked down their noses at us. It was not all that unusual, given how they approached most situations, but I certainly hadn't expected to find them here when I was out with Luna.

Mother's gaze raked over Luna's outfit, her nose scrunching in distaste. I didn't know why. Luna's dress fit perfectly with all old fae standards. I wished Luna had worn something she felt more comfortable in, but I knew this whole clothing debacle was my fault. Luna noticed Mother's appraisal too, and I hated it as she glanced at her plate.

How could they be here? This was such bad luck. I tried to meet Luna's gaze, to tell her...something, but she was clearly embarrassed by Mother's stare. I was horrified but also wanted to give way to the giggle building in my throat. I'd been about to say I'd had the perfect examples of what *not* to be in my parents, a topic I was sure I hadn't broached with anyone, ever. And now, here they were. Now, we had to face them.

I had no idea what to tell them about Luna.

"Vincent," my father said. He and I looked very similar; I'd been told so for as long as I could remember. His dark brown hair was thick around his face. I knew he spent a great deal of time taming his wild waves. I'd given up on that when I moved out of Andiveron House. Luna reaching across the table to brush some from my face tonight was proof enough that I'd made the right decision. Father's dark brown eyes were the same as my own. Even our clothing styles seemed to match. We both wore white shirts under long, dark brown jackets. The main difference was my jacket had more gold embellishments. I liked that differentiator. It reminded me of Luna's wonderfully obnoxious outfits. At the thought of her, my gaze returned to her worried face.

"Hi, Mother, Father, this is Luna." I hesitated over her surname. The softening of the worry lines on her brow told me she appreciated the gesture.

They barely glanced in her direction as the server returned to gather our empty plates. "Yes," Father said, dismissing her. "We looked for you at the paper this morning and you weren't around. I wanted to check on your upcoming feature."

I put forth my practiced smile and replied, "We'll need to talk about it some other time, Father. As you can see..." I gestured again to Luna. "I'm occupied at the moment."

"I'm sure she understands," Father continued, not even bothering to address the comment to Luna. "You're an important male with responsibilities. That is simply the way of things. She may not understand the requirements of an old fae family, but I'm sure she respects them."

I stood, pushing my chair back a little louder than I intended. "Father." My whole body flushed. Had it been only moments ago that Luna considered me nothing like this kind of old fae? After this display, I was reasonably confident her attitude about me would change. I wouldn't even be upset if she decided not to continue with our bargain. "That's incredibly rude. Luna's time is just as valuable as mine, and I won't allow you to disrespect it."

I pulled out some coin and left it on the table. We were foregoing dessert, which was usually my favorite treat here, but it couldn't be helped. I offered my hand to Luna; she stood with me, her shoulders trembling ever so slightly.

"Vincent," my mother cut in. "He only meant that we don't know your friend. We're sure she's nice"—her nostrils flared—"but she's not exactly serious relationship material."

"Mother," I hissed, "you are completely out of line."

Luna's face was as white as a sheet. This was so much worse than the pink that bloomed on her cheeks when she was embarrassed. I realized too late that my hand was still outstretched for her. I was sure she had no interest in taking it, given Mother's last comment. Not wanting to embarrass her or myself further, I pulled it back. She snatched it before it got too far away.

"I'd like to leave," she said steadily.

My heart kicked in my chest. "So would I."

Before we took a step, wind blew through our alcove, and the wine glasses on our table fell to the floor, shattering. This was officially a disaster. I couldn't believe my parents would do such a thing, but I was sure the wind wasn't natural, or mine. Father's face was red. My bet was on him being the culprit.

Mother squeezed his hand. "Vincent, don't make a scene."

Luna glanced at me with confusion. I imagined she knew my wind well enough by now to realize that wasn't me.

"You already have," I whispered. "We'll leave you to it."

Hands clasped, we wound our way through the maze of tables as quickly as we dared, trying to get as far from my parents as we could in as little time as possible. I wasn't sure what to say to Luna once we were clear of the restaurant. How many ways could I say I was sorry? How could I explain what

I'd been about to say before they arrived? I'd only look like a liar now. She'd never believe I had intended to tell her their behavior had embarrassed me my entire life.

I took a deep breath as we pushed through the doors. At some point, she'd taken the lead, pulling me—probably when I'd lost track of how precisely to get away. Now that I watched her, though, I saw that wasn't quite right. Was she limping? The air was cool against my heated skin. I had opened my mouth to say something, unsure, when I realized what had happened.

"My gods, Luna, your foot is bleeding. Did you step on the glass?"

She peered down. "Yes, I'm so stupid. I forgot I wore these flimsy slippers instead of my usual boots." She shook her head. "I didn't even think."

"Absolutely none of this is your fault," I said, my anger at my parents falling away as I realized she must still have glass stuck in her foot. I looked around. We were in Central Circle. I needed somewhere to remove the glass and clean the wound. Unfortunately, there was only one location that made sense. "We can go to my place. I can clean it and wrap it there."

She nodded. I wasn't sure that was consent for what my wind did next, but she didn't object as it swept her into my arms.

"This is a little much." Her laugh unknotted something in my chest.

I shrugged as I started walking. "Maybe, but you're entitled to hazard treatment after that experience." My head tilted back toward the restaurant.

"That wasn't your fault," she said, but I was already shaking my head.

"I'm so sorry for their behavior. I'll get this out of your foot, and then I'll understand if you never want to speak to me again."

Her hand wrapped around a fold of my jacket as I walked.

We were almost there, but she pulled on the fabric, demanding my attention. I glanced down at the beautiful woman in my arms.

"They are not you, Vincent. Don't you remember what I asked you right before they arrived?" I stopped walking, her blue eyes demanding I meet them. I was going to run us into a building being this distracted.

"I know...but that was before..."

"Before what?" she pressed. "Before your parents made asses of themselves? I, more than anyone, know that children aren't their parents."

I hated that example but knew she meant it. Freeing myself from her gaze, I started walking again. "We're almost there, and then I can have the glass out momentarily," I said, ignoring her comment.

"Where..." she didn't finish the question, but I knew what she was asking.

I sucked in a breath. It was too late, now, to change my mind. I wouldn't have her walk home with glass in her foot. "This is my apartment." I glanced down briefly before walking up the steps to the front door.

Her eyes widened in understanding. "You don't live in Andiveron House," she said, now understanding what I'd shared about my morning walks during our meal.

My lips pressed into a thin smile, and I opened the door, letting my first-ever guest into my home.

16

Luna

The rough outline I had sketched of Vincent was becoming clearer. The new lines were crisp, and the colors were filled in.

He didn't live in Andiveron House.

When he'd told me of his morning and evening walks in the park, I'd questioned the proximity to his family home, but then I'd decided the distance of the walk might be the appeal. I hadn't even imagined this scenario—his own apartment. It was too foreign a concept for old fae.

Vincent seemed to freeze as we stood at the entry to his home. It was as if he took it in with fresh eyes while I hung in his arms. After everything I'd learned about him in the last ten days, it really shouldn't have surprised me as much as it did. It was just that no member of an old fae family left their home. I didn't count, as I hadn't ever been invited.

The door opened into a pristine living space. There was no way he'd intended to have me as a visitor today, but not an item was out of place. A brown leather sofa sat against one wall, and a sturdy wooden table and chairs were along the other. The kitchen, with a wood-burning stove, was beyond a half wall, and the apartment seemed to extend farther back, presumably to a bedroom.

I pursed my lips as his wind set me on the sofa. After meeting his parents tonight, I could imagine a few reasons why he'd want to leave.

It wasn't done, though. He was old fae; he didn't have some complicated half-fae heritage like me. I thought of his sister, Skye. They seemed so close. I would have never guessed they didn't live under the same roof.

He mumbled something soft, putting a pillow under my foot to lift it, and disappeared into another room.

Feeling safe and completely mystified by my surroundings, I replayed the evening. No matter my attempts to dissuade us, the meal had felt like a date. We'd barely discussed the bargain or any comparable ways Vincent could position the inn to match the restaurant's success. After my initial attempt at distance, talking about Darius, we'd slipped into easy conversation.

It hadn't only been easy; it had been engaging. Vincent intrigued me on every level. He'd been so dismissive and rude at our first meeting—I remembered clearly that he hadn't engaged with most of Earl's attempts at conversation; he'd only done so when the opportunity to insult the tavern presented itself.

I had to believe he hid behind that dismissive distance because it was far from the male I'd gotten to know since making our bargain. Vincent was accustomed to being used for his family name and taste-maker status. It seemed even his parents weren't above suggesting his next article. My body warmed in embarrassment at how easily I'd fallen into that same pattern—what he must have thought of me.

His wind whipped around me as he returned to the room with an armful of supplies. The wind was the most confusing thing of all. It didn't seem to match any other part of him. Even if I ignored Vincent's initial arrogance, he was still a fae of propriety. He often seemed embarrassed by its actions. As his wind wound through my hair, it had no such compunction. I liked it and was dying to know how much was within his control.

"How much does it hurt?" he asked.

I shook my head, not sure what he was referring to.

"Your foot." He gestured.

"Truth be told, I'd forgotten about it."

He flushed at my words. I reached toward my foot. My slipper was still on, but I winced as my toes wiggled. A piece of glass was still lodged through the slipper into my skin. Vincent had a bucket of water, a rag, soap, and strips of cloth with him. He set it all down and kneeled beside me.

"Let me." His hands were warm. He must have run them under warm water when he'd filled the bucket. I held my breath as he lifted my foot, examining the damage. "It doesn't look too deep, but I'll need to pull it out and remove the slipper to be sure."

I nodded, not remembering the last time someone had worried over me quite so needlessly. "It's a small piece of glass."

He glanced sideways at me. "I'll pull it out on three. One." His fingers wrapped around the large sliver. "Two." He held my gaze, his brown eyes saying too much. They were so apologetic. His guilt was apparent, even though there was no conceivable way this was his fault and the damage was minor. "Three." He glanced down and pulled.

I didn't even feel it come out. He placed it on the table beside him, then tugged off my slipper. His brow furrowed as he leaned in to consider the slice. He brought the bucket of water closer to my foot and pulled out a rag, wringing it before using it to wash the cut.

"Vincent, you don't have to do that." I swatted at him and reached for the cloth. "Give that here."

He held it back. "Just let me. You won't see if you've cleaned it from that side."

I wasn't sure if he had a point, but he looked so intent on washing my foot as he rinsed the rag and scrubbed gently again, this time with soap. I let him continue, leaning back against the armrest as he worked. His movements were careful, like I was a fragile thing to cherish—the opposite of everything his parents had said about me.

"Vincent." He glanced up through long lashes as he knelt at my feet. Warmth bloomed in my chest, and I wasn't quite sure why. "What were you going to say before your parents arrived?"

His chuckle was low, almost dark. "It doesn't matter now."

I reached for his chin before I could stop myself. My fingers lifted his gaze to meet mine. "It does to me." I swallowed. "They proved my question even more true than I could have realized."

He winced.

"Sorry," I said, realizing that sounded harsh. His parents *had* said I wasn't significant enough to matter.

"Don't be." He wrung the rag again. The water was a brownish red from the dirt and my blood, but he kept going. "Funny enough, I wanted to say I had perfect examples of how *not* to act. My parents have always been that way. The more society changed around them, the more they clung to harmful and inaccurate beliefs about magic."

"That's why you left?" I asked, my voice almost a whisper.

He seemed satisfied with cleaning my foot. "The bleeding has stopped, but I will wrap it anyway." He pulled the strips of cloth from his pile of work items. Before I could protest, he continued, "That's not the only reason I left."

A light breeze swirled around the room, and I thought I knew. "Your wind."

He looked up, something close to awe in his gaze at my inherent understanding. Of course it was his wind. It was the most unique thing about him. Any old fae family would find it odd, especially if it was so playful all the time.

"So, it's always like this?" I raised my hand and let the breeze wrap around it.

He laughed. It was the first real one I'd heard since his parents had appeared in the restaurant. "Not quite."

His wind swept through his hair as if to sass him.

"It's always been...energetic, but its infatuation with you is new." The tips of his high cheekbones pinked, and I wanted to lean forward and press my lips to them.

Where did that come from?

His words sped up as he realized what he'd said. "My parents never appreciated that my wind wanted to be used. They believe magic should be powerful and present but more like a status symbol than an actual part of life. Mine strongly disagreed."

The wind whipped around the room in a frenzy.

"I can understand that."

"At some point, it all became too much for us. My parents not only punished me when it acted out, but they did everything they could to control it. When I was old enough to figure out how to provide for myself without them, I left." He swallowed. "I tried to take Skye with me. She didn't want to go. She may disagree with my parents, but she isn't one for confrontation." He tilted his head. "Neither am I, but my magic left me no choice. Hers is...much more naturally what's expected of old fae family magic, so it was never a problem."

I didn't even know what to say. He'd finished bandaging my foot, but his hands were still wrapped around the arch, like he didn't want to let go. I understood the feeling.

He looked around the room again as if suddenly becoming self-conscious about where we were. "I'm sorry, I've not had anyone here before. I don't think I have anything to offer you." He glanced down to where he still held my foot and startled as if he'd forgotten what he was doing. Setting it down gently on the couch, he cleared his throat. "I can get you a carriage home."

His befuddlement was beyond adorable. It was another part of him that didn't mix with the rest. I wiggled my toes to check for pain. He'd done more than was necessary for my foot. I wasn't even sure it required this. Slowly, I sat up, pressing my foot to the floor to test it.

"You shouldn't—"

I held up my hand, checking my weight on my foot. I didn't feel a thing. Satisfied, I stood and reached for him where he was still on his knees before me. He glanced up, and I wasn't prepared for the look that crossed his face. Desire dared to be there, and I couldn't deny it also throbbed in my chest. I wanted to respect his wishes and get out of his private space, but I wasn't quite ready for the night to end if he wasn't.

"I think we should get a drink," I said, smoothing my dress back into place. Hesitantly, he took my hand as he stood. "I want to take you somewhere. A place where we don't have to think about the column, my father, or our bargain. In fact, we both should promise not to think of those things at all."

"Another bargain, Miss Pierce. Didn't we learn our lesson the first time?"

"I'm not sure what lesson you've learned, but our first bargain has only left me wanting more." Maybe that wasn't entirely true. We'd been spending so much time prepping for my thing—the article—I hadn't had to consider the price of our current agreement. I pushed away the thought, wanting to enjoy this moment, this side of Vincent I'd only started to glimpse.

"A bargain of only benefits. We both agree to have fun in the city by the bay."

He looked at me like he didn't think he deserved the offer. Like he was ready to refuse.

"Before you say no, please remember your parents said terrible things about me today."

He looked horrified, his face paling. I smirked, squeezing his hand tighter as he tried to snatch it away.

"I'm kidding." I tilted my head. "Well, I'm not kidding. They did that, but I would never hold it against you. I'm teasing. You can, of course, say no if you want." He opened his mouth, and I rambled: "If it makes a difference, I really don't want you to say no."

His smile lit up the dark room. "What about your foot?"

I waved my hand. "It's fine, and I'm sure your wind will help me if I need it—maybe even if I don't."

He laughed at that. "Indeed. Alright. Where are we going?"

I shimmied with glee as I slid my foot back into the slipper. "It's a surprise," I said, not letting go of his hand as I dragged him back into the night.

17

Luna

We walked hand in hand the few blocks to my chosen establishment. I'd considered Parkview Tavern, but everyone knew me there. I wanted somewhere where we'd both be strangers. His wind wrapped around my foot with each step I took, creating a gentle layer between it and the ground. It acted to propel me forward without putting any weight on the cut. I gave him a heavy dose of side-eye, and this time, he shrugged. It was as much an acknowledgment as any that he and his wind were aligned in this.

The night was dark; a new moon hung above us, and I found I missed its glow.

Companionable silence lingered between us as I opened the door to Elemental Tavern and ushered him inside. He glanced around, taking in the boisterous atmosphere that was unlike anything we'd been to together. This place was...loud but alive. It was somewhere I liked to go to disappear. There was always music, and the later it got, the more entertaining the patrons. This was one of the only taverns in Sandrin that didn't prohibit the use of magic. Fae flocked to it for that reason. It was easy for fae magic to get out of hand while they were drinking. Yet, even as a non-magic user, I felt safe here. The rules were clear: all magic that bumped into other guests must be consensual. Once I'd realized that the rules were enforced, I'd come often to see the fae with their magic.

They were at their least pretentious here, no matter what court or family they belonged to. Everyone seemed like they were here to have fun, to let loose. A part of me liked being around the magic without the weight of someone's disappointment that I didn't have any.

"What is this place?" Vincent asked.

"It's a magic tavern." I wasn't surprised he wasn't familiar with it. I didn't think many of those from old fae families came here; at least, I'd not seen any I recognized. This place was for the fae who didn't come from high society—those who worked in the city like the humans.

"They're allowed to use magic?" He sniffed the air. Fae had an excellent sense of smell regarding other magic being wielded, even magic outside their element. The scent signatures of each wielder's magic were unique.

"They are," I said. "They won't use it on you without your consent."

His gaze followed a couple across the tavern. A woman, human by the looks of it, was being lifted in the air, her partner rushing toward her even though his magic held her in place. She squealed in delight as the magic dropped her, but he caught her in his arms.

"That's a little much for a tavern," Vincent said as we found seats at the bar. We ordered drinks that were magically delivered to us moments later. The bartender must be wind fae, too.

Vincent sipped his drink as if trying to adjust to our new surroundings. "Isn't that something that should be done...in private?" His gaze found another couple. I could only assume the wielder was of the Norden Court; the female with magic kept turning her partner's drink to solid ice and then back. They both giggled every time she did so.

I laughed as his wind swept through my hair. "I'm not sure you're in a position to judge." His fingers tightened around his drink glass, and his wind retreated.

"Some displays are more suggestive than others," I said. "The later we stay, the more the scales tip in the risqué direction." I took a sip of my drink. Maybe I hadn't thought this through. I'd thought his wind would like it, but somehow, this place had brought forth his propriety.

His wind rushed along my skin, wrapping around me with more than a bit of possessiveness, consuming me in a way Vincent's sensibilities didn't seem to allow. When I looked at him in question, he was glaring at a male on the other side of me. The fae looked me over appreciatively but seemed to smell Vincent's magic in the air. He raised his hands in surrender, returning to his drink.

"Seems like you fit in here fine." I smirked. He looked a little flustered as he pulled his wind back to him. "Is magic still such a private thing for you? If you left Andiveron House to be able to use it as you please, I thought you'd like it here."

He tilted his head from side to side as he took another sip. "As I said at the apartment, my magic has been free around you."

My body warmed. I wasn't sure whether it was from the sip of spirits or his words.

"It's not usually so bad. Letting it assist me with everyday tasks has been enough."

"*Not so bad* doesn't sound like a satisfying way to live."

He smirked, running his fingers through his hair. It reminded me fleetingly that I'd done the same at Timeless Classics before the food was served. I wanted to do it again.

"I may have left Andiveron House, but I haven't rid myself of everything I was raised to be," he said.

"What do you mean?"

"I'm not as free as you are."

I laughed loudly. "Obviously."

He leaned forward. "No one knows I've split with my family. So, I keep up appearances in public. Again, I'm sure that sounds ridiculous to you, since my wind tries to sweep you away at every opportunity, but..." He shrugged.

"I don't think you're out here lying to my face, Vincent. If I thought you were that kind of fae, I wouldn't have even made the bargain, no matter how much I like your column."

He grinned at that. "While I may use magic for everyday tasks, using it for something like this is...different. I'm never sure how someone will react if they see me acting differently than what's expected."

His wind was in my hair, and from the glint in his eyes, I knew it was no mistake. It hadn't slipped free.

"This seems like something unexpected." I gestured to my hair.

"Well, you brought me here. You only have yourself to blame." He seemed so focused on me that the rest of the tavern fell away. "As you say, I'll let you determine what kind of male I am. You seem more than capable."

I wanted to reach across the space between us and put my hand on his cheek. I wanted to press my lips to his. I wanted so many things that couldn't be because we'd chosen this path. We still had weeks yet before Long Night. I still hadn't tried to get Darius to invite me to Pierce House. I wasn't even sure one invite would be enough. What if we didn't find anything? I couldn't wait until the last second, either; I needed Vincent to publish his article before Long Night if I was going to fill the inn in time.

Tomorrow. I resolved to send a message to Darius tomorrow. I'd update him on my progress. Maybe if he met with me somewhere neutral first, he would agree to a meal at the house for me to present my long-term plans for the inn. That could work.

Vincent stared at me. I'd been lost in thought for too long.

"Did you say something?" I asked.

He shook his head. "I think you might be breaking our bargain."

My face fell. How could he know that? I was going to do everything I could. I hadn't failed yet.

"Not that one." His hand rested on mine, concern in his brown eyes. "You promised me at the apartment that we wouldn't think about the column, your father, or our bargain on this adventure. I don't think you're holding up your end."

My smile was tentative, and I turned on the stool to face him. As I did, his gaze slid down my body with appreciation. The look was far different from the one he'd given my colorful shawl. This look had me reaching for the empty drink glass, anything to steady myself. I wondered if he found me more attractive in these old fae styles. No matter how carefully his sister had selected the pieces, they still weren't quite me. As much as I pretended I was fine with our approach, with appealing to the fae of Sandrin, I couldn't say I enjoyed the idea that he might want to change me.

I was comfortable in my skin, even though my skin was somewhere in between fae and human. When Mom had passed, I'd found friends who accepted me for who I was. I'd decided I didn't need to be accepted by everyone; a few who cared for me would be enough.

I was changing that with this plan. I told myself it was temporary, a plan to save the inn that would keep it mine past Long Night. If I didn't do this, I'd have to find a new home. The memories of Mom that I'd carefully tucked away across the property would be lost to whatever new establishment Darius sold to. I didn't want that to happen—apparently, more than I didn't want to change myself to get customers.

Vincent's gaze met mine and held. He leaned in, and something jolted through my body. His lips were at my ear. To the rest of the bar, it might look like he was leaning in to be heard above the music. We hadn't been this close since I'd pretended to be his lover at the boutique.

"It looks like you require assistance freeing your mind," he said.

I tilted my head, unsure what he meant, though I knew he was correct. My mind was still spinning over everything I had to do. Over every way he and I didn't fit together because of the separate worlds from which we came. I'd learned tonight that we weren't as far apart as I thought, both from old fae families but not living on the estate. I wasn't sure that left us anywhere helpful, though. He still didn't seem to appreciate things that broke the mold. And no matter how much he seemed to sincerely enjoy my company, I wouldn't change for him.

"Excuse me, miss," a voice asked over my shoulder, "would you care to dance?"

I turned to look at the fae in question. Water circled his hand, showing he intended to use his element if I said yes. He was tall, with long blond hair knotted at the base of his neck. A quick glance around the room told me the hour was later than I'd realized. Vincent had fended off the first suitor, but plenty more fae were looking to show off their magic. It appeared that Vincent and I were almost the only two in the tavern not locked in some magic display. No wonder this male had felt bold enough to approach. I opened my mouth to turn him down.

"Apologies, sir," Vincent cut in. "I was about to request a dance myself."

I gave the Norden a halfhearted smile, wishing him the best, and turned to look at Vincent. I was sure he'd only said that to get the fae to back off, but when I met his gaze, he was already standing, draping his coat on the barstool. Unsure about everything, I couldn't shake free from the part of me that wanted to know what Vincent's wind would feel like under his control. I was sure I'd regret this, but I wouldn't pass up the opportunity. Taking Vincent's offered hand, I let him lead me to the dance floor.

18

Vincent

W*hat did I say?* I had no time to reconsider the words that had shot from my mouth unapproved by my brain. Luna took my offered hand, and regret was the furthest thing from my mind when my hand closed around hers and I led her to the edge of the dancefloor. She was right; the magic usage had become more pronounced the longer we stayed. What had originally been a few couples showing off was now nearly every couple in the tavern experimenting with something.

My wind thudded in my chest. I wasn't ready to let it out, but it swirled there as I considered that she'd chosen this place for me—for my magic. She had thought I'd enjoy the freedom. Truth be told, I probably would if I could get out of my own way. I was on edge from seeing my parents, from everything they'd said, from Luna getting hurt and taking her to the apartment, and the confusing way I felt around her. No wonder my magic was eager to play.

Now, I'd gone and let my pride take over. I hadn't liked the first male leering at her, nor the second asking her to dance. It was incredibly unhelpful, though.

She wasn't mine.

Maybe that doesn't have to be true. The thought stopped air from flowing into my lungs.

"Vincent?"

I'd held her hand at the edge of the dance floor for too long. She probably thought I was hesitating, that I didn't want to dance with her. Nothing was further from the truth. Luna's big blue eyes looked up at me.

"Did you actually want to dance?" she asked. "Or were you trying to save me from rejecting that other male?"

She was so charitable, even in this. I'd had no idea she was planning to reject him. Everything in me hadn't wanted them to dance together, so I'd acted. I wasn't sure if I wanted to dance, but I knew—absolutely knew—that I wanted to be with her, even if only on the dance floor for the length of a single song.

"I'd like to dance," I leaned toward her ear, ostensibly to avoid the noise but mostly because I liked that she let me so close. "If you would."

My wind chose that moment to whip around her, ensuring she was wrapped up in me. She laughed, and I sighed. "You did agree to dance with my wind, so I guess this is what you signed up for."

"I have a question," she said quietly, her hands moving into position for me to take. It was as if she feared I didn't know how to dance even though I'd been raised in an old fae estate, with balls and celebrations that required such things.

"Ask it."

The music was slow, and most couples seemed more focused on their magic than the rhythm. I took her offered hands and swept her into my arms. One hand was carefully on her waist, and the other held hers. I swallowed my nerves and pulled her a little closer. She fit against me so well, and my wind swelled in my chest.

She sniffed the air as if she could sense it trying to escape. "How often does your wind…" She seemed to struggle to find the words. That wasn't like Luna. She usually had more words than she needed. "Act on its own?"

I laughed. Of course she'd ask. My wind had done nothing but harass her since we met. I leaned in close, my nose brushing lightly across her cheek, before my lips settled at her ear. "That's the secret, isn't it? My wind and I are one, but sometimes it does things I lack the courage to."

Her radiant smile threatened to bring me to my knees. As if proving my point with flair, my wind slid through her hair. She leaned into the gesture, and something warm infused my chest.

This felt too good. I distracted myself, looking around the dancefloor. It was magical simply to see the pairings. Fae and human was common, but more unique were the pairings between fae courts. Nearly every combination of the four elements could be found on the dance floor. A female behind us created a water vortex around her and her partner. A male off to the side shook the ground beneath them with each step they took. None of it made sense—it was magic for magic's sake. My wind thrummed with excitement.

"You don't have to do any magic if you don't want to," she said. "This is nice."

She sounded like she meant it, but I'd promised her a dance with wind, and my magic had heard me. It was itching to slide around us again. "Would you…" I cleared my throat. "Would it be alright if I used it?"

The smile that lit up her features was all I needed. "Yes, if you're comfortable."

I was decidedly uncomfortable, but I liked that about her.

She didn't hide herself from the world like I did. She was unapologetically her in everything she did. Her curiosity was intoxicating. How she spoke whatever was on her mind had me hanging on her every word. And her energy—the confidence she exuded simply by being herself—was more attractive than I was prepared to ignore.

I broke our rule as my mind wandered to our bargain. She made it seem like I was doing her some big favor. It had upset me to think that was all she wanted me for. Now, I wasn't sure either was true. Her research had been as helpful as mine. She knew how to tell a story and how to make people comfortable. I knew she'd do fine with the inn if she could get visitors in the door, which I would do with my column.

The locked door had had me stewing for the days we'd been apart. I wouldn't allow myself to think of her, so I focused on it instead. I wondered how much of the vacancy was her fault. Sometimes, magic like that did more than was inherently obvious. It might be stopping customers from arriving as much as it prevented us from opening the door. My magic may not be up to solving that problem, but I knew someone who could. I'd sent him a message earlier that morning.

Our movement brought us closer. My fingers stretched to wrap her tighter in my arms, and all thoughts of the inn and the article were gone again. Before I could think too much about it, my wind swept around us and pushed us ever so slightly closer together. She looked up at me and smiled as it wove through the blonde strands of her hair. Then it created a little vortex around us, similar to the way the water had for another couple on the dance floor. I was content to continue moving like this, but my wind had other ideas.

It wrapped around our joined hands, and then I felt it slide up her arm, wind against skin as it blew beneath the material of her navy-blue dress. I sucked in a breath, wrangling my wind back. "I'm sorry."

Her eyes danced with mirth. "I think your wind likes me more than it likes you."

"Undoubtedly. Have you seen yourself? There is no competition between the two of us."

She looked down, and I realized she was still uncomfortable with the outfit. It was according to our plan that she'd dressed like this tonight.

"You like me in this fae fashion?" she asked.

I almost stumbled. Her words caught me off guard. My wind tipped her chin up so she met my gaze. "Luna, let me be clear. I find you beautiful no matter what you wear, and I'd happily drop this part of the plan if you'd let me."

We kept moving, my wind circling.

"Have you ever recommended something half-fae?" she asked.

I shook my head. "Not to my knowledge. I'm sorry." I wasn't sure what to say. My success had been with the fae; they were who I appealed to.

"It all feels the same. The same colors, the same cuts, it's like you all want to blend in." She glanced up at me. "Well, not you—not all the time."

"What do you mean? I fit the mold perfectly."

We spun again, and she gestured downward. "Every part of you but that jacket."

I'd thought about this at the restaurant when my father had showed up. It shouldn't surprise me that she'd noticed. It was such a slight distinction from the standard fashion. Like all the others, it was a dark jacket, but the ties were gold.

"I like the fasteners," I replied with a quick glance at the jacket. "They're different but usually not noticeable."

She laughed. "Please don't mistake me. I love the fasteners. They're perfect."

"I will accept your love of the fasteners if you accept my

prior compliments as having nothing to do with this dress," I said, pulling her closer.

Her cheeks flushed, and I took a little pride in her reaction to me. My wind decided it wanted a turn, and it swept across her cheek in an attempt to cool her flush.

Her gaze met mine, a little sad. "Do you ever wonder what would have happened if we didn't need each other the way we do?"

I let out a breath. "I'm sure that's one of the topics we're not supposed to discuss tonight."

She laughed and bumped into me as we danced. What did I say to that? We hadn't had the most graceful first meeting, but she was right; we'd had a chance at...*something*, at the end. Before I'd learned her last name. That thought had me shaking my head. We'd never had a chance because she'd been planning to use me the whole time. She'd always wanted to ask for the recommendation, like everyone else.

That assumption no longer felt right, though. The answer was only a breath away if I dared to ask. *Do I want to know?* I slid my hand down her arm, leaning close and whispering into her ear before I could stop myself. "I think about it all the time. I wonder when you knew I was the author of 'Benefits of Magic.'"

She stepped back and I stopped breathing as her bright blue eyes widened.

"I didn't know until after you left, Vincent." She stopped moving, but stayed in the circle of my arms. "One of my regulars...his wife works with you at the paper. They told me later that evening."

I let out a shaky breath. It was what I wanted to hear, but why did it make me feel so terrible?

"I think I need to go." I let her hand drop.

She nodded and followed me from the dance floor. Paying the tab, we left the tavern. The night was chilly, a cold wind sweeping across the city from the sea. She shivered, looking up at me like she wanted to say something. I wasn't sure I wanted to hear anything else. Why had I asked? I hadn't really wanted to know the answer. I'd convinced myself to push her to spy on her father because I'd been sure she was using me for my column. Had I really believed she orchestrated our meeting? It didn't even make sense. She'd thrown a drink at me; it was hardly a move to win my affection.

It worked, though.

My wind tapped against my forehead in a pattern that said I should know better. That my thoughts were incongruent with everything else I'd known about her. The more I got to know her, the less I could cling to the lies I'd told myself. If I accepted the truth that her regular had mentioned what I wrote and she'd decided to ask me what she considered a harmless favor, our bargain, what I asked of her, made me a bit of a bastard. She couldn't have known how often people asked to have things featured. She was nothing like the rest of them. I wasn't sure she had a disingenuous bone in her body.

"Luna," I started. She'd been watching me closely. I had no idea what she'd seen on my face.

"You can't take it back now," she said, and they were the last words I expected.

"Maybe we shouldn't—"

"No." Her hands were on her hips. "I don't know how you convinced yourself to agree to our bargain in the first place, but I see your regret." She stepped closer, her chin rising slightly. "It's too late. You agreed. We both still need this."

She was right, of course. I still wanted to write feature stories. I still needed a way to get to her father. But did it have to be through her?

As if hearing my thoughts, she continued. "I'll send a message to Darius, and we'll get to work on your side of things. I'll buy a few more stupid dresses"—she waved her hand down her body—"and we'll both get what we want by Long Night. You will have your investigative piece, and I'll have saved my inn."

I swallowed my response. There wasn't much I could say, even if, truthfully, I wasn't sure that was what I wanted any longer.

19

Luna

Days later, I was still venting my frustrations with Vincent on the dough I kneaded. In the safety of my cottage, I stewed on his question from the magic tavern. *How dare he show regret*? I pushed my palms into the dough and folded it. *How dare he realize he was the ass in this whole bargain.* I could admit I realized now why he'd been so sensitive to my request for a recommendation. That was what everyone did. That was how everyone saw him.

You saw him that way, too, before you knew better.

That was the problem, wasn't it? I couldn't have known how people used him for his recommendations without knowing him.

Couldn't the same be said for him and your relationship with Darius?

I shook my head and folded the dough again. No. He'd known there was strain between me and Darius. He'd said he went to the court records office. Vincent would have seen where my name was in the Norden book.

Why is this bothering me?

I didn't know what had come over him, but his hesitation to continue our bargain had been plain as day on his face. I could still see it with perfect clarity. I gritted my teeth and folded the dough again.

That couldn't happen. No matter the complexities of my feelings for Vincent, I needed to save this inn. We'd come so far already. The only way I could keep him from canceling our bargain was to plow forward with Darius. I had to hold up my end, and then he'd have no choice but to continue.

I'd sent Darius a message the morning after seeing Vincent. I had yet to hear back, but that wasn't abnormal. I didn't expect an immediate response, or, at least, that is what I told myself. What would it be like if my father actually wanted to hear from me? Or spend time with me?

Well, it didn't guarantee things would be better. I remembered how Vincent's parents had approached our table at the restaurant. The entitled way they'd claimed his time and attempted to dictate his actions. He'd fought them off the best he could, but still. It was clear they treasured him in their own way. Maybe more like a precious stone to look at and value instead of a living, breathing fae with his own thoughts and opinions, but...it was something. They had their own ideas and requirements for what his life should look like. I wasn't sure that was any better than my father completely ignoring me.

I pressed my palms into the dough again with more force.

When a knock on the door sounded, I silently thanked the gods for distracting me from the thoughts of Vincent and our bargain. "Come in!"

Evelyn entered, balancing a stack of books precariously in one arm. A folded piece of paper lay across the top. I reached to help her but my hands were still covered in sticky dough.

"Sorry, Evelyn, I can't help you at the moment."

Evelyn grunted. "I saw this on the inn's doorstep, so I grabbed it." She set the folded paper on the counter. "The rest are mine." She gestured to the stack of books. "We have a good starting point for opening that door."

I hadn't seen Evelyn much in the last week, given I wasn't working at the tavern often. Seraphina, the friend she was, hadn't given me shifts, knowing I had things to do for the inn. That hadn't stopped Evelyn from reporting on her progress. She'd sent me her notes on the magic after I stopped by the tavern; it was a treatise I could only understand every other word of, but Evelyn was its author. I'd known she was brilliant, but I couldn't believe she'd been hiding such a big part of her life from us. She seemed obsessed with solving this problem. It was as if the magic sealing the door personally offended her.

Rinsing my hands, I toweled them dry and grabbed the note. My breath came up short. It was from Darius. I broke the seal and read it.

"He wants to meet for the evening meal." I coughed. "At Parkview Tavern." My eyes continued skimming the page. "Tomorrow."

Evelyn stepped closer to read over my shoulder. "That was quick. What did you say to him?"

"I said I wanted to report the inn's progress. I also told him I had a favor to ask." I flipped the page over to see if he'd written on the other side. "He didn't even ask about the favor. Or the inn."

Evelyn's hands went to her hips. "Well, at least if you meet him at the tavern, Seraphina and I will be there if it goes to shit."

I laughed. "Yes, that will help."

It was still strange. Even the fact that Parkview Tavern was where he wanted to meet. I'd expected Darius to be more like Vincent's parents. It wouldn't have surprised me if he'd suggested the same restaurant Vincent had taken me to. Just as quickly, another unwanted thought jumped in. *Maybe he doesn't want to be seen with you there by anyone important, anyone he knows.*

Honestly, I wished I didn't always think the worst of him. I wished there was some place in the middle where we could meet. I'd love to believe he'd invited me to the tavern because he knew I was comfortable there, but that would require him to know anything about my life—which he didn't. I sighed.

"Are you going to accept?" Evelyn asked.

"Yes, of course. This is part of the deal with Vincent. For him to write the article, I must get him into Pierce House."

Evelyn looked like she'd say something but shook her head instead. "Have you decided on the favor that will get you and Vincent invited to the house?"

I hadn't. I really should have come up with something in my original note to Darius, but another small part of me had wanted to see if he'd respond if there was nothing in it for him. He had, which I guessed was to his credit. I wasn't great at lying. I'd need something close to the truth, or he'd never believe it. At least I had until tomorrow to workshop ideas.

"You could tell him you want to see Pierce House?" she offered.

"I'm not sure that's enough. He's never offered to show it to me before. Why would he now?"

Evelyn's gaze darted between me and the letter. "He's never offered to meet for a meal before, either, until you asked to speak with him. Maybe that's the difference."

"Me asking?" I had said this to Seraphina weeks ago, but I was still surprised Evelyn mentioned it. I'd never asked Darius for anything. Maybe he'd been waiting for me to do so. I shook my head. "I don't think he cares what I want. He didn't care when I was a child and had no magic. Nothing has changed." My words were too harsh for Evelyn. This had nothing to do with her. "Sorry." I brushed my hair back from my face.

She smiled. "It's fine. You know him better than I. Do you want to walk over to the inn and test some of what I've found?"

"Yes, that'd be great. Let me bring this." I picked up the bowl where my dough was resting. My instincts told me I'd soon have more emotions to work out on it.

We entered the inn, and I headed to the small kitchen while Evelyn went upstairs. Rolling the dough into twist shapes didn't work out the same energy as kneading, but it was soothing nonetheless. These pastries were my favorite, perfect for adding a little sugar and cinnamon. As I finished and slid them in the oven, a knock sounded at the door.

I opened it to find Vincent and...someone else.

"Hi, Luna," Vincent said. "I hope we're not imposing. This is my friend, Ambrose. He might know something about the magic on your locked door."

As I studied Vincent, any lingering anger seemed to rush from my chest like a retreating tide. We hadn't made plans to speak again until I could uphold my side of the bargain. I wouldn't risk him trying to back out again, and spending time together only seemed to weaken his resolve. Mine, too, if I was honest.

Now, here he was, trying to solve one of my problems that had no part in our bargain. Something prickled behind my eyes. I blinked rapidly and turned my focus to his friend. Ambrose was tall, with auburn hair pushed back from his face. It was messy, as if he consistently ran his hand through it.

"Hi, Ambrose. Thanks for coming by." I glanced nervously at Vincent. "But I already have someone here working on the door."

"It's Evelyn Knowles, isn't it?" Ambrose, as I expected, ran his fingers through his hair, waiting for my answer.

My eyes narrowed, and I folded my arms over my chest as I held the door, ready to close it. What did this stranger want with Evelyn?

As if recognizing my concern, Ambrose held out his hands. "I work with her at the Vesten Library." He sounded regretful as he continued. "She's the only other person in the city who could help with this if it is as Vincent describes."

Appearing like she was summoned, Evelyn padded down the stairs to stand at my side. "What are you doing here, Ambrose?"

"I was asked to help. It sounded interesting."

Evelyn glared at him, her hand on her hip. "It only sounded interesting because you knew whoever solved it would be better positioned for our paper."

Ambrose folded his arms over his chest. The move showed off oddly defined biceps for an academic. My gaze hadn't lingered for more than a moment when a familiar wind swept through my hair. I shivered, glaring at Vincent as the conversation continued.

Vincent noted my glare, smirking as if to say he and his wind had no regrets. I remembered his words from the dance floor. *My wind and I are one, but sometimes it does things I lack the courage to.*

"And I noticed you didn't tell me about it at the library yesterday." Ambrose tapped his chin. "Or maybe it slipped your mind."

"She is one of my best friends." Evelyn gestured to me in a way that would have been sweet if she hadn't sounded so exhausted by the announcement. "Must you vex me even in my extracurricular activities?"

My attention left Vincent and returned to the researchers arguing at the door. I wasn't sure I'd ever heard Evelyn speak this way to someone. It was clear that Ambrose only wanted to be here because Evelyn was. Evelyn seemed to understand no such thing. I couldn't help but laugh at the tension.

They both glared at me.

"Vincent asked if I could help. And this is his..." Ambrose paused, his cheeks heating. He must have realized he didn't know the extent of my relationship with Vincent. He shot a panicked glance at Vincent, who didn't look like he was doing all too well himself with completing the sentence.

I decided to put them both out of their misery. "How do you two know each other?" I asked, gesturing between Ambrose and Vincent. Now that I sensed a collegiate rivalry between Evelyn and Ambrose, I was beyond entertained by the coincidence.

"We met when he wrote a piece earlier this year on the Compass Points' visit to Sandrin." He glanced at Vincent. "That one never got published, did it?"

"No, it didn't," he said stiffly. "But that's not why we're here." He gestured between Evelyn and Ambrose. "As they've both attested, they are the only two scholars capable of solving the issue with your door. I suggest we let them work. You and I can chat in the kitchen, where I smell some sugary sweetness we should discuss serving at the inn's announcement weekend."

I wasn't ready to be alone with Vincent so quickly. What if he wanted to dissolve our bargain again? I knew he had his reasons, as I had mine for wanting to keep it. The comment about the piece he'd worked on with Ambrose was an easy reminder. He didn't want to write recommendations forever, and I was his ticket away from them. All he needed to do was write one final recommendation—mine.

"The rolls have a little time before they're ready," I hedged. "Let's see what these two will get up to first."

He pursed his lips as if he might try to argue, but then

shook his head and followed us as we marched up the steps to the locked door.

"You've been holding out on me," Ambrose said as he knelt before the door. He turned to glare at Evelyn.

"I had it under control." She crossed her arms over her chest.

"Of course you did, but you should have said something." Ambrose turned to me then. "Do you know anything about the magic on this door?"

"No. I didn't even know it was magically locked until..." I glanced at Evelyn for help. "Two weeks ago?"

"What were you going to try today?" Ambrose asked Evelyn.

She glared at Ambrose but shot a worried look over her shoulder at me. "Ambrose, can we...confer?" I couldn't imagine what I had done wrong, but I shrugged and stepped back to give them space. I didn't realize until too late that this left me in the same position I'd attempted to avoid downstairs.

Vincent smiled at me. It was too charming, the way his thick brown hair fell over his right eye. My fingers twitched to reach for it. I straightened my spine. "I wrote to my father. I'm meeting him for a meal at the tavern tomorrow."

The smile on Vincent's face disappeared. "You didn't have to do that."

I held up a hand. "Yes, Vincent, I did. We have a bargain. I'm only following through on my side."

His eyes shifted back and forth, though whether in thought or panic, I wasn't sure.

"Do you...need me for anything? I never meant to put you in that position. Well, I did. Obviously," he muttered. "And I knew it would be painful. I just..." He sighed. "I just didn't know...I'm sorry."

He seemed unable to finish a thought, but with his apology, my shoulders fell, and with them my defenses. I thought he meant that he hadn't known me when he'd made his original ask—hadn't known the extent of Darius's dismissal. The same way I hadn't known the extent to which requesting recommendations bothered him.

"Thank you for the offer. I don't need anything. I'll ask him, and we'll see what he says."

Vincent hesitated. "May I meet you at the tavern after the meal? I don't care about Darius's answer. I want to ensure you're well after the conversation."

My whole body heated. Of course, Seraphina and Evelyn would be there, but the idea that Vincent wanted to check on me warmed something deep inside. I don't know what that said about the rest of our arrangement, but I couldn't stop my lip from tilting into a smile. "That would be fine."

At that moment, Ambrose cleared his throat to regain our attention. "We..." Ambrose started, then glanced at Evelyn. "We need to talk to you about a sensitive matter."

"Me?" I pointed to myself, unsure what I had to do with this.

He nodded. Evelyn stepped forward. "We need to talk to you about magic," she whispered. "Do you want them to go?" Her gaze shot between Ambrose and Vincent.

"Magic? I don't have any magic. Why would they need to go?"

She frowned, and I immediately knew I wouldn't like the words coming from her mouth.

"I know you believe that." She gave Ambrose and Vincent a sideways glance. "But the magic on this door, well...it's connected to *something*. I'm confident it's your magic." She ran her fingers through her hair nervously. "Only your magic can open it."

20

Vincent

I didn't know much, as I continued to prove with Luna, but I knew this wasn't a great way to approach the topic of her magic.

Luna had magic—I fully agreed with that point, but my one attempt to discuss it with her had left me unwilling to broach the subject again without more evidence. I had yet to find any. I knew the look on Evelyn's face, though. Ambrose got it sometimes when he was deep in an experiment. Luna's inability to acknowledge her magic was now a blocker in Evelyn's research.

"I don't have magic," Luna said coldly. She folded her arms over her chest.

"I'm not sure that's strictly true." Evelyn matched her pose.

I let my head tilt back and stared at the ceiling momentarily. Not how I would have approached the conversation, but Evelyn had known Luna far longer. I hoped her angle would work.

"What do you mean? Not strictly true?" The knuckles on Luna's fists turned white as she clenched them tighter.

"I mean that you *do* have magic. It's...not always accessible."

Ah, well, at least that helped me understand what I'd seen. After the night I'd met Luna, I would have bet any amount of coin that she had magic. The water had responded to her call. I was sure of it. But her reaction when I even mentioned it had left me confused. My gaze shifted between Luna and Evelyn. Was it possible Luna hadn't known? And Evelyn had?

"Not always accessible?" Luna repeated the words like they were a curse. "What does that mean?"

"I don't know," Evelyn said, throwing her hands in the air. She was most definitely not equipped to speak with her friend right now. She was discussing an experiment that wasn't going her way. I had to step in.

"Luna." Her glare turned on me, and I regretted my decision immediately, but as Evelyn let out a breath and rubbed her temples, I knew I was best to handle the rest of this conversation. "Are there ever things you do that can't be explained?" I searched for an example I could give her, and immediately, the pieces clicked together in my mind. "Like when you threw my drink at me?"

Her frown deepened.

I held up my hands, begging for patience. "You said you didn't throw it, right? But you were angry at me."

"You were being an ass," she said matter-of-factly.

My palms were still face up in supplication. "Yes, and I smelled moonflower and juniper when the drink struck my face. Those scents shouldn't have been present in the drink."

Her brow furrowed as she tried to follow my logic.

"I smelled the same thing outside when the water rippled around you." Then, the item in the locked room popped into my head. The moonflower. I remembered her quiet voice when she'd given me the tour, admitting that she stole the moonflowers when they bloomed.

I had known then. I'd also known she wasn't ready to

discuss it. My wind swirled in my chest as I broached the forbidden topic again. I lowered my voice. "You said the moonflowers bloomed for you?"

She tilted her head. "Yes...I told you I stole them from Byrd."

Ambrose's eyes lit up as he heard the words and got a little too enthusiastic, jumping back in. "Moonflower can only be kept by water fae."

I glared at Ambrose, and his head hung as he stepped back next to Evelyn.

"What do you mean?" Luna replied. "This whole place is the property of water fae. Darius is of the Norden Court, and so was Byrd."

"Yes, but the flower can only be picked by a water fae."

She bit her lip. "I'm half water fae, but that doesn't mean I have the magic. Maybe it's just a technicality."

She had a point, but I was also sure she was wrong.

Ambrose couldn't help himself, stepping in again. "The flower requires magic. It's how they distinguish water fae from others. It doesn't require intentional usage, only the presence of the magic. You could even be wielding without realizing it."

"Seraphina and I found it odd that you wouldn't admit to throwing the drink at him," Evelyn said. "We thought you were embarrassed because he was handsome."

My wind preened.

"It makes more sense that you were unaware of the magic but that it still acted on your behalf. I've read about such things, especially in long-repressed power. It makes itself known eventually."

"This is crazy," Luna said.

Her gaze found mine and hung on like a lifeline. No matter what she said, I could see her considering it. Right when I thought she'd admit it, water rimmed her eyes, and I knew what she would say next would break my heart.

"Darius didn't want me because I didn't have any magic. He checked."

My hands balled into fists, the nubs of my nails digging into the skin to keep hold of my emotions. This wasn't the time for me to overreact to what she shared. There would be time for that later. I couldn't believe Darius would have said such a thing to her. Then I thought of my parents and realized I could easily see them saying the same thing to me if I hadn't had visible magic. I took a step closer to her in the hallway. I raised my hand to reach for hers, and then I realized she might not welcome it. I dropped it, but when I found her gaze, it was fixed on my fallen hand. Why was everything so difficult between us?

"I'm sorry he said that to you," I whispered. "I'm sorry the fae are so terrible, and that he was a terrible father on top of that for making you feel like your magic was the only part of you that mattered. I assure you, it's not."

She was still staring at my hand clasped into a tight fist at my side. Should I reach out again? See if she took it?

I don't want her to feel alone.

"I do have to admit, Luna, I was sure you had magic the night we met. It didn't occur to me that could be the reason behind the drink in my face. I was pretty sure I'd earned that myself. Outside, though, the water in the moat came to life around you. I'm not sure what triggers your magic. I understand it can be different for many half-fae, but I think you have it somewhere."

Her eyes widened. "You thought I was fae that night?"

I let my eyes close momentarily as I tried to think through how she'd react to that. "I did." I'd continue to be honest with her, no matter where it got me. "I knew you were half-fae when I went to the court records room. I figured it out with where your name was in the book." I didn't want her to think I hadn't known what I was doing when I'd asked her to speak with

Darius. While I might not have known the extent of the pain it would cause, I'd known it wouldn't be good.

I stepped closer to her and lowered my voice again, hoping Ambrose and Evelyn couldn't hear. My fingers reached for hers, brushing against them, and with it, my wind circled where our skin met. "I followed the scent of your magic to the moat. It was heavenly. No matter how much you disliked me, I had to know more."

Her big blue eyes widened farther, and a faint blush touched her cheeks. Hopefully, that meant she believed me. Only time would tell.

She held my gaze. "You think I have magic."

My wind circled her hands as she pulled them away to stare at them. She smiled softly, looking at them like she'd never seen them before. "I don't know how to use it."

I smirked. "You have some magic experts here that might be able to give you instruction. Be careful, Luna. Don't push yourself too hard. Half-fae magic is unpredictable. It's different for everyone." She knew this, but I felt it bore repeating before she got her hopes up. "Some have full access, some have one day a year. Others only with the seasons. It's entirely unique, like the individual."

She gestured back to where Evelyn and Ambrose stood. "I understand, but I don't know how to attempt to open the door."

"I'm sure they can explain it to you. In overly long, dry detail."

Her laugh surprised me, and it looked like it surprised her, too, which I liked. At the sound the scholars jumped back into action, scurrying to the door, their gazes locked on us.

Evelyn spoke first. "Your magic is the connection between the lock on this door and whatever magic it holds. Someone close to you must have cast it."

"Why do you say that?" I asked when it looked like Luna wouldn't.

"Well, it's someone who realized she has magic. It's no accident that her power is the connection to the lock." She glanced at Ambrose. "But if we're correct, it's a memory that keeps the door sealed."

"Memory?" I asked. "Isn't that Suden magic? And very few Suden, at that?"

I remembered the memory stone in the packet Patricia had given me. There were more ways to hold memories than Suden magic.

"Blood magic could work, too," Ambrose said as I realized the same. "It's becoming less taboo now that all the Compass Points have learned about it. It was always available previously, if maybe a little looked down upon." He waved his hand. "As were many other things that didn't make much sense. The fae courts may have been unwilling to recognize it as valid, but that didn't mean it didn't exist."

We all stood in silence at that.

"So, do I need to find my magic or the memory?" Luna asked, pulling us back to the conversation.

"Your magic," Ambrose said. "The magic is required to unlock the door. We suspect the memory will reveal itself once you get inside."

"Then what's the point of the memory?" I asked.

"Well..." Evelyn tilted her head. "She'll have to decide what to do with the memory. I assume it's one she's a part of." She glanced apologetically at Luna, then spoke to her directly. "I suspect the memory is simply the intention used to fuel the magic. Blood magic works from intention. The memory will be a strong one, something that drove the need for the magic in the first place."

"If I'm a part of the memory, would I remember it?" Luna asked.

"Not necessarily," Evelyn replied. "We're in an inn. I presume this room has a bed like any other." She shrugged.

"Maybe you were asleep when the driving memory happened."

Luna gasped. "There was only one night I slept in a room at the inn." She glanced down the hall as if realizing where she was. "It was in this room."

Evelyn seemed to understand what she was saying, though Ambrose and I did not.

"You really think something happened that night?" Luna asked.

"It's the only thing that makes sense right now." Evelyn said. "I want you to prepare for the worst."

Ambrose ran his fingers through his hair again. "I obviously don't know the memory." He shook his head. "It doesn't matter. I agree with Evelyn's assessment. I know Evelyn didn't confirm it earlier, but the other item we've failed to discuss is the full impact of this magic."

Luna's gaze shot to Evelyn's. "Your hypothesis. You've confirmed it?"

Evelyn nodded slowly. "The magic makes the inn...unappealing to travelers. If we don't remove the magic, I don't think even Vincent's recommendation will help the inn."

21

Luna

They all thought I had magic. I hadn't been ready to start testing it yesterday, even with Vincent's quiet and confident examples. He knew the topic of my magic was uncomfortable for me. I remembered the first time he'd brought it up on the beach. His explanation made more sense than I was comfortable with. He'd assumed I controlled water the first night we met. Though he'd been quick to say he eventually found out I was half-fae before coming to me with his request, it was an interesting piece of information nonetheless. When he'd first heard my name, he thought I was fae.

I wanted us to get past these first impressions, no matter how good- or bad-intentioned.

Now, my mind was spinning, I hadn't slept, and I was a jumble of nerves. It was safe to say I wasn't sure what to do about the inn or Vincent when I opened the door to Parkview Tavern to meet Darius.

A dull roar of conversation greeted me as I entered. Most chairs and barstools were occupied with excited patrons. I should have come earlier. If Darius was rude and dismissive, I'd rather be at a table so fewer people could hear the disaster in progress. I sighed and slid through the crowd, moving toward the bar. This was yet another reminder of how I was failing. The influx of travelers continued. More visitors arrived every day, but still, none made their way to Cliff House Inn. I clenched my teeth.

We still had two and a half weeks left until Long Night. I could figure this out.

I'd put in words with Winchester and Earthbend inns when I did my initial research. I'd given them each a generous tip of the money Darius had provided for repairs to send customers our way once they were full. They'd said they were happy to help when they had no occupancy. With the volume of unfamiliar faces in the tavern today, I had a hard time imagining their inns weren't filled, but still, not one inquiry had come my way.

I had to face facts. Evelyn was right. My inn was cursed by blood magic.

Another question for my absentee father: did he know? I wasn't sure now was the time to broach the topic when my ultimate goal was to get Vincent and myself invited to Pierce House. I should focus on being charming, but I had never been good at hiding my feelings. And I was feeling frustrated.

Approaching the bar, I waved at Seraphina. She gave me a nod in return and gestured to a table on the left. I assumed she needed me to take a quick order; Evelyn was busy with a customer while someone else flagged her for more drinks. I could help. It was still early, and we'd have to wait for a table anyway, even once Darius did arrive. As I turned, though, my brows raised in surprise. Darius sat quietly where she'd gestured. He had a book propped open before him and something in a mug steamed by his hand as he turned the page.

He was here already?

I had arrived fifteen minutes early and thought that was a lot, but he was all set up like he'd been there for a while. Like he'd known the place would be packed and wanted to procure us that table. Someone could have knocked me over with a feather. This was maybe the last thing I'd expected tonight.

I rolled my shoulders back. I had asked for this. It was time to go through with it. Slowly, I pushed through the crowd again to get to him.

He looked up at my approach. "Luna!" he said brightly, marking his page and closing the book. "This place is packed! Looks like business is good for your friend."

That caught me off-guard on multiple counts. I was still spinning from the fact that he'd arrived early—how did he know Seraphina was my friend?

"Yeah," I said hesitantly. "Thanks for grabbing the table. I had no idea it would be this bad."

He gestured for me to sit. "Cliff House has been keeping you that busy, then? You haven't been working here, too?"

His smile seemed harmless enough, but with Darius, I was always trying to figure out what he could do with the information I provided.

"I haven't. Seraphina said I was essentially fired until the Long Night; then we could talk."

He chuckled. "Sounds like a good friend."

Seraphina showed up at that moment. She set a Solstice Sip on my side of the table and gestured to Darius's drink. "Do you need a refill?"

"No, thanks. What did she bring you?" Darius asked, examining my drink.

"It's the Sweet Solstice Sip," I said. "Or, at least, it's the recipe and the honey liqueur from the original. Have you tried one?" I wanted him to be at ease when I finally worked up the nerve to ask him my questions.

He shook his head. "That's from the Andiveron boy's column?" His nostrils flared as he asked, but I nodded. It shouldn't surprise me that Darius knew who wrote the supposedly anonymous column.

"Ah, I don't keep up with fae trends too well," he said, but I heard something between his words, like maybe it wasn't so much fae trends he didn't keep up with as much as Andiveron trends he didn't care for. I wondered if inviting Vincent and me to Pierce House would be a bigger ask than I'd realized. Was there something between Vincent's family and mine? Other than animosity from being in different courts?

"Do you two want food?" Seraphina asked.

"Yes, please," I said.

Darius ordered the soup of the day. Seraphina disappeared.

"You didn't order," he said.

I raised my glass and smiled. "She knows what I like."

Darius raised his mug, and I found myself clinking our glasses together.

"Thanks for meeting me," I said.

He tilted his head as if in question. "I'm always happy to do so, Luna. I hope you know that."

I absolutely did *not* know that and wasn't sure how to respond. If that was true, I wanted to know why. I took a sip of my drink, considering. I decided the only way out was through. Darius had no reason to do what I asked, but if what he said was true, if he was always happy to meet, then he would be happy to host Vincent and me.

At this point, there was only a tiny chance our plan for the inn would work, given that I had no idea how to access my magic. Magic necessary to save the inn. My eyes met his. They looked so much like my own, bright blue and welcoming, although I'd never once felt welcome by him.

I took a deep breath. "I didn't know that. Why would I know that?" I asked, trying not to sound confrontational. I wasn't sure it worked; I was too caught up in hearing the answer.

He sat up straighter. "I guess that's a fair question." He took a sip of his drink. I was more than surprised by his assessment, by the careful consideration of my question and his open response. "Maybe it's easier if we start fresh. I'd like you to be able to come to me with anything. I want to help you in any way I can."

My fingers wrapped around my glass again. "Why give me such an impossible task with the inn, then? If you want to help me?"

He laughed, but it didn't sound joyful. "I'm pretty sure you're the only one that can save it. And if you're not interested in doing so, there is no point in me holding on to it."

I lifted my glass to my lips again. His words were similar to Evelyn's. They made me wonder if he, too, was aware of the blood magic. I wasn't ready to ask him about that, especially considering the memory.

Starting fresh was also a concept I didn't know how to address. Were we to pretend the last twenty-five years hadn't happened? That he hadn't abandoned me? Was this some misalignment between humans and fae? Twenty-five years probably seemed like nothing to him. It might not be much to me in the span of my lifetime, either, but those years he'd ignored me still hurt.

"So," he started when he must have realized I couldn't find the words to say anything else, "do you have plans for your name day?"

I cleared my throat. Then took another big gulp as I desperately tried to understand his question. "What?"

He licked his lips like maybe he was reconsidering. I was sure I'd heard him correctly. I didn't know why he would be asking.

"Do you have plans for your name day next week?" He swallowed hard and tapped his fingers against the side of his drink. "I wondered if we could host you at the house. Your grandmother and I would be thrilled to have you for a meal."

I sucked in a breath. Exactly what I needed was falling into my lap, and I wasn't entirely sure what to do about it. Thankfully, Seraphina arrived at that moment to deliver the food. She brought Darius his soup, and for me, a meat pie. I couldn't even get excited over one of my favorite dishes as I contemplated how to respond to Darius. Seraphina gave me a weak smile as if she wanted to offer me some support but couldn't interrupt my meal.

"You two need anything else?" she asked.

Yes, I need answers that make sense. But that wasn't her problem. I smiled and shook my head, and she was gone. Once again, I was alone with Darius—my estranged father who wanted to host a name day meal for me. No matter how inconceivable the offer, I couldn't waste this opportunity.

"I'd like to come," I said as I cut into the pie, letting the steam burst out through the slit, "but I'd like to bring someone."

Darius made a noncommittal "Oh?" sound, like a question. It was like he expected me to provide more information. I figured I needed to. What was I going to say? I'd had plenty of time to develop a story but had failed. I knew I was a lousy liar, and my lack of relationship with Darius wouldn't make me any better.

"I'd like to bring Vincent Andiveron," I said carefully, tasting the name on my tongue.

Darius's eyebrows rose. "You know him, then? It's not just enjoying his column?" He gestured to the drink near my plate.

"Yes." I took another sip.

Darius waited for more. I wasn't sure I had more to say. He clearly wanted to know what Vincent and I were to each other.

I honestly wished I knew, but I had no idea. Unfortunately, Darius seemed content to wait, lifting a spoonful of soup to his mouth with a patient smile in place.

He was fae. Who knew how long he could outlast me here? I let honesty reign as Darius's quiet patience defeated me.

"I know you're waiting for some explanation, but I don't have one. We've been...seeing each other," I said hesitantly. I knew that had connotations that weren't precisely true to Vincent and me, but it felt true enough that I could say it with a straight face.

Darius's eyebrows raised farther.

"He's important to me, and therefore it would be nice, if I was to come to a family home that I've never been invited to, to have someone familiar...someone who will look out for me should things not go the way I expect."

I hadn't realized what I would say until the words were out. Now that they were, they felt like the ones I'd been searching for all along. I might not be sure Vincent and I could have a romantic future after all the pain of this bargain we'd made, but I knew I cared for him. I believed he cared about me as more than a means to an end, too.

Even if we were visiting Pierce House to see if my father was up to some nefarious activity, I wanted Vincent by my side when I found out the truth. Though I hated to admit it, I wanted to know if my father was attempting to keep half-fae like myself from learning about their magic, especially with this recent change of heart. This whole discussion was a total turn from everything I'd expected. I was getting exactly what I needed, so I wouldn't press, but my curiosity was more than piqued. Why now? I hadn't even given him the report about the inn. I hadn't had to ask for my favor—he'd offered me exactly what I needed. It was too good to be true, I was sure.

But I wanted to save Cliff House, and this was our ticket to do so.

I let out a breath and met Darius's steely blue gaze. My confusion must have been apparent. He was no longer smiling, but he nodded. "If that's what you wish, we'd be happy to have you both."

I took a bite of the pie, unable to enjoy it.

What had I gotten myself into?

22

Vincent

I was drawn to Luna as I entered the tavern, like the tide to the shore. She and Darius were finishing their meal. I slid through the mass of people to get to the bar. Someone was settling up, allowing me to snag an empty stool. Seraphina gave me a look as I sat.

"I didn't know you were coming." She glanced pointedly at the table where Luna sat with Darius. There were no tears. Luna looked concerned, but that was to be expected. Maybe things were going better than anticipated.

I shrugged. "I wanted to be here if she needed me."

Seraphina's brow furrowed. "If she needed to tell you she failed? So you can decide not to write her recommendation?" Her hands moved to her hips as she continued. "Or if she needed you because she's in tears, since you're the one who made her confront the father who abandoned her?"

Her words stung, but they were no more than I deserved.

"I told Luna, and I'll tell you, I didn't know how bad her

relationship with Darius was when I asked." I held up my hands at her skeptical look. "I knew it wasn't great, but I had no idea…" I waved my hands in a general gesture of the mess Darius had created. "I tried to get her to drop it, but she wouldn't even discuss it. So now I'm here to do what I can for a person I care about, who I put in a terrible position."

Seraphina's eyes were still narrowed in my general direction, but the words that came out of her mouth made me feel like I'd passed a test. "What can I get you?"

"A Solstice Sip, please."

She shook her head. "Now you're sucking up."

I laughed. "I wouldn't have recommended them if I didn't think they were good."

"You're saying not all your recommendations are purchased with a bargain?"

"Not all." I hedged, not wanting to relive the painful details to Seraphina. "Desperate times and all."

"Fine," Seraphina said, mixing the drink.

"How did you two meet?" I asked. Seraphina was awfully fond of Luna for a boss. She also seemed to know quite a bit about her.

"She ended up here her first day in town. People weren't traveling, and business wasn't good." Seraphina shrugged. "We chatted all day. Luna is the most welcoming person I know, which is why it bothers me so much that someone has been anything less than welcoming to her."

I nodded in understanding. "I get that."

"This is the first time he's come here, though," Seraphina said almost to herself as she passed me my drink. "He only met her for moments at the inn when she arrived in town. He didn't even take her to the cottage when she accepted. He let Byrd take care of it, a man who hated that anyone was there to watch him fail Cliff House."

"Well, here's to him being more welcoming and Luna deciding if she'll accept it."

Seraphina glared at me as I raised my glass. "She *has* to accept it to keep her deal with you."

I sighed and took a drink. She wasn't wrong. I'd tried to discuss breaking our agreement, but Luna hadn't been interested. I didn't know what to say to her. Part of me wanted to tell her to drop the whole thing. I'd still write the article if we could get the blood magic taken care of, but as Ambrose had said, the article wouldn't help if there was magic driving people away from the inn. I didn't need her to do this thing with Darius for the article. I could find another way or wait for another feature piece.

When had I become so protective of her? I'd been so incensed when I'd thought she was using me for the recommendation that I could admit I hadn't cared what it would cost her to uphold her side of our bargain. But I'd known I'd misjudged her even before I gathered the courage to ask her about it. Luna wasn't the type to so blatantly use people. The memory of her slipping her arm around me in the dress shop came to mind. All it had taken was a desperate plea from my sister, and Luna had feigned feelings for me to save my pride. I'd never met someone so genuinely interested in helping others, sometimes at the expense of herself.

I was glad she had someone like Seraphina looking out for her. Someone who helped keep her level while pushing her to take risks, like with the inn.

The light touch of a hand rested on my shoulder, pulling me from my thoughts. "I wasn't sure you'd make it," Luna said.

I glanced at the table she'd been seated at with her father. He was gone.

"I told you I would." I searched her gaze. She seemed alright, if a little dazed. I wanted to know everything they'd spoken of. I wanted to know everything about her life. I swallowed. That was new. I'd been semi-aware that my feelings for Luna had shifted throughout this bargain, but I didn't think I'd contemplated how drastically.

She smiled at me, and I knocked my glass backward, almost spilling it. Seraphina laughed to herself as she cleaned a glass behind the bar, a knowing look in her eye. I ran my hand through my hair, trying to gather my scattered thoughts. I still had no idea where Luna stood.

"I'm glad you did," she said earnestly. "I need to talk to you." Her face shifted. I wanted to say it was with embarrassment, but I couldn't be sure.

"Do you want to sit?" I asked, offering her the stool.

"No, I'll wait for another to open." She shifted on her feet.

"You can have mine, Luna." An older man sitting on my left stood.

"Thanks, Earl. You sure?"

"Yeah, Daisy is expecting me." He patted her shoulder while giving me a suspicious glare reminiscent of Seraphina's.

I didn't connect the dots until he was already gone. "That's Daisy's husband? The Daisy I work with at the paper?"

Luna nodded, and Seraphina slid her a Solstice Sip. Then Luna turned to me, her face serious.

"What is it?" I asked. "If it didn't work, it doesn't matter. We don't have to try again." Her lip curved into a hesitant smile, and she twisted one of the silver strands around her finger. I'd never seen her look so nervous.

"You're killing me, Luna. What happened?"

She laughed, which seemed to finally break her nerves. Taking a big gulp of her drink, she explained, "Well, he offered exactly what I needed before I could even ask. My name day is next week, a day I've never spent with him, but he asked me to come to Pierce House for a celebratory meal."

"That's great, right?" I asked. Seraphina was listening over Luna's shoulder. I glanced at her. "Isn't that great?"

Seraphina's glare still cut deep, even with our tacit peace.

Then Luna's hand was on my cheek, pulling my face back to hers. "Focus, Vincent." She seemed to realize she was touching me quite familiarly and snapped her hand back to her glass.

My hand raised of its own accord to touch the place her palm had been.

Seraphina groaned. "Keep telling the story before I lose my appetite."

Luna's face reddened. "Well, I said I'd accept, but I wanted to bring someone. He seemed to know who you were, or at least your surname. Anyway, he asked who you were to me that you'd be invited to this event." She coughed, her nerves showing again. "And, well, I told you I was a terrible liar. The only thing I could come up with was to say you were important to me and that you would be reassuring to have with me when I didn't know what to expect from him and my grandmother." She paused, taking another long sip of her drink. "Anyway, I'm pretty sure he now believes you and I are seeing each other... romantically."

Seraphina laughed, leaning forward on the bar before I could say anything. "Why does he believe that, Luna?"

The glare Luna leveled at Seraphina was just shy of adorable. She tried her best to look menacing but couldn't hide her affection for even a moment. "Fine!" She waved her hands around. "He believes that because *that's* what I told him. I told him we've been seeing each other."

Seraphina's cackle echoed off the rafters as she headed to the kitchen, likely to check on an order. This left Luna and me staring at each other. I didn't say anything, and her cheeks flushed again. Words still eluded me. I knew I needed to find some soon but couldn't decide which ones. She said she didn't like to lie, so she'd said we were together because it felt close to true.

What did it mean that saying we were seeing each other

didn't feel like a lie to her? Hadn't I been thinking the same? Too many words were fighting for space, and none of them made it out.

"It's fine if you don't want to go under such circumstances," she stammered. "I can look for evidence for you."

I reached for her hand and her gaze focused solely on where our skin touched.

"You will not go alone," I said. "I will happily take you—be your date for your name day meal. Are you sure you want to search his office? We don't have to..."

She squeezed my hand. "I have to. He said he wants to start fresh." That was nice, but it seemed oddly out of the blue given what she'd told me about the last twenty-some years of her relationship with him. She must have seen the questions on my face. "I need to know if I can trust it."

That, I understood.

"If he's trying to change the course of our relationship, I need to know if he's secretly working against half-fae and their magic."

"Of course, Luna. We'll do whatever you want."

Her returning smile was shy as her hand fell to her lap, breaking our contact. I hoped my intention was clear, but I also was not prepared to scare her off with some declaration of my feelings. That was what I'd been trying to get to the first time I'd tried to break our bargain. I wanted to tell her that she meant more to me than our stupid deal. If we could move past our disastrous first meeting, whatever we might have was worth more. She'd had no interest in the topic then.

You didn't say any of that. My wind swirled in my chest as if helping me see the obvious.

Well, that was a good point.

I didn't think I had any better words now to express myself, and I didn't have time to find them as she continued.

"Wonderful," she said. "The meal is next week."

I nodded. "Are we still good to come by and test your magic tomorrow?" Ambrose and Evelyn had made this particular plan with her, but I wanted to be there. As before, I wasn't sure either of the academics were best suited for tests where the expected outcome was outside their control.

"Yes, I'll have a fresh loaf of bread ready for everyone, and we'll see what we can do." She smoothed her skirt as if in reassurance. "Now, if you'll excuse me, I'll head home. It's been a long day."

"Do you want me to walk with you?"

She waved me off. "No, you stay. It's a quarter moon tonight. I need the walk and the moonlight to clear my head. I'll see you tomorrow."

I wasn't sure how things had worked out the way they had, but I couldn't help but think they'd gone entirely in my favor. It only occurred to me after Luna left what we'd actually need to do at Darius's house. She was bringing me to snoop. At least, that had been the original plan. We'd need to get into his study and search for any evidence of his attempt to bribe the governor to stop the school from being built. Luna said she still wanted to do it, no matter her father's apparent change of heart. That part, I understood. I'd want to know, too, if he were being nice to my face but secretly tearing down everything I believed in behind my back.

Luna's words about wanting me there with her warmed my heart as much as they sent chills down my spine. She wanted me there in case she learned the worst. She wanted someone who cared about her to be with her if the worst was true.

I downed the rest of my drink. I'd do it, of course; I'd prioritize her, but if that occurred, it would also mean I had what I needed to expose him.

23

Luna

When we're nervous, we make bread. I kneaded a batch of dough the following morning. My cottage was usually my refuge. The hanging plants and ocean scent were usually a calming balm. Ever since I'd realized the problem may be inside me—with magic I apparently had, and my inability to use it—my nerves had followed me everywhere.

Even Darius thought I had to be the one to save the inn.

I wasn't sure what to make of that. I hadn't wanted to press him on it when I was still learning so much about the magic myself, but it appeared he at least suspected something. What did that mean about who had placed the magic on the inn? If Evelyn was right, there could only have been two people in the supposed memory. I didn't like where the evidence was pointing.

So many of my questions had no answers, and the only thing I knew to do was knead the dough until it no longer stuck to my fingers.

As of late, I'd been lucky to make bread when I had visitors, either Evelyn and Seraphina to help clean or the group arriving today to test my magic. I wasn't sure what I'd do when I was back to much less company at the inn.

Or maybe there won't be a cozy cottage here for me to work in. Perhaps it will be sold and repurposed, so it won't even matter. More unhelpful thoughts slid into my mind as I worked. The thoughts might be a possible future, but dwelling on negativity gave me nothing.

Instead, I'd focus on how to test my magic.

I remembered when Darius visited the village where Mom raised me. I'd been young, but he had been such a novelty in my childhood that the memory stuck with me.

"We're going to play a game," he'd said.

Our house had been small, with only one bedroom for me and Mom. He'd led me outside to play. Mom stood with her arms crossed on the step, but she gave me a tight smile before looking to the sky.

Darius had a bowl of water with him. He asked me to grab it and pull it to me. When I tried to do so physically with my hands, he laughed. "No, sweetie, with what's in here." He patted his chest. He spoke so warmly then. What had changed?

I looked at Mom, but she was determined not to watch. She stared steadfastly into the distance.

"I..." I stumbled, not wanting to disappoint him—not wanting our game to end. "I'm...I don't know what to do."

He set the bowl down as he glared over his shoulder at Mom. "You are half-fae, sweetie. That means you might have magic like me." He tipped his palm up, and the water from the bowl leaped into it, swirling around like a self-crashing wave, never leaving the confines he gave it. My mouth opened wide.

"I can do that?" I glanced at Mom, who still refused to meet my gaze. She didn't stop him, though. Mom was near enough to hear his words, to intervene if she thought he was saying something wrong. She didn't.

"We don't know, Luna. Since you're a mix of me and your mom, you might not, but if you do, I want to help you learn to use it."

I nodded, pretending to understand things that I couldn't comprehend.

"So, close your eyes and focus on something in here." He pointed to his chest again. "Magic comes from the heart of ourselves. You must feel it inside before the water will listen to you."

"What does it feel like?"

He tilted his head, a reassuring smile crossing his face. "I think it's a little different for everyone, but maybe like peace? Something calming?"

I looked at the wave crashing in circles on his palm. "That is calming?"

He shrugged. "It is to me. Now you try. Once you find the spot inside, ask it to come to you."

With a final, unmet glance at Mom, I did what he said. My eyes closed, and I felt around inside for something peaceful.

But I wasn't calm. I was very much not calm.

What was happening here? Mom wasn't helping. Darius was my dad, but he was a stranger, telling me I had magic. No part of whatever was going on was calming. If I had magic like he said, would he take me away? Maybe I better not look too hard.

I was curious, though, so I searched. He said I'd have to call it if I found it, but I could skip that step if necessary.

I didn't even find it.

Darius was patient. He took me farther down the street to the stream to try there. He thought more water might help me connect with it. Still, I didn't find anything. It was almost dark when Mom came down the road and told him that was enough. Her hands were on her hips. "You've tried. Now leave her be."

He glanced at Mom, then back to me. "What if I don't want to?" he said over my head. I could tell he tried to speak quietly, but I could hear every word.

"That's not...that wasn't—"

A warm calm spread through me as I stood ankle-deep in the water. I felt it then, I thought—what Darius was looking for.

Mom glanced at me as the moonlight shone, panic in her eyes. "Luna, go back to the house. I have to speak with Darius."

My mouth opened and closed like I was a fish out of water. The feeling grew stronger—the calm, the command of the water around my ankles. I'd found what Darius was looking for; I was sure of it. Then the cold cut of Mom's voice brought me back to reality. It made me think my fears were confirmed. If I did what Darius wanted, if I found the calm, called to it, and moved the water, he would take me away.

I wouldn't leave Mom.

At her command, I'd jumped out of the stream and run back down the road to the house. I never heard the rest of their heated conversation, and Darius didn't visit our village again.

Dough finally fell easily from my fingers, and I was ready to let it rise. My trip down memory lane had done nothing to ease my anxiety, but at least it had helped me finish kneading. I carried the bowl to the fire and placed it on the hearth. There was nothing else to do but try and find the warmth.

Thinking about the test with Darius reminded me that I *had* found something that day. I hadn't doubted Vincent's assertions about the night we met. His explanation, especially about the drink, made too much sense, but finding the calm that Darius had asked me to seek was something I hadn't let myself remember.

I wondered how different my relationship with Darius would be if I'd said something then—if I'd explored whatever I'd felt. Would he have known how to help me call it? I hadn't tried because of the look on Mom's face—terror, sadness, desperation. I'd thought we could avoid these things if only I didn't do what Darius asked. I'd trusted Mom to know what was best.

Why had she thought not having magic was best? It was a question I should have asked myself much sooner, but none of these pieces had fit together before.

I considered the test again, how Darius had tried to find my magic. He'd had me stand in the water when nothing else helped. I'd been doing the same the night I met Vincent. Maybe I needed to be standing in the water for it to work.

There was still a little time before everyone showed up. I could go down to the sea and try it. The pattern was too much to ignore. I'd feel more foolish with all of them standing there with me, watching. With a prick of anxiety, I walked toward the steps.

I still thought of Mom often, but never these memories. My life with her had been full of love, energy, and community in our small town. The humans had looked out for each other, even as the continent changed. As much as I hadn't wanted Darius to steal me away, I wondered if that was what he would have done. My child's mind had made up so much to fill in so many gaps.

And so much of what I knew of Darius was through Mom's lens.

The waves rolled along the beach as I walked to it. Each crash was another memory of Mom's disdain.

"He only cares about power. If you don't have any, he won't

want you," she'd said a few years later when I asked about him again.

Another crash.

"Fae are selfish and cruel. Don't count on them for anything." It had been her warning mantra whenever a fae arrived in our small village.

It hadn't occurred to me until I was much older that this also partially applied to me: I was half-fae. Mom liked to pretend I was fully human. There was never any evidence to the contrary. The only noticeable difference would be my aging, but as I was in my mid-twenties, it was nearly impossible to tell that my aging had slowed.

Waves continued to roll in, the tide rising as I slipped off my boots and stepped into the water. Perhaps Mom had done me a disservice? I wasn't blaming her, just questioning my relationship with my fae heritage. I'd always lain all the blame for my distance from it at Darius's feet, but...that picture now felt incomplete. I didn't want to think I'd been so easily charmed by a man who'd ignored me for twenty-five years, but he'd seemed so genuine yesterday. He'd had no answers to my questions, but he'd focused on starting fresh, on starting over. Even how he worried about Vincent's place in my life was confusing.

Last night, I'd been too focused on getting what I needed for Vincent's story—an invite to the house—and now, next week, I'd be at Pierce House, and could ask what I wanted to know.

Part of me wanted to hear his side of the story. The pain of his absence wouldn't disappear, but we could only start fresh once I understood his perspective of these childhood events. Not knowing why he'd changed his mind would eat at me worse than not having him around.

Waves crashed against the shore, but the sound was soothing. I was only ankle-deep in the water, but each roll of waves brought it a little higher on my skin. The current's pull reminded me of the night I'd been swept away. My pulse elevated. I glanced up, breathing deeply. The sun was high, with few clouds covering it. This wasn't the same as that night. The one night I'd slept in a room at the inn.

I focused on my magic and evening out my breath. There was no need to get worked up about the memory before I had proof. The water rolled against me, but no core of magic flared to life. My gaze roamed the horizon as I wondered what it would be like to feel the breadth of the sea with water magic. It had to be empowering to know that something so vast and encompassing was yours. I bet it was connecting, in a way, too, knowing others of your court felt the same.

If only I could make the connection.

I felt nothing.

The beach was unsurprisingly empty, so I started walking along the water. The loose skirt of my brightly colored dress blew in the breeze. I walked with no agenda other than clearing my head. Wind wrapped around me as I did. It was lovely how well the wind and water worked together. Some might think they were constantly competing for control, but I thought they had more of a partnership than we realized. The wind circled tighter, bringing an uncommon warmth that took me a moment to recognize. When I did, I glanced over my shoulder to see Vincent standing at the bottom of the steps.

24

Vincent

I was lucky she hadn't turned a moment earlier, when I'd stumbled down the final step after catching sight of her. She was picturesque, walking in the water; serene like a still pool but poised and confident like a wave crashing against the cliff. This place, with Luna, was exactly what I wanted after the day I'd had. Patricia couldn't complain too much. The weekly features summarizing prior recommendations were doing well. Visitors were flocking to the taverns, the shops, and the restaurants we featured. It was clear from her questions, though, that she wanted a yes or no on the Darius article soon.

I'd told her I'd have an answer before the end of the week—either way. There was a part of me that felt like I was failing at this assignment. It wasn't a feeling I was used to. My wind swept through my hair and circled my temples as if to remind me that wasn't the case. I wasn't failing. In this particular assignment, I was deciding something was more important. Luna was more important.

My gaze returned to her as the water rocked against her ankles. She belonged there. I couldn't explain it. I'd thought that the night we met, too. Not because of the magic she displayed but because of the resilience in her gaze. The determination to hold on to the peace she sought, if only for another moment. I saw it here again, and it knocked the wind from me.

More aptly, it set my wind loose. It encircled her before I could tamp it down. I was confident that bright red tinged my cheeks when she turned and acknowledged my presence. At least she was smiling as we walked toward each other.

"Sorry," she said when we met at the shoreline. "I must have lost track of time."

I shook my head. "I should apologize to you."

Her head tilted in question.

"My wind..." I coughed as it swirled her ankles again, where her skin met the water.

She appraised me with a gaze I wasn't sure I could decipher. "Your wind and I have an understanding that it seems you and I do not." She placed her hands on her hips. "Even though you and your wind are allegedly one in the same." A smirk was firmly in place on her lips, and I knew my wind's imposition was forgiven.

I didn't have time to ask exactly what the understanding was before Evelyn and Ambrose charged down the steps.

"Any progress in our absence?" Ambrose called as they came toward us. He had his quill poised to note anything she said in a small journal he was carrying for the occasion. I glanced to the sky, wishing they would disappear for another few minutes.

Luna touched my arm, squeezing it gently before she went to greet them. My gaze lingered on the spot, cursing my sleeves for existing. It was warm today, and I'd left my jacket up at the inn when I'd gone to search for her on the property. Whether I acknowledged the decision or not, I started rolling up the sleeves, exposing my forearms. If she touched me again, I wanted to grant her direct access to my skin.

I was a goner.

"No progress," Luna said as she greeted Evelyn and Ambrose, "though I do remember finding the feeling of calm once before."

"Feeling of calm?" Ambrose asked, pen poised to write.

Luna looked between the two of them. Evelyn, too, gave her a blank stare. She turned to me. "My...Darius...when he came to test me as a child. He described finding my magic inside me as a sense of calm."

I nodded, reassuring her. "Everyone is taught a little differently—especially the first part. Most fae arrive at the court schools with the ability to call their magic, taught in some fashion by whoever raised them. The school is more about how to control the element long-term."

"How were you taught?" she asked.

I cleared my throat. "I'm not sure it—"

"My parents called it a quiet place," Ambrose jumped in. I hoped Zrak, god of wind, blessed him for it. He was one of my only friends who knew the lengths to which my parents had gone to ensure my magic was as powerful as they'd expected. Granted, he'd also asked to study it after discovering their methods, but his heart was in the right place.

Luna's bright blue eyes were still on me, even as Ambrose continued. As much as I wanted her attention, I didn't want it on this. I wanted her magic to be a calm or quiet place. Not the loud and angry pressure I had started with. Sometimes, I wondered if it was why my magic was so expressive. It blew through my hair at the thought.

"So, you did find the calm or the quiet place once?" I asked, steadying my voice.

"I think so, but I was too afraid that Darius would take me from my mom if I had magic." She ran her hand through her hair and sighed. "I didn't know anything about him. My mom had only taught me to distrust the fae. It's not a good reason, but it's what I have. I went back to the house while they fought about my future. He didn't return, and I only saw Darius at the inn after that, so Mom must have won."

Evelyn must have known most of this because she nodded stoically at Luna's words. Ambrose stopped writing, thankfully. And I...well, I stared at her like an idiot, transfixed by the idea that her mom would have kept her from part of herself. Luna hadn't spoken much about her mom, but I understood they had had a good relationship before she passed. I knew I shouldn't judge, but it didn't seem helpful if her mom had asked her to deny part of herself. It was terrible that Darius had ignored her because she didn't have magic. It would be as bad if her mom had taught her to ignore her power or pretend it didn't exist.

"I'm sorry to hear that," I said. "Is there anything from that experience you want to try and recreate?"

She bit her lip. "That's what I was doing down here. When Darius tested me, I was standing in the water when I felt the calm. I did the same the night we met." She gestured to her boots left on the beach. "So I thought standing in the water might help." She shrugged. "No luck so far."

"Do you want to keep trying down here? Or go back to the door?" Ambrose asked.

"I don't think it's worth going to the door until I know how to harness the magic, do you?" She looked at me.

I glanced helplessly at Ambrose.

"It's hard to say not knowing what the magic's intention is on the door."

"Let's give it a try," she said. "I've gone as far as possible with this assumption." She gestured to the water. "We might as well try something else."

"Alright." I waited for her to step forward before starting up the stairs.

"You two go ahead," she said. "Evelyn and I will catch up."

It hadn't escaped my notice that Evelyn hadn't spoken about her magic. I had been too focused on Luna to consider what it meant. Before I turned to go, I noticed Evelyn had a more fragile look on her face that made me wonder how long Luna had been trying to be rid of us.

"Do you know anything about Evelyn's magic?" Ambrose asked quietly as we walked up the steps.

I shook my head. "No. Aren't you the one who works with her?"

Pink touched his cheeks. "Yes, but that's very much on the theory of magic and history. Nothing about our own. It's in the Vesten Library. I doubt they'd be so progressive as to hire a non-Vesten, but I know nothing about her power." He gave me a sideways glance. "Speaking of, your magic is looking pretty familiar with Luna."

My gaze darted to my feet.

"It's good. I think. I've never seen it so familiar. So inquisitive?" He couldn't seem to find the word he was looking for. "I'm saying I'm happy for you. I was sure your parents' methods of forcing it to show would have lasting impacts."

I grunted in acknowledgment, certain that they had and that he observed the impacts.

"So, are you and Luna..." He didn't fill in the ending, obviously hoping I would.

"I don't know what Luna and I are," I replied, running my hands through my hair. "I told you we made this bargain."

He clapped a hand on my back. "It seems you're well past that, though, aren't you?"

I took a deep breath. "I want to be, but the last time I tried to talk to her about it, she brushed me off."

"She is taking you to a meal at her estranged father's house.

To celebrate her name day," he said pointedly. "I don't think you've been ruled out entirely."

I huffed out a laugh. When he put it that way, it did sound like I had a chance. "Thanks, Ambrose. Now, any idea what we will try when we get to the door?"

His lips pressed together in thought. "I've always got theories to test. Not sure any of them will be useful, but we've got tests."

"That's definitely what I'm afraid of."

"I can't tell if her magic has a physical or mental block," Ambrose continued. "From what you two have said, she hasn't been aware of the times she's used it. Maybe the water has something to do with that, but still, she's triggering it without thought." He tilted his head as we walked through the trees. "It seems she's taken the calm thing to heart." He sighed. "But from what she said today, if her mom was against magic, it might be something she doesn't want to access, subconsciously. Her mom is gone, right?"

I nodded.

"This could be lingering guilt over using what her human parent never wanted her to."

I'd thought the same thing after hearing the story of her first magic test. I couldn't imagine a parent so adamant that their child not present magic. In the fae courts, the strength of an element was everything. It was so important that the strength of the element, not lineage, was how our rulers, the Compass Points, were determined.

"What is the physical, then?" I asked, wanting to get all the information I could from Ambrose.

"Well, it's not uncommon for half-fae to have unique circumstances in which they access their magic. I met another Vesten who has a human parent, and he can access his fire all the time, but he can only shift when he sees the color black. I also met a Suden with a human parent who had to touch the earth with his hands to wield the element. That's not a requirement for most Suden. They can access the magic without touch."

"And you have no idea what unknown requirement Luna might have to meet?"

He considered it and shook his head. "She would know better than I."

She seemed on the right track with her feet in the water. "Is there any limit to what the requirement could be?" I asked.

Sympathy covered Ambrose's features. "Not really. Usually, it has some significance to the wielder so that they can figure it out. The magic inside of us wants to be wielded. It wants to be at peace with its wielder. The requirements would be such that they wouldn't tax the fae to complete them."

I scratched my jaw in thought even as he changed the subject.

"Have you made any more progress on your research into Darius Pierce?"

We were approaching the inn, about to break through the tree cover.

"Not much," I said. "I've been hesitant to do anything else without Luna. I don't want to feel like I'm sneaking behind her back to investigate her family."

Ambrose laughed. "You've got it bad."

I swatted at him, even though I knew it was true. "Didn't she say she wanted to know?" he pressed.

"Yes," I sighed. "I just don't know if she meant it. We'll have to talk about it soon since we're going to have a meal there next week. She said she'd help me sneak into his office while we were there. I don't know what we'll do if we find anything that says he's bribing the governor."

"You'll have to trust she knows what she's doing." He patted my shoulder sympathetically. "Are you so sure you'll find something?"

"I have no idea. I hope he isn't doing this, especially since he wants to make amends with Luna, but..."

"But you know what it's like to have parents obsessed with court tradition?"

I hung my head as we entered the inn. "That I do."

25

Luna

We'd learned a lot about what *didn't* call my magic yesterday but had no luck with anything that did. I admired Evelyn and Ambrose's dedication to their extensive process. They had a list of tests, and for each one we completed, Ambrose recorded the outcome.

They were all listed as failures.

Vincent was quiet but reassuring. I liked that about him. It was almost dark when we finally finished the experiments, and Vincent walked me back through the woods to my cottage. Something in my heart warmed at his consideration. That same something inside me wanted to reach for him, wanted to entwine our fingers as we walked, and maybe not let go. He'd squeezed my arm before he left, saying we'd figure it out and that he'd see me in a few days for the meal with Darius.

I wanted him to stay, but my mouth wouldn't open to say the words. His wind wrapped around my arm in its own farewell as he walked back through the trees until they hid him from sight.

It was for the best. Probably.

Even as I thought that, days later, my mind still wondered why. Yes, he'd been an ass when we first met and then made the stupid bargain that forced me to confront Darius. I wasn't exactly innocent in our meeting. Magically fueled or not, I'd thrown a drink at him. Then I hadn't hesitated to ask him for a favor once I'd found out who he was.

I wanted to believe we could be more than our first meeting.

He'd tried to get out of our bargain. I knew that's what he wanted, but no matter how much our feelings for each other might have changed, we still wanted the outcomes we'd bargained for. I still wanted to save the inn. He still wanted to write a piece that wasn't a recommendation. And some part of me wanted to know if what Darius was accused of was real. Now that I'd heard the accusation and Vincent's overheard conversation, I needed to discover if it was true. Forging some new relationship with him would mean nothing if he secretly tried to deny half-fae a right to learn magic.

I'd complicated matters by being so honest with Darius. It appeared he didn't think much of Vincent from his initial reaction. I chalked that up to court politics. The Norden and Osten Families were still getting used to their leaders' friendship. It was understandable after hundreds of years of animosity.

Two outfits lay across my bed. Vincent would be here soon, and I didn't know what to wear. The first, a plain black dress, was one of the outfits Vincent and I had purchased for my new fae look. Whenever I left Cliff House property, I'd been trying to stick to the new look we'd come up with so that if—*when*—the inn was featured in Vincent's column, readers would remember me as a respectable fae from a respectable family.

The second outfit was louder, a gold skirt and a white off-the-shoulder blouse.

I should stick with the plan. The black dress is fine.

My gaze flicked between the two outfits, and my heart rate sped up as I reached for the fae dress. No, that didn't feel right. This was my first time entering Pierce House. I wanted to do it as myself. If Darius was genuinely going to accept me, I wanted him to accept me for who I was, not the front Vincent and I had constructed for his column.

The black dress went back into the closet. Moments later, as I put the finishing touches on my coronet braid, leaving the peeks of silver out and twisting them around my face, Vincent knocked at the door.

His smile was huge when he saw me, his gaze running the length of me. "You look amazing."

He didn't look so bad himself, but he always looked good. He wore his favorite dark brown jacket and a plain white shirt beneath.

"You don't want to chastise me for not wearing the black dress?"

The smile flattened. "I've told you multiple times, Luna"—he stepped into my space—"you are breathtaking the way you are. Others may expect the more traditional dress, but I regret the purchases in that dress shop every day. It's a failing of the fae that you tame yourself for them."

He was so close.

He smelled so good.

His lips were right there.

My body was moving before I could overthink it. I'd wanted to know what he tasted like since the day we met. Then, we'd been more whipping wind and quick judgments. Now, when my lips met his, wind swirled around us, blocking out everything else, like a safe harbor from the storm.

The rest of him took a moment to catch up to my snap decision.

His lips were firm, unyielding, as I'd caught him off guard

with my advance. It only took a moment for his hands to follow the wind's path. Strong arms wrapped around me, and my own arms slipped around his neck to reach for the thick locks of hair that continually drew my attention.

I may have started this, but Vincent and his wind worked in tandem to escalate it. His lips turned searching as his tongue pressed against the seam of mine. The cyclone of his wind pressed us closer together. I didn't mind, suddenly wanting nothing between us. My lips parted, granting him access and meeting him stroke for stroke. Our tongues tangled in a dance we'd waited too long to start. I didn't know if it was his hand or his wind that slid up the length of my ribs, and I didn't care. They were both him—both sending waves of want crashing through me.

Breathless, I pulled back. He stumbled forward, following, nipping my lip, unwilling to let me go.

"Luna," he said in a gruff voice that had my insides melting.

"That was the perfect start to the evening," I said. My gaze roamed my cozy cottage, flipping between the couch and the bedroom. He followed my gaze with interest. Then I sighed, resigned. "But should things escalate further, we will be late."

"Right." He tugged on his shirt sleeves and tried to compose himself. The plants were still swaying in a light breeze from his wind. I couldn't help but smile in satisfaction.

He cleared his throat and handed me a small box. "Happy name day."

"Vincent, you didn't need to get me anything. I can't thank you enough for coming with me. This could prove to be an unfortunate evening."

I opened the box. It was a necklace, a pendant in the shape of the moon's phases. The pendant was silver, perfectly matching the color of my moon-stricken hair.

"You looked so fierce the first night we met, glaring at the full moon. It didn't stand a chance against whatever you demanded of it. That look—it was power and grace, beauty and strength in perfect harmony."

I wasn't sure I could speak. My throat was thick with emotion. I wanted to think I communicated everything I couldn't say as our gazes held. "Will you help me put it on?" I asked, turning my back to him.

His fingers skimmed across the curve of my shoulders like a light breeze. It was even more satisfying than when his wind did it. *Sometimes, it does things I lack the courage to.* His response to my question had gooseflesh pebbling my skin. He and his wind working in tandem would put me in the eye of a storm. It was a thought that had me tingling with anticipation. As he fastened the clasp, I shook my head free of images and the desire to continue our kiss. His fingers lingered, his touch soft.

I needed us to reach Darius's house before things got out of hand. The way we were headed, I'd have him in my bed in moments, and we wouldn't leave the cottage for days.

I turned to face him. The heat in his eyes made my knees weak. As if he knew, his wind was there, steadying me.

"Perfect," he said.

"Thank you, Vincent." I attempted to compose myself.

"We should probably go." He looked wistfully over my shoulder toward the bedroom. I laughed, knowing that our thoughts were aligned in this, too.

VINCENT HAD PROCURED us a carriage for the ride to Pierce House. I sat beside him on the bench but didn't touch him. Our kiss had left me more than a little flustered. I didn't know what to do with my hands. They folded in my lap, then flopped uselessly at my sides as I searched for a place to put them. Should I reach for Vincent's? Did he want to kiss me again? I knew it was silly to wonder as he snuck glances at me, too.

Where might that kiss lead once we made it through this evening? I was abuzz with anticipation.

His wind blew the blond strands of hair from my face, growing frustrated when it realized the rest of my hair was braided. I laughed as I toyed with the charm he had given me. It was what I needed, something to keep my thoughts from the heavier ones—the reason I'd got us invited to Pierce House to begin with, fulfilling my end of our stupid bargain.

Part of me knew if I said I didn't want to search Darius's office tonight, Vincent would let me off the hook. He'd say it wasn't necessary, even though I was sure he wanted to write features as much as I wanted to run Cliff House Inn. My hand fell to my skirt, smoothing it. That wasn't the only reason we had to do it.

If Darius wanted to mend things between us—if he wanted some semblance of a relationship—I needed to know who he was. Maybe I could ask him instead of sneaking into his office? I dismissed the thought. Inviting me to the house did not mean he would openly confess his sins. I had to know if he was trying to stop half-fae from learning magic. I couldn't be part of his family if he were doing that.

Vincent's hand covered mine, lifting it to his lips. "Second thoughts?"

I gently bumped his shoulder. "I knew we'd get here."

He gripped my hand tighter. "You know I don't need the information."

First, I wasn't sure that was true. One thing we hadn't talked about was how much longer his boss would wait. He must be facing pressure to report on his findings. It seemed very Vincent to keep that pressure to himself. I shook my head. As much as I wanted him to succeed in his career goals, this wasn't only for him.

"*I* need it." I turned my hand to meet his, intertwining our fingers. "Out of the blue, Darius wants to start fresh. That's what tonight is...trying to forge a relationship with my father." I cleared my throat as I tested out the title instead of his name. "If I think there is any chance of it succeeding, I need to know that he is not involved with this."

"I'm sorry that I made you doubt him at all."

"You didn't create and submit the evidence!" I said. Vincent's face turned pensive at that, but I continued. "Here is the plan. I'm sure tonight will be a formal meal. He even said my grandmother would dine with us. I'll excuse myself when they move us from the dining room to the family room for a digestif. You will find a reason to follow me. I can leave my bag there. Say I needed it and chase after me."

"You're giving this a lot of thought," he said.

"Well, I'm nervous. I ramble when I'm nervous. You should know that by now."

"You're beautiful when you ramble. I support your decision to play spy in your father's house, but can we discuss what we might find?"

"I know what we might find, Vincent." I sighed. "That is why I must do this. If I were sure he was uninvolved, I'd say we could skip it, but I'm not. Mom was so sure he only cared about pureblood fae and power. He never came back to see me after deciding I had none. That doesn't speak to someone with no motive to stop others from being educated in magic." I'd worked up steam on my argument. "If that is the kind of male he is, I don't want anything to do with him. Even if he is finally ready to act like my father." I nodded more to myself than anyone, but Vincent's dark brown eyes were molten when I'd finished.

"You really shouldn't look at me like that," I said, and yet I couldn't help but wiggle in my seat as I spoke. The attention was indecent, to say the least.

"I wish I'd kissed you the first night we met," he said. "When you complimented my wind while insulting me."

"You could make up for it now." I smirked.

His lips were on mine before I took another breath. He picked up right where we'd left off in the cottage. His tongue stroked mine as it invaded my mouth. His hand was at my neck, tilting my head to grant a better angle. A chill ran up my spine, the cold thrill mixing decadently with the heat pooling low in my stomach. Wind danced along my neck and shoulders, and I shivered in delight when his arms pulled me closer to him as he drew away with a last, lingering press of his mouth to mine.

He shifted in his seat, and I did the same. He set my senses alive in a way I had yet to feel—an unspeakable excitement mixed with a perfect calm in my chest at what the night would bring. I knew I was taking many risks. Coming into my father's house was a big step. Dining with him and my grandmother, who I'd never met, was another. Determining if he could have such animosity toward half-fae as to work against us was icing on the cake.

"I'm glad you're with me," I said, holding Vincent's gaze.

"There is nowhere else I'd rather be."

26

Vincent

Pierce House was in the Norden District. It was right on the water where the bay curved to the sea. It was almost unfair that Darius got the best of both views in Sandrin. I was sure his water magic felt right at home here. As quickly as the thought crossed my mind, my hand balled into a fist at my side as we approached the sprawling manor.

I couldn't believe he'd kept Luna from this.

I'd never been to Pierce House. It was not a big surprise, given that the truce between fae courts was new. It looked like my parents' home—the one I'd grown up in.

I reached for Luna's hand again as the coach rolled unevenly onto a large, circular path. I stepped down, releasing Luna momentarily only to offer my hand again as she exited. It was safe to say I was obsessed with her touch.

She craned her neck to take in the brick building. It was all a single story. This pointed to its age. Newer buildings in Sandrin were two or even three floors. More citizens than ever wanted to live in the city, so vertical space was necessary. Only the original homes, claimed by old fae, still took up so much land. I shook my head, wondering what he did with all the space. I'd told my parents years ago that they should downsize. They'd tutted and patted my shoulder like I knew nothing. I probably didn't when it came to the status symbol these old houses were to the fae.

As an old fae family, multiple generations of Pierce's lived here. I stewed again as I remembered that Luna had never been granted that privilege. Darius had a small family, from the court records I saw. He was an only child, so in reality, he and his parents lived in this massive building, although it was common knowledge that Klein, Darius's father, was in the north doing some Norden magic research.

It seemed like such a waste. I truly hoped we'd find nothing tonight that supported the tip received by the paper. Part of me wondered if there was any chance that Darius's isolation from Luna had anything to do with her mother. The more she spoke about her, the more concerned I was with her mother's efforts to disregard part of her nature. Luna was fae and human. Half of each, and wholly perfect. I wished she'd had more people in her life who made her feel that way.

She hooked her hand around my arm as we strolled toward the door. I glared at the coat sleeve preventing her hand from reaching my skin. Instead, I let my hand rest over hers while my gaze roamed the scenery. The grounds were beautiful. One of the perks of water magic was that he could pull water directly from the sea to ensure all his plants were properly hydrated. The lush grass, growing ivy, and full copse of trees made it seem like we might be in the park.

"Ready?" I asked, raising a hand to knock.

She nodded, thankfully, because the large wooden door opened before my knuckles even rapped against it.

"Luna! I'm so glad you made it." Darius answered the door himself.

I was sure this was abnormal. Even if only he and his parents lived here, there would be household staff. My parents and grandparents lived in their house and employed ten people to keep it up.

He gestured us in. "Happy name day."

I let Luna's hand slip from my arm and pressed my hand briefly against her lower back as I urged her to follow her father. I'd be right behind her, but this was her night. Maybe if things went well enough for them now, she wouldn't want to break into his study before drinks.

The house was beautiful, as I'd expected it would be. Marble floors and stone pillars decorated every room. Large portraits filled the hallways and rooms we passed. Many appeared to be of members of the family line, or pictures of Sandrin as it progressed. The Pierce family had been here since its founding. Darius greeted me courteously but seemed to appreciate my willingness to follow as he led Luna through the halls. She glanced back at me occasionally, and I smiled each time in reassurance as Darius kept chattering about the family and the house.

He didn't sound like a fae intent on keeping magic from his daughter, but what did you really know of someone raised in polite society? They were so good at being what they needed to be in the moment. It was how I'd been raised, too.

"Vincent, your parents' home is much the same as ours, no?" Darius asked as he led us to a formal dining room.

"I see many similarities."

He offered me a seat and pulled the chair next to it out for Luna.

"I hope you don't mind. We'll eat first. The cook has said it's ready, so I'd hate to let it get cold. We can have drinks in the parlor after the meal if you have time."

I glanced at Luna, letting her know it was all her show.

"We'd love to," she said.

Darius went to the corner of the room and grabbed a bottle of wine from a cart. "Eloise should be here momentarily. They'll serve the food as soon as she comes down. Wine while we wait?"

Luna nodded, and he filled her glass. I accepted the same.

"So," Darius said as he sat with his own glass, leaving the bottle on the table. He finally turned his attention to me. "Any new recommendations I should know about?"

My shoulders tensed, as I wasn't exactly sure how to answer that. The next new recommendation would be Luna's. I'd started working on it earlier this week. I looked at her helplessly.

She shrugged. "He might be working on a piece for me, for Cliff House, if we can work some things out." She let the sentence hang there. Her words broke my heart a little. I told myself not to panic. She might be referring to the fact of the locked room and whatever magic prevented visitors from coming to the inn. She couldn't still be worried I wouldn't write the recommendation without her upholding her side of the bargain. Nothing could be further from the truth, but sharp fear slid down my spine as I replayed our conversations and realized I hadn't told her that.

My wind thrashed in my chest as if to say *You still have time.*

Darius's eyes narrowed like he wasn't sure how he felt about her statement, but suspicion was absolutely on the list of emotions appearing on his face. "Is he now?"

I coughed. "It's a beautiful property. I can't believe it doesn't get more attention."

"Neither can I," Darius said flatly, lifting his wine glass to his lips. He paused and glanced at me like he had me in checkmate, though I had no idea what game we were playing. "Don't you only feature fae establishments?" His words sounded almost pained, but his eyes narrowed in anticipation of my response.

Luna frowned, and Darius flinched, catching her reaction out of the corner of his eye. He must have realized how the question sounded to her. "I didn't mean—" he started. "Luna, I meant he only featured establishments that obviously cater to old fae, not that you weren't fae."

Well, he had not minced words with that one. However, I couldn't fault him for clearing things up so directly for Luna. I laughed as I brought my wine glass to my lips and sipped. "Tell me how you really feel, Darius." It felt odd to speak so frankly with him. I was, after all, the fae—how had she phrased it?—seeing his daughter. His estranged daughter, all things considered, so I wasn't sure how much his opinion counted.

I glanced at Luna as I thought the word *seeing*. How close to the truth did that come for her? It had felt that way when we visited my past recommendations together, even through our missteps. It had felt that way when she kissed me today at the cottage and again in the carriage. This was another item I needed to clear up as soon as possible. I wanted to be *seeing* her.

She reached for my thigh under the table and squeezed. It was more than reassuring.

"I won't apologize, Vincent. Your family's opinions are well known. I want to make sure my daughter knows that."

"You'll get no complaint from me if you decide to start being protective of her. I'd say it's up to her if she'll allow it, though."

Darius flushed and opened his mouth, no doubt to respond harshly.

"Father." The single word brought the male to a standstill. Luna must have realized its effect but was merciless as she wielded it. "I told you Vincent was important to me. I'd appreciate it if you at least tried to get to know him, separate from what you know of his family, before jumping to conclusions."

Darius looked chastised in a way I could never imagine my father being by anything I said. In fact, I couldn't imagine my father and I ever having a conversation mirroring this.

"You're right, Luna." He raised his glass. "I apologize, Vincent. We're here to celebrate Luna. I will refrain from any further outbursts."

"*You* might, but I certainly will not." A voice sounded from the doorway. The older female's words held a command I was sure she took full advantage of. She wore the deepest blue from head to toe, and large diamond earrings hung from her ears. Eloise must be the power of the family. I could tell the moment she stepped into the room. Water wasn't flying from her hands, but her magic smelled like a storm brewing. I sat up straighter in my seat. She must be older than I'd realized because her age was showing. Wrinkles lined her face, and more than streaks of silver like Luna's covered her hair. I wasn't sure what came over me, but I stood, dipping my chin as she took her seat at the head of the table.

"You think manners will impress me?" Eloise tsked. "It's been twenty-five years, and we finally get Luna into our home only to have an Andiveron escort her?"

I took my seat and glanced at Luna. Her brows furrowed in confusion. I thought she'd caught the same part of that speech that I had. *It's been twenty-five years, and we finally get Luna into our home.*

They'd wanted her here all along.

27

Luna

We *finally get Luna into our home*. The words felt like a brand on my skin. I didn't know who to look at or what to think. Vincent's hand squeezed my thigh gently under the table, returning the support I'd recently shown him. My gaze met his, and those deep brown eyes were my calm in the storm. I knew he was trying to communicate with me. Did I need him to jump in? Distract? Press?

No, this question had plagued me for as long as I could remember. I put my hand on top of his where it rested. All I needed was his support.

"What do you mean? You finally get me into your home?"

Eloise, my grandmother, turned her fierce gaze on me. "Precisely what I said."

A scent flowed into the room with her, like the sea before a storm. I was sure many would find it intimidating, but it evoked a sense of calm in me.

"Mother..." Darius started.

Thankfully, the meal was brought out at that moment. As Darius indicated, the staff had been waiting for Eloise, and all at once, a roasted meat dish and bowls of vegetables were served. A quiet moment passed among us before whatever truths Darius and Eloise would unleash. As soon as the staff disappeared behind the kitchen doors, Darius and Eloise held each other's gaze in a wordless battle.

"We'd love to get to know you and celebrate your name day," Darius said, still not looking at me. It appeared he was waiting to ensure Eloise agreed.

"Fine," Eloise said, picking up her fork and moving toward the filled plate.

I looked down at my own plate, wondering if I should let this go. Vincent's hand had left my leg, as it was needed to tend to the utensils and food on the table, but his wind wrapped around the same spot his hand had been. The slight pressure was comforting.

Darius's nostrils flared, and I had no doubt he realized Vincent was using his magic. The scent of magic was noticeable to other fae. I found it interesting that I could scent Eloise's magic, and Darius's when he'd rescued me, but I hadn't grasped the scent of Vincent's yet. Maybe it was a half-fae thing. Darius opened his mouth like he would say something, maybe tell Vincent off for using his magic in Pierce House. It wasn't exactly polite.

But the support of his wind emboldened me, so I jumped in, interrupting whatever Darius would say. "I'd like to know. I've believed you wanted nothing to do with me since you came to our village and tried to test me for magic."

The pressure around my leg strengthened as if the increased weight was Vincent's way of saying he was with me.

"I told you," Eloise said primly, glaring at her son.

Darius took a long sip of his wine. He put the goblet down completely before holding my gaze. "I'm sorry, Luna. I never wanted that." He sighed, his hand coming to his temple as he seemed to be working through some internal decision.

"Your mother didn't like it here." He glanced around, then gestured.

"Here, like...Pierce House?"

"Yes, but also fae society in general." He paused. "I don't blame her. We did everything we could." He glanced at Eloise. "We even banished Klein, my father, but I'm afraid it was too late. Your mother realized the uphill battle that being human in fae society would bring."

"I thought Klein was studying some unique properties of Norden magic that are only available in the north," Vincent said.

"Sure," Eloise said, glaring at him. "He could be doing that. We didn't care. He held views much like your parents', so we wanted him gone." Her tone was sharp, but Vincent didn't flinch at the comment. I'd only met his parents once and agreed the impression they made was less than stellar, but Darius and Eloise seemed very against them. Maybe even more than fae court rivalry dictated.

"You banished your husband to try and make Mom more comfortable? But she still left? Why not let him return?" I directed the question to Eloise.

"Please understand, ours was a union of power. Many with magic make matches based on strengthening elemental lines. When I realized the type of male he was, I did all I could to distance us. Some could argue it took me longer than it should have to realize." She dabbed her mouth with her napkin. "His opinions have no place here, dear. Even though your mother took you away, we always treated this home as yours. Anyone who would not welcome you was not someone we welcomed."

My throat tightened, and something prickled at the corners of my eyes. Even the constant pressure of Vincent's wind on my thigh was not enough to calm the swell of emotions rushing inside me. I could all too clearly imagine Mom having a bad experience here. Every angry word she'd said about the fae was likely based on some fact. They'd been too passionate not to be. She'd been tricked, harassed, and threatened. I knew she'd believed this was not a safe place to raise me, but with how Darius and Eloise expressed themselves now, it didn't seem like such a permanent separation had been required.

"When did he leave?" I asked, my throat constricting around the words.

"Too late," Darius replied. "Maybe weeks before you did."

They'd sent him away when she was still here. Any excuses I'd made that they weren't listening to her, that she hadn't given them a chance, crumbled. It still may have been too late for Darius and Mom, as he said, but if they'd proved willing to change the situation for us, why deprive me of a father?

"I need a moment." I excused myself from the table. A chair beside me scooted across the floor, and I knew Vincent was rising with me. He stopped briefly to accept directions to a private room from Eloise and Darius while I wandered aimlessly ahead. When his hand was on my back a moment later, he guided me into a set of closed double doors. "Eloise said this was private."

It was Darius's study, and my mind instantly fled from the weight of what I'd been considering—the choices Mom had made on my behalf. "This is his study?" I asked, looking around.

"Luna," Vincent warned. "Don't you want to talk about—"

I was behind his desk, looking at the sprawl of papers before Vincent had time to finish his sentence.

"I don't think now is the best time for this," he tried.

"I'd rather search these papers than think about what Mom let me believe for over twenty years."

She'd taken so much from me. I was sure her experiences had been terrible. Eloise and Darius had admitted as much, but hadn't they done something about the problem? Part of why I'd been so surprised about Vincent's apartment was because old fae families didn't leave these estates. Kicking Klein out was no small thing. Mom and Darius hadn't needed to remain together for me to have a place here. I shook my head, wanting desperately to discuss Mom's choices with her but knowing it was impossible. Something wet hit my cheek.

Vincent's lips pursed in thought, and then he came around the desk to help, brushing the tear from my cheek as he did. "I'm here to talk when you're ready."

I squeezed his hand before my gaze skimmed the desk—all the papers of running an estate, everything I needed to distract me from what I'd learned. Financials and correspondence, all splayed out for me to peruse. I almost wondered if he'd sent us here on purpose. That didn't seem like him, at least what I was coming to know of him, but it *did* sound like Eloise. They couldn't have known my original plan, though.

The warm palm pressing against my back drew my gaze to Vincent's. "Are you sure you don't want to talk while we search?"

I shook my head.

"Do you mind if I talk to you?"

I glanced up at him. "Now?" I splayed my hands.

His lip tipped into an irresistible smile. "I won't slow us down, I promise."

I knew this would be an attempt to pry my feelings free, feelings I was determined to avoid, but he looked so earnest, and I wanted so badly to know what he would share. "Please, go ahead."

"I'd like to talk about my parents," he started.

I gave him a sideways glance. "You think talking about your family will make me talk about mine?"

He smirked but shook his head. "To be fair, your father brought them up, so I have an excuse to discuss them. You had the unfortunate pleasure of meeting my parents. I feel you got a good glimpse of who they are, but I'd like to tell you more."

I stopped my search and turned to face him. "I don't lump you along with them like Darius. You don't have to do this."

His smile was devastating in its own way. "I'd like to all the same."

My nod was brief, and then I returned to searching, letting him share what he would.

"They are as prejudiced as he says. It's not even bound to half-fae or human, honestly. It even applies to fae who don't have what they consider to be the right amount of magic for a pureblood family." His hands stopped searching. I was sure they were running through his hair, though I didn't look up.

"I didn't tell you how I learned to call my magic."

"It didn't escape my notice that Ambrose jumped in." I shuffled a few papers as I skimmed them. "You don't have to share anything you're uncomfortable with."

His wind wrapped around my wrist and glided up my arm. It sent a chill down my spine, and I shivered in delight.

"It wouldn't have been helpful in that situation. The way I learned wasn't one I'd wish on anyone else." He swallowed. "Finding my magic was never calm like you described. It was always a storm. My parents wanted to ensure my magic was strong. An old fae belief said that the more your magic is tested—truly tested—by elders, the stronger it will become. So, it was never a quiet stillness in which I learned."

My throat tightened again, this time for what I was sure would come next from Vincent's lips. I paused and turned to look at him.

"Please, keep searching," he said.

"They used their wind on you to draw yours out?"

I didn't return to searching the papers, and he kept talking, holding my gaze. "They sent their wind at me at every opportunity, hoping mine would rise to defend me. I guess I was never really in danger from it." He paused. "But it made for an unpleasant association with my magic." He laughed without mirth. "It also led to my wind acting out in odd ways as I aged."

My hands were on his arms, squeezing in reassurance the same way his wind had. His wind swept along my cheek, clearing away more tears I didn't realize had fallen. This information made me cherish his wind's attention even more.

"Unfortunately, their methods worked. One day, my wind sprang forth and pushed them both away in a display they've not forgotten. I'm stronger than the two combined, and they credit themselves for that."

It made me sick to my stomach. "I'm sorry they did that to you."

He shrugged. "I just want you to know that anything Darius says about my parents is probably true."

"I'm not trying to build a relationship with your parents," I said pointedly. "I'm trying to build one with you."

His smile was small. His wind pushed our hands together, wrapping around where they joined. "As we sat at the table, I was thinking of everything I wanted to tell you—to make sure you knew. It all fled my mind."

"I assure you, we have time. You can tell me when the thoughts return."

He gestured back to the desk. "Let's keep looking." He opened a few drawers and rifled through each.

"I think I found something." He handed me a piece of paper that looked well-aged. It had been folded and refolded many times. The paper was thin with wear. Unfortunately, I knew who it was from before I read the contents. The handwriting was as familiar to me as my own. This was a letter from Mom.

28

Vincent

My brow furrowed as I passed the letter to Luna. This was everything I'd feared. I hadn't read the entire thing but I'd seen the words we were searching for: bargain, donations, half-fae education. I tried not to hold my breath as her eyes roamed the page. Tears welled in her eyes, and even my wind hesitated to wipe them away. How could this be where the story ended? Darius had seemed so genuine in there. He disliked me for everything he thought my family to be. How could he be the same? Eloise, too, in a terrifying sort of way.

She passed the letter back to me. "You should read it. I don't think it says what you think it does." Her voice was soft and a little wobbly. I was sure that must mean exactly what I thought it did, but I'd take her word for it. We could cause a scene on the way out if we needed to.

I started reading, and my heart broke with each sentence I processed. Luna was right. This was not what I'd thought it was. My eyes locked with hers, and tears streamed down her face.

"He's been donating to the education of half-fae since you were born?" I asked. "Your mom used that as blackmail for him to stay away?"

This was...well, I didn't know about worse, but I knew it was more complicated.

"How could she have done that to me? She knew what his dismissal did to me." Luna pushed her silver strands back and tried swiping tears from her cheeks, but they kept coming. My wind drifted to her cheeks, letting the tears fall but drying them before they dripped onto her blouse. She laughed at the gesture even as her face remained pained.

"I don't think we get to know that for sure, but based on what Darius said, we can guess."

Luna nodded. "Protecting me from the fae is one thing, but actively blackmailing my father to stay away from me is another."

I agreed, but I also knew what Luna's mom meant to her. Luna needed to formulate her own opinions on this before I weighed in. It would be even more difficult since her mother was gone. She couldn't answer for what she'd done, though the blackmail was clear as day in this letter. Darius had wanted to spend time with Luna. He had wanted to be in her life. Luna's mom had not only said no, but she'd also ensured that if Darius ever approached Luna, his family would be punished.

Sponsoring half-fae education was a heated debate now. The new Norden Point had changed all the rules since she was of two courts herself. It would have been much worse when this letter was written almost twenty years ago. The previous Norden Point had had strict rules about fae education. I wasn't familiar enough with the penalties of the Norden Court, but I could easily imagine that this knowledge in the hands of the prior Norden Point would have been cause for exile.

My wind caressed Luna's skin. I realized I wanted to do the same. I wanted to be there for her while she processed so much information in so short a letter. Reaching for her, I wrapped my arms around her shoulders, squeezing. All I wanted to do was reassure her. Families were messy, and this would be painful to process. As much as her mom had blackmailed Darius, he had still gone along with it. The Pierce position in the Norden Court had been more important to him than his daughter. There was no good news in this letter. She sagged into my arms, and I let her collapse against me, wrapping my arms around her completely.

"This is such a mess," she said.

I nodded as my head rested on her hair, and I tucked her in even closer as if that could keep her safe from the feelings assaulting her now.

A knock on the door to the study reminded me we were still in Pierce House. Darius and Eloise were still out there. Did Luna want to speak to them about this now? She'd been overwhelmed by the idea that they had tried to see her before. They had done so much to ensure she'd be welcome in Pierce House if she ever came. This letter complicated those assertions.

"Come in," Luna called. Her voice was muffled as she spoke into my chest, her face pressed against it. I released her, but she didn't let me go. She stayed right where she was as Darius and Eloise entered the room.

"We wanted to check on you," Darius said, his gaze not missing much as he skimmed the room. It was apparent we'd disrupted most things on the desk. We hadn't returned any papers we'd pulled from the drawers.

"Were you two looking for something?" His gaze finally fell to the crumpled letter on the desk. I assumed he knew what it was by the wear and age. "Luna, I can explain that."

She pushed herself from my arms and turned to face him. "I don't know what is worse. To learn that the father who has ignored me my entire life wanted to spend time with me, or that my mom, the woman who raised me, blackmailed him to stay away." The tears started streaming again. I let my hand fall to the small of her back in reassurance. "It's another thing entirely to realize that your father could be blackmailed. That something like court affiliation would be enough to keep you from me."

Darius raked his hand through his hair. "I didn't want you to find out this way." He gestured to the paper. "I'm sorry, but I have little defense against everything you say. You have the proof there. Even when your mom convinced me you didn't have magic, that changed nothing for me. I was still your father and wanted to be present in your life."

"You were donating to people who would teach magic to half-fae?"

He nodded. "No matter how much the fae tried to pretend half-fae weren't a part of our world, they always have been. And there have always been people willing to break the rules to help them understand that part of their heritage. I'm sure you know the magic side you inherit is never straightforward."

Luna laughed, but with her tears, it came out garbled. "I'm well aware."

"I hoped you would be interested in studying when you finally came to Sandrin. But"—he shrugged, looking a little ashamed—"all I could sense was your anger at me for abandoning you." He gestured again to the letter. "And for that, I have no excuse."

"Was the court position so important?" I asked. I didn't mean to insert myself, but Darius didn't seem the type to cow to blackmail. If there was something else in this, Luna deserved to know it.

He glared at me but relented. "I didn't give a shit about the court position, but the last Norden Point was dangerous. Rumors spread that he was searching for those with magic who weren't pureblood fae. If it came out I was helping half-fae, the natural conclusion would lead him to find you." His gaze held Luna's before turning to me. "He was unstable at best. I couldn't risk Luna being in his crosshairs."

It didn't change the result, but the explanation fit much better with the picture of Darius I'd been assembling.

"Everything in this house is yours. I want you to feel that way, Luna, but can I ask what made you decide to start rifling through drawers now?"

She tensed in my arm and glanced at me with wide eyes. I read everything in them. She would find a way to forgive her father and would want to have a relationship with him. However, she did not want to start that new relationship with lies. I sighed. I would do this for her. I would do anything for her, though I didn't want to contemplate that too hard at the moment. "I'm afraid that's my fault."

Darius's gaze snapped to me like I'd finally proved to be the weasel he expected.

"I had a tip at the paper that you were doing the exact opposite of what this letter says. So, before accepting everything you said tonight as truth, I wanted to ensure you weren't lying to Luna."

"A tip," he said through clenched teeth. "That I was..."

"Bribing the governor to stop development of the magic school for half-fae," I said.

Darius snorted. "I've done many things I regret in my relationship with Luna, but stopping her from exploring her magic has never been one of them. Stopping any half-fae that wants to from exploring their magic is never something I could abide."

"Where did this tip come from?" Eloise asked with narrowed eyes. She'd been quiet so far, letting Darius explain himself to his daughter, but she was ready to pounce on me the same way Darius was.

"I'm not sure, hence why I needed to investigate it."

She opened her mouth to retort, but I got there first.

"I admit, I thought it was farfetched until I heard Darius in the stairwell at the governor's office. He was talking about a payment and the magic school." I let the information hang there, hoping he would take the bait.

He laughed, but it was dark. "Yes, well, the tip has some truth to it. Not about me." He strode farther into the room, pulled more papers from the desk, and handed them to me. "Someone is paying the governor to halt her decision on the school in Sandrin. I've been trying to figure out who and matching the bribes on the opposite side." I could feel his glare as I perused the documents. They were everything I needed to prove his innocence. It was the entire letter, of which the packet I'd been given had only snippets. This clearly stated his intention to see the school's development proceed. I met his gaze as I handed the items to Luna. Something in this stare felt knowing, accusatory. I bristled, unsure what he was trying to say.

"Vincent is being overly kind, making it sound like he was the only one with questions, but I had them, too." Luna lifted her chin. "I wanted to know for sure before accepting any kind of relationship with you."

As Darius's gaze turned from me to Luna, it softened. "I understand." He waved his hand at the documents. "Take them if you need them. Are there any other questions I can answer for you about it?"

"Was Mom's time here so bad," she asked quietly, "that she'd want to deprive me of a father?"

Darius's face crumpled, but he found a way to answer. "It wasn't good. I don't fault her for leaving. Klein was cruel, as were his guests. They spoke down to her, belittled her, and treated her as less than. I don't fault her for wanting to protect you, either. I only wish she'd remembered that I wasn't like my father. I wasn't like any of them, and I like to think it's what drew her to me in the first place."

Luna chewed on her lip before responding. “I think we should go. I need to...” Her words trailed off as she gestured around the room. “Process all of this. I’m sorry we went through your things,” she added sheepishly.

“You’re welcome here anytime, Luna.” He held her gaze. “I want you to know that.”

She nodded and slipped her hand into mine, interlocking our fingers. “Let’s go.”

29

Luna

I told myself I wasn't running—I was processing. Cliff House Inn was finally visible through the carriage window. The full moon's light cast a gentle glow across the pines. I wanted to run into the tree cover, to my cottage. I let out a sigh of relief at our approach.

"It makes you feel safe," Vincent said.

I turned to look at him. He'd been quiet on the ride, giving me space. While I needed it from my family, I didn't want it from him. He and I, no matter the initial bargain we struck, had always been honest with each other about what we wanted. I hoped to eventually be more honest with him about how much my feelings had changed, about what he meant to me now. When everything I knew collapsed like a house of cards, Vincent refused to let it fall—his wind would hold every piece in place until I was ready for my next move. He was solid ground, even as the continent tilted beneath my feet.

Maybe he made me feel safe, too.

"It does," I said as he hopped out of the carriage and offered me a hand. I took it, lacing our fingers again as we walked toward the property.

I glanced at the sky and the glowing orb above us. I fingered the necklace he'd given me. The phases of the moon meant more to me than I realized.

"I want to show you something." I tugged him forward, a smile finally breaking across my lips, maybe for the first time since the meal at Pierce House began.

He looked hesitant but let me lead. "Are you sure you don't want to be alone?"

I shook my head and pulled. He didn't fight me.

"I told you about the moonflowers I'd borrow from the property."

"Yes," he said cautiously. "It was another reason I was convinced you had magic."

My steps halted, and I turned. "Because they only bloom in the presence of Norden magic?"

He nodded, then glanced up. "Norden magic and the light of the moon. Guess we're in luck."

"They've always bloomed for me. Even when Mom and I visited on our vacations." The words constricted something in my chest, as saying *Mom* reminded me of all she'd kept from me.

"They have good taste." He pulled my hand to his lips. They were warm against my cold skin. I shivered as his wind slipped across my hand, encircling it with the touch of his lips. He laughed. "I guess I'm my own competition. This is going to take some getting used to."

I smiled in return. "Don't worry, I'm a lot." I gestured vaguely at everything that had happened since we met. "You might need the backup."

He stepped closer, his wind working to unbraid my hair so it could slide through it. I was more than a little amazed when it dropped the pins holding my braid in place into Vincent's pocket, freeing my waves. "We are eager for anything you choose to give us."

"I might need you to prove that."

His wind skimmed my arm and danced across my exposed shoulders. My body flushed, heat shooting straight to my core. The smile on his handsome face said he knew precisely the effect he was having on me.

"My wind and I will do so on my knees every day you allow it." His grin turned feral. "In any way you require."

A stilted sound escaped my lips. The wind was gone in the space of a breath. I gasped inadvertently at its retreat.

"I was simply illustrating my enthusiasm for the task, Miss Pierce," he said primly. His gaze held mine, daring me to contest his dedication. "Now, about those moonflowers."

His fae beauty was always on display, but in the moonlight, it was devastating. His hand still held mine, and I used it to push him back against the nearest tree, bringing my body flush to his. My face was inches from his, our breaths mingling as I said, "The moonflowers can wait." His wind wrapped around us both at my words. I knew there was something I wanted to show him, more I needed to consider about all I'd learned tonight, but none of it seemed important as his lips pressed against mine. He pulled me closer, and I fell against him, wanting to deepen this growing connection. His hand slid up my side, gently caressing the curve of my breast. I couldn't breathe; I couldn't think. I only wanted. I tilted my head, opening myself to kiss him deeper. Our tongues tangled as our kiss intensified. When his hand touched the skin of my neck, I was alight, my body on fire even as a wave of pleasure shot through me.

Light from the full moon snuck through the canopy of trees. The press of Vincent's body against mine was a warmth on the chilly night. Scents of leather and mint wrapped around me. It felt like home. Suddenly, I gasped as I made the connection. I should have known Vincent's quiet strength would help me locate it. I pressed my hands against his chest, pushing myself back, and worked to catch my breath. Our kiss revealed the quiet calm lurking beneath the surface, one I'd been searching for all week. "Your magic smells like leather and mint."

He shook his head, coming out of his own daze. Then, my words must have registered. "What did you say?"

"I think I found it. The quiet, the calm."

He ran his hand through his hair. "You can smell my magic?"

My lips tilted into a smile. "Come with me."

Only those with magic could smell the scent of another's. With how much Vincent's wind had lavished attention on me, I'd yet to know its signature scent. But out here, under the light of the moon, in the safety of Vincent's arms, I finally understood. I took his hand, pulled him behind me, and we ran toward the inn.

The bed of moonflowers, tucked against the southern side of the building, bloomed with our approach. I paused, not wanting to disturb them.

Vincent's hands rested on my hips as he stood behind me. "I think they know you're here." His lips pressed against my neck.

I reached inside for that quiet place. The moonflowers always bloomed for me, but there was also a lingering warmth beneath my skin as they did. I felt it now, so I stepped away from Vincent and fell to my knees before the flowerbed. My fingers pressed into the dirt, which, as I was beginning to suspect, was damp.

"I think I water them without realizing it."

Vincent's head tilted to the side when I glanced over my shoulder. "You used magic?"

"I think so," I said hesitantly. "Maybe unconsciously."

He fell to his knees beside me, his hand reaching for the soil. He sniffed the air. "Yes, of course. Moonflower and juniper is the scent of your magic." He searched the area around us as if it would give us clues as to what provoked the scent.

I glanced up. My fingers found their way to the pendant he'd given me—the moon's phases. Then, I met his gaze. "I know what it is."

I felt his eyes on me even as my face lifted to the moon's light—the caveat to my magic. "I love being out at night. As a child, it was always my favorite to stay out late enough for the moon and stars to shine. Here, it's one of my favorite times of the day." I hesitated. "I only have one negative memory in the moonlight. The night Darius saved me from drowning." I canted my head in thought. Like so many with my father, that memory needed to be re-examined in a new light. It had never made sense to me why he'd been on that beach. It had also been the only night I'd stayed at the inn. I feared what else I would learn from the memory holding the door shut.

"On one of my last trips here with my mom, we went to the water late at night. The current was strong," I recounted. "It pulled me from her. I only remember waking in the center of the cyclone near the beach I first took you to."

Recognition flashed in his gaze. "I suspected that beach meant something to you. Sorry, I didn't know."

I shook my head. "It was important for me to remember. Darius pulled me from the water. I always assumed I'd gotten lucky, that his water magic had saved me. Now I wonder...if I saved myself."

"Maybe we should go check it out?" Vincent suggested.

I shook my head. "No. Let's go to the locked room."

He took my hand and followed me to the door that stood between me and saving the property I loved.

After our visit to Pierce House tonight, I knew my father would give me more time for the inn if needed. We hadn't had time to discuss it, but something had triggered him to try and establish our relationship now. Mom had been gone for a few years. I didn't know why he chose now—maybe because Byrd had quit—but I knew if I told him my progress, he'd give me the time I needed to fix the inn.

But I felt so close.

I wanted to do it now.

I knelt before the locked door with the moonlight streaming in through the window at the end of the hallway. Vincent stood a step away to let me work. The calm was there —quiet and comforting. It rumbled to a low roar at my command, like a rushing wave ready to crash over the shore. I pushed away the fears. Tonight, I'd learned so much and hadn't let the weight of it crush me. Whatever the memory, I could face it. My water magic surged. I wrapped my hand around the doorknob and twisted.

I WASN'T sure what I was seeing, exactly. Like many others I'd cleaned over the last few weeks, the room was just a room. What confused me the most was that my parents stood in it. They looked muted, toned down from the vibrancy of life. This was a memory. I wasn't yet sure whose.

"Why did you bring her here?" Mom asked, hands on her hips. She was soaking wet and spitting mad. The plummeting feeling in my stomach told me I could no longer avoid admitting that I knew exactly when this was. My gaze raked the room, and I noticed a figure shifting under the covers. She was small and tucked in tight like someone had taken the time to swaddle her in as many blankets as they could find, but her blond streaks were visible from here.

It was me. asleep in the large bed.

"I didn't know where you were. My priority was getting her dry and making her feel safe," Darius whisper-hissed at Mom. "When were you going to tell me, by the way," he asked sardonically, "that she has magic?"

Mom stepped back, eyes widening at his words. "She doesn't."

"I think she does, Meredith," he said pointedly. "And it saved her life."

"Don't say things like that," Mom hissed.

Darius leaned into her space. "I found her in the water on the other side of the cliff. She had created a whirlpool and set herself at its center." He held her gaze. "I don't even want to think about what would have happened if she hadn't." He ran his hand through his hair. "What were you thinking?"

Mom exploded. "I won't have you questioning my parenting. You wouldn't survive one full day with her on your own—"

"You never gave me the chance!" Darius cut in. "I will happily take as many as I can have!"

"That's not the point," Mom said. "She doesn't belong with you. She belongs with me."

"That was your argument when you said she had no magic. I didn't believe it then. I certainly don't believe it now."

"This is all irrelevant. I'm taking my daughter and going back to the cottage. We'll leave in the morning."

"Our daughter, Meredith." He breathed heavily from the heat of the argument. "And I think it's time she got another chance to know her father." He glanced around the room. "I want to give her the inn."

Mom looked confused. "Give her the inn?"

"Yes." He waved his hands around. "This would all be hers.

She could run it eventually. Not now," he added as Mom opened her mouth to protest. "When she's ready."

"Absolutely not."

"Why? She loves it here. You said it yourself."

Mom shook her head. I was surprised smoke wasn't pouring from her ears. "Loving an annual vacation to the city and living here are very different." Her head was still shaking as she continued. "I won't even get into the layers of what you owning the property and lording it over her would be like."

"That's not what I meant, and you know it. It would be hers free and clear. Whether she wants to see me or not."

"You can't buy her affection!"

"I wouldn't have to try if you'd let me see her."

He sounded so tired. So did Mom. I found it hard to believe they had ever been a couple. They were talking past each other at every point. Mom seemed ready to assume the worst of Darius, and the worst part was that I didn't know why. He'd said her time at Pierce House had been bad, and the fae had been cruel. Was all of this to protect me from the same experience?

"This isn't happening," Mom said. "We'll be gone in the morning." She moved to where I was in the bed, ready to scoop me into her arms and carry me back to the cottage.

"Don't disturb her. You two can have this room tonight."

Mom nodded.

Darius stood at the door. "I know I hurt you, Meredith, but you're hurting her. She needs me in her life, especially if she has magic. If not me, she needs someone to train with to understand it."

"She does not have magic." Mom bit out every word.

Darius shook his head. He'd been holding a flower stem in his hand. A moonflower. He laid it on the desk in the room as he walked toward the door. "That bloomed for her tonight." He pointed to the flower. "I've walked this property a hundred times, and they've never flowered for me." He shook his head again. "She has magic, whether you want to acknowledge it or not. It will make itself known eventually." He left, letting the door shut behind him.

The memory continued, and I feared I had my answer about whose it was.

Mom dried herself off and got into bed next to me, her hand stroking my hair gently. "You're not one of them, sweetie. You could never be as evil as the fae," she whispered. She reached for something in her trouser pocket. It was a vial of liquid, and it was deep red. As she tipped it side to side, the slow viscosity with which it moved made me realize it was blood. "We'll see if this was worth what I paid for it. He won't give you the inn if it fails."

I couldn't believe what I was seeing. Mom hated magic but was ready to wield purchased blood magic. It didn't make any sense…yet it made perfect sense. Blood magic was something humans could wield—it didn't have the legacy of snobbery existing with fae elements. If Klein and other fae had dismissed her in her time at Pierce House, it would only make sense she was ready to fight fire with fire now. She unstopped the bottle and let the drops fall to the floor. The wood soaked them up immediately, and the room began to glow.

Suddenly, I lurched back, no longer watching the scene unfold. Strong arms wrapped around me.

"Luna, are you alright?" Vincent was with me. I was in the present. The door was open. The moonflower Vincent had found last time was still lying on the desk, preserved like it had been the day Darius left it there in the memory.

Somehow, I knew what I had to do. The moon was still bright. Power flooded me as I moved into the light it cast through the window. Water flowed from my hands with little thought. "You can wait outside," I whispered to Vincent.

His only response was to wrap his arms around me more tightly. "I'm with you."

The water rushed over every surface, cleansing Mom's thoughtless blood magic from the space. It scrubbed and dried as it went. There was no way I could have accomplished the removal by simple cleaning. My element penetrated the deep layer of blood magic in the space. I felt the moment the magic lost hold, the moment my water broke through. The how of it didn't make sense—there was so much about my magic that I didn't understand—but in the quiet calm within me, I knew the inn was free.

30

Luna

The task was finished, the room and blood magic cleansed by the water magic that flowed through me under the moon's light. I wanted to crumple. My body swayed as if it might, but the scent of mint and leather hit my nose, and those strong arms that encircled me when I flung free of the memory still held me tightly—still held me up when I was ready to fall.

Vincent was still with me.

"Mom used blood magic on the inn," I said, falling farther into his waiting arms, knowing he'd bear whatever burdens I gave him. I wasn't used to wielding magic, at least not with such intention. It hadn't been enough to know Mom had used blood magic. I'd needed to fix it. I'd needed to cleanse, to undo everything she'd done to keep me from my fae heritage. Resting more fully against Vincent, I let my magic wander the room a final time.

His hands trailed down my arms in reassurance. The blood

magic was gone. I still couldn't believe she'd done it. No matter Mom's intention, she'd taken things from me, taken a relationship with my father, and I was having a hard time reconciling that with the woman I had known.

I wished she was here to ask. From the memory, I knew she'd been trying to protect me. I could feel that as firmly as I was sure she'd felt it the day it happened, but just because Darius had let her down didn't mean he would let the same thing happen to me.

"Darius tried to give the inn to me. I could have come here more regularly and had a job when I was ready to move to Sandrin." I swiped a tear from my face. "She thought he would use it to control me."

Vincent squeezed my shoulders again. "You cleansed it? Do you need to do anything else here?"

I was dead on my feet, and I so badly wanted to lie down. Cleaning up this mess left by my parents' relationship was exhausting. Before my chin fully dipped in a nod, wind swooped me into Vincent's arms, and he carried me down the staircase.

"I can walk," I said half-heartedly. It must have been unconvincing because my head was leaning against his chest. He pulled me closer to him. Collapsing against him shouldn't have felt so good, but cradled in his arms, I felt safe.

"I know you can, but you don't have to," he whispered.

My heart melted, and I nuzzled in farther, taking pleasure from the increasing beats of his heart. The moon's light was still bright. His wind slipped away, unfurling from its place around me as we entered the forested part of the property. When we were at my cottage door, the wind returned, wrapping around me again as it pushed the door open and handed me a moonflower.

I smiled, smelling the flower, until Vincent set me on the couch and turned away. "Vincent." I sat up immediately and tracked his movement. He went to the kitchen instead of the door. I was so afraid he would leave in some misplaced attempt to give me space, leave me alone with my thoughts. I'd need to process them, that was true, but they were not my immediate concern. There was nothing I could do about Mom's choices. And I'd already taken steps to reconcile with Darius. I'd made decisions with the new information presented. I'd continue to do so in the future. All of that would take time.

The one thing I hadn't done was discuss my feelings with Vincent.

He'd taken off his jacket, hanging it by the door. "I'm here," he said, rolling up the sleeves on his shirt and exposing his forearms. "You look like you could use some tea. Did you say you make your own moonflower blend?" Wind swept around the flower stem in my hand, and I smiled down at it.

"There is some in the cupboard." Now that I knew he wasn't leaving, I slumped across the back of the couch, watching him. "They were such a mess—my parents."

Vincent smiled softly as he continued his work, boiling water and searching my cupboards for the promised tea. His silent acknowledgment urged me to continue.

"I knew Mom didn't like Darius, but this seemed excessive. She was so ready to see him as the villain of my story. It was a role already cast for him since he'd turned into the villain in hers."

"He did say he didn't protect her from the fae. I know you've only had glimpses of what that can be like, but imagine how my parents treated you at the restaurant...but even more direct, every day."

I considered this. "I know she was trying to protect me, but I can't help but wonder if she ever would have come clean about his intent. When would she have let me decide if I wanted to have a relationship with him? Now she's gone, and I'll never know."

"As you said, I don't think we can know, but it felt like you fixed whatever she did?"

"I think so." I shrugged. "It's also good to finally know what triggers my magic."

He smiled. "It makes perfect sense that it was moonlight. When I saw you standing in the moat at Parkside Tavern, I thought you were a goddess of some unknown moon court. It was like the moonlight was drawn to you. I should have known then."

My cheeks heated. "You were too confused about whether to be taken with me or angry at me to be responsible for such details."

"You have no idea," he replied. The water boiled, and he poured it into two mugs, adding the moonflower tea. He handed me a mug and sat with his on the other side of the couch. "Then it seems like we're ready to feature the inn," he said. "Which is good because Long Night is in two weeks."

"I don't think Darius's deadline was real," I said. "I think he was trying to motivate me to figure out my magic in his own way."

He laughed. "Yes, well. Doesn't mean we can't still accomplish our original goal."

I scooted closer to him on the couch. "I don't want to use you for the thing everyone else seems to. You're worth more to me than promoting the inn."

He reached for my moon-touched strand of blond hair, twisting it around his finger. "I know. That's why I want to do it for you anyway."

I took a sip of the tea. "What about your end of our bargain?" It seems I'd been granted everything I wanted, but the opposite could be said for Vincent.

"The tip is obviously false. I'll find another story to get into feature work."

I pursed my lips. "Darius did say someone was doing what that tip accused him of, it just wasn't him."

"I noticed that, too. I'll search more and see if there is anything else in the documents my editor gave me." He shrugged, and his dark gaze held mine. "It's not what's most important to me right now."

"I'm sorry," I said.

He smirked. "Sorry that your father wasn't bribing the governor to stop the magic school's development?"

"Well, no." I laughed and placed my hand on his forearm. They were very nice forearms. A muscle flexed beneath my touch. "I'm sorry we didn't find the story you wanted."

"That wasn't precisely our bargain, was it? You needed to help me access Darius, which you did well beyond the requirement."

"So our bargain is complete?" I asked a bit cheekily.

"I'm not sure our bargain was worth the paper it was written on."

"We didn't write it down, Vincent."

"Exactly."

I leaned forward, setting my cup on the low table next to the couch. "I want you to stay." I wanted a lot more, but I figured I'd start with this.

He set his cup down, and I crawled into his lap as he did so. "All I want is to be here for you, Luna. I won't leave unless you ask me to."

My face was inches from his, and I was finding it difficult to concentrate on his words. His wind was already slipping around my wrist and across my arms. "I can sleep here, though." He motioned to the couch. The wind paused the progress across my skin with his words. "I can imagine you've had a trying day."

I bit the inside of my cheek. "I have, but the decisions they made on my behalf are past. I can only choose the future I want." I cleared my throat, suddenly nervous, though I wasn't sure why. "Before I learned any of this, I was sure of the future I wanted with you. I still am."

His brown gaze devoured me before he moved. I saw the moment his resolve snapped. His wind rushed forward, and he kissed me like every second he kept his lips from mine was a disservice to us both. I'd felt the touch of his lips multiple times already. This was different—this was more than mutual attraction and sweet stolen moments. His kiss was chasing, grasping, claiming all in one.

The two of us, reaching for the future we wanted—together.

He pulled me to him, erasing any distance between us. I purred in satisfaction as my chest pressed to his. My hands rested on his shoulders and slid around his neck as I sank into the kiss. I went for his hair first. My nails scraped his scalp as they freely perused the thick locks I loved. I resolved to run my hands through them every day I could.

"Luna," he breathed, pausing as if unable to say more.

"Bedroom. Now," I replied as I regretfully removed my hands from his hair. A squeal of delight slipped from my lips as his wind responded to my command. It lifted us both and swept us toward the bedroom. We didn't even have to untangle.

"I've never lifted two people before," he said curiously as we landed on the bed in a mess of limbs. My lips were on his neck, and his words jumbled together.

"Maybe worry about that later." I ran my hands over every inch of him I could find.

His wind swirled around the hem of my blouse as if asking permission. I raised my arms in response, and it pulled the shirt over my head, tossing it to the floor. Vincent was there as it fell away. His hands slid up the sides of my body, heating every part of me that he touched. He tugged at the band around my chest, loosening it and banishing it to the corner of the room with my top. His hands cupped my breasts. I gasped as he bent forward, his mouth following his hands. When his lips closed around the peak, he hummed in satisfaction at my moan.

My body burned, even as his wind swirled around us, pressing us together. "I need this off," I said, between breathless pants, pulling at his shirt.

He obliged, revealing a lean frame and honed, wiry muscle. His forearms had only been the appetizer. I wanted to lick him from head to toe. He must have seen as much in my gaze. His smile was sinful as he said, "You'll have to wait your turn," and then bit down on my nipple.

I could feel his smile against my skin as I moaned. His tongue followed the bite, lavishing attention as his hands roamed my skin.

We fumbled out of the rest of our clothes, eager to have nothing between us. Finally, we fell back together onto the bed. I straddled him. His hands reached up behind my neck, pulling me down to him as he drank in his fill. "You're perfect."

His kiss was molten, and his tongue slipped into my mouth with familiarity. I could easily imagine we'd been doing this for years instead of only a few stolen kisses.

"I don't deserve you." His hand cupped my cheek, and I turned my head to nip at his finger. "But I won't continue to question why you seem so willing to have me." He chuckled as he flipped us over. His wind lifted me higher than necessary for the motion and shot butterflies through my stomach.

"More than willing." I stared up at him from where I now lay on the bed. "Demanding."

He growled in pure male satisfaction, a sound so at odds with the persona he presented to the city. I loved this wild part of him that felt like it was just for me. I ran my hands up his chest, twisting my fingers in the hair at the back of his neck.

"Your obsession with my hair is intoxicating," he breathed, letting my hands rake through it.

"It's not only your hair I'm obsessed with." I attempted to pull him toward me again, urging him to satisfy the need that had been growing since the day we met.

He smirked, gently resisting my pull. He tilted his head in consideration. "I never expected you to be impatient."

Heat spun inside me, shooting straight to my core. I was beyond impatient. He seemed to realize as his hand dipped lower. Anticipation flared with each caress of his fingers over my stomach, my thigh, and finally, where I needed him most. He expertly stroked my center, circling my clit. His attention was rapt as he worked, like he sought to memorize each sound I made and each movement that brought them forth. A finger slipped inside me, stealing a gasp from my lungs. Another followed, plunging into the heat of my core, curling and building my pleasure.

"Vincent," I rasped. His name on my lips was the only reason I could cling to. My mind spun in all directions, my hands gripping his chest, the sheets, his hair, anything to hold me to this moment. I didn't want to let it go.

"I've got you. Always." His strokes didn't slow, and his words stoked something else inside me. The image of a partner with whom to share my burdens. A friend with whom to share my joys. And a lover with whom to share my heart. My release crashed through me like a wave of power. My eyes closed, and my limbs liquefied with the future his words promised.

I knew he was right. He had me. He wouldn't let me go.

He leaned forward to press another kiss to my lips. I chased him as he pulled back. His laugh was a light on the darkest night, like the moon's light for my soul.

"My turn." I reached for him. His length was hard and ready between us. I pumped him, lining him up with my entrance.

"Luna," he spoke through hitched breaths as I worked him.

"Kiss me."

He granted my request, leaning down into another scorching kiss. As he did, I guided him to where I needed him. A gasp slipped from my lips as our bodies connected—a rightness filling me as I stretched to accommodate him. My head fell back against the pillow.

"Are you alright?" Worry laced his voice.

"I'm fine. Just let me enjoy this for a minute."

Somehow, I could hear the smirk curve his lips through his chuckle, though I refused to lift my head to confirm it. "Take all the time you need." I clenched around him, and his lips were on mine again. My hands reclaimed their place in his hair. "I'm going to start believing you only want me for my hair," he said between kisses.

"It's quite perfect. I'm not sure how you manage it." His wind slid over my clit, stealing my breath as he started to move.

"Wind-assisted perfection," he replied, as his wind assisted in ways that had nothing to do with his hair. It stoked the building heat as he thrust deeper and deeper inside me.

"I could get used to this," I breathed.

"Good." His lips were on mine again, and there was no more space for words as our bodies united in building pleasure. His hand was on my breast, mine in his hair. Our tongues slid against each other at every opportunity. I was at the cliff's edge again, looking over, and this time, I knew Vincent was with me. We may have started this relationship with our own goals and desires, but they'd merged somewhere along the way. A joint desire to stand with each other. To support each other. To partner together through whatever life brought. It was intoxicating to know someone was as focused on my pleasure as I was on theirs. Before I finished the thought, the warmth of his wind applied perfect pressure, sending me barreling over the cliff. He followed, his wind circling us as we fell together.

31

Vincent

The scent of moonflower and juniper lingered in the bedroom the following day. Luna's magic must have rolled off her in waves under the full moon. It would make sense; it had to make itself known somehow. My arm was draped over her hip, her back to my stomach. I pulled her closer, burying my nose in the wild curls of her hair splayed across the pillow. I couldn't believe how lucky I was. She wanted me, maybe as much as I wanted her.

"Vincent." The soft sound of my name on her lips had me brushing her hair aside to grant myself access to her skin. I pressed a kiss to the place where her neck and shoulder met. She scooted farther into me, tilting her head to expose more.

My wind stirred, a warm breeze stealing through the strands of her hair. She was mine. I dragged my lips over her skin. Her taste was a flavor I would savor. A taste I hadn't come close to fully exploring.

She wiggled against me as I paused my exploration to nip and suck the column of her neck. "Don't start what you can't finish."

"Try me," she said, her voice teasing as she wiggled again.

I didn't think, only moved, rolling her to her back as I slid down her still-naked body. My hands caressed curves I'd only begun to map. My gaze raked over every inch of her, staring up at her through hooded lashes as I took in all she offered.

"So beautiful. And all mine." The words were an offering to this woman who'd splashed into my life and for whom I'd fallen deep and fast.

"All yours." Her hands were in my hair again, and though I teased her, I'd never grow tired of the attention. I leaned into her touch even as I planted kisses at the curve of her hip and her stomach and nipped her thigh. Nails scraped my scalp as I journeyed lower. I felt the moment her head fell back against the pillow, her fingers stretching and flexing in my hair—both relaxing and tightening their grip all at once. It was the exact moment my tongue slid across her center.

She shivered beneath me, her body already greedy for the next stroke—one I desperately wanted to provide. One hand held her steady as I tasted her again, a long, slow exploration of every movement of her body. She almost vibrated in anticipation as I paused, letting the suspense build her pleasure.

"You're teasing me," she breathed.

"I'm savoring." My tongue plunged into her heat, unable to show further restraint.

Her answering moan had my wind lifting her body from the bed, angling her right where I wanted her while preventing her movement. I feasted then, relishing her taste along with every noise I wrung from her.

"Vincent," her voice was shaky from the inability to catch her breath. "More."

I smiled smugly while continuing my ministrations. My fingers worked her along with my tongue.

Her hands raked into my hair again, directing me where she wanted me. I followed, cataloging her likes, wanting nothing more than to have her languid and satisfied. Even suspended in the air, she bucked with her rising pleasure. My wind spun tight, holding her firmly as her hips chased my tongue, demanding more, demanding everything I wanted to give.

"Right there," she said, and I needed no further direction. Her body coiled even as my wind held her in place. Her heels reached for something to push against, and her hands searched for sheets to wrap around, everything building to the final stroke of my tongue, the final plunge of my fingers, before I sucked hard on her clit, granting her the friction I knew she sought. Her answering cry was a beautiful melody, one I hoped to recreate time and again. I didn't stop, didn't slow as I worked her through her climax, sucking and licking as she rode her release.

With my wind wrapped around her, I could feel her muscles uncoil, her legs straighten as her body went soft from pleasure. I released her from my hold, setting her back down on the bed.

"That was..." She struggled to push herself to her elbows to look at me. "That was perfect."

I knew my smile was broad enough to show all my teeth. "I'm happy to be of service."

She pushed farther forward, where I still hovered on my knees, and kissed me. My cock twitched at the thought of her tasting herself on my lips. She was reaching for me before I could form another thought. Each stroke of her hand along my shaft sent reason farther from the surface. There was something I had to do—somewhere I had to be. None of it seemed to matter as her hand slid against me.

"I—" Words escaped me. I swallowed, realizing the

meaning of the smile playing at her lips and the shift of her body as she worked to flip me over. "As much as I'd like to continue," I choked out, glancing at the sun streaming through the cottage window, "I need to get to the paper."

She let her hand fall, granting me a semblance of focus. Her smile was sinful, as if she realized her effect on me. I took a deep breath, clearing my lust-addled mind, though a distant part of me knew this was more than that. "I have to turn in the recommendation piece today. It's not ready yet." She didn't look worried, but I didn't want to disappoint her.

"You know..." she started, but I cut her off.

"I know you don't need it before Long Night. I know everything you would say, but please." I leaned forward. "Let me do this for you." I kissed her deeply.

She pulled me down against her, wrapping her arms around my neck. "If you insist," she whispered against my lips. "Come back to me as soon as you can."

"I will." I kissed her again, using all my willpower to pull away. I wanted to do this, though. It meant a great deal to me to help her this way. We would have a future full of mornings like this. I could spare one to do this for her.

I SWIPED my quill back and forth across my face, and my leg moved restlessly in my chair. Usually, the newspaper office was a welcome place of energy and ideas. Today, I could only think about getting back to Luna's cottage.

At least I hadn't wasted the day. I'd gone back through the memory stone and the other documents Patricia had provided when she gave me the assignment. They proved to have no other helpful information. Even when they'd been pointing directly at Darius Pierce, I'd said they were vague. Now that I knew he wasn't against the school, they were all but useless.

On top of everything, I was struggling with the draft to recommend Cliff House Inn. I'd started it the same way I'd done all my other recommendations, with an eye on why the fae would find it an excellent establishment. It hadn't taken more than a few paragraphs to realize I hated it. No matter what Luna said and how ready she was to go to any lengths to save the inn, I hated portraying her this way. I hated trying to fit her unique flare into the box of fae propriety.

It felt wrong.

Crossing out another line, I finally gave up and crumpled the paper. I pulled out a fresh sheet. I would write this the way I should have from the beginning.

This draft came much easier. A few hours later, I was tweaking the final words, ensuring they communicated everything I wanted. This piece was certainly different, but that made me like it all the more.

"Vincent, do you have a minute?" Patricia called from her office door.

I needed to talk to her anyway. Today was the day I owed her my answer on the feature. Darius wasn't guilty, and I had no other leads. Nodding, I strode across the room.

"Have a seat." She closed the door behind us and took her seat behind her desk.

"Do you have the school bribe piece for tomorrow's paper?"

I crossed one leg over the other, taken aback. That wasn't what I'd said I'd deliver today. "I've verified that Darius Pierce is not trying to stop the school's development." I ran my hand through my hair. "Unfortunately, I don't have any new leads."

Her eyes widened. "You couldn't have verified."

"I did. I found the full letter to go with the scraps in the folder."

"There's no way you—" She looked worried now, and I didn't like it. I had been about to tell her about Luna, that I had a source on the inside, and that she'd helped me verify the information, but I knew a look of determination when I saw it. Something in Patricia's features had me on edge. She was surprised I had anything. Had she expected me to fail so completely?

Probably. But why? Why would she give me something she didn't want me to complete?

"Do you have the letter?" she tried again.

"I don't have it here with me, but I can get it today if required." I used my unshakeable fae confidence voice. I had lost track of the documents when we left Pierce House, but I was pretty sure Luna had them. I'd had other things on my mind when we returned to Luna's cottage, but to clear Darius's name, I'd brave returning to Pierce House if we'd left them there. I held Patricia's stare. She was acting incredibly suspicious about this.

She waved her hand at my comment. "Don't bother. We're printing the tip anyway. Have it written up today."

I shook my head slowly, wondering if I'd misheard. "Excuse me?"

"You heard me." She glared at a document on her desk like it did her personal harm. "We're printing the tip. Write it up. You wanted a feature piece."

"Not one I know to be untrue."

"Someone is paying to hold off the school development," she said.

Darius had said as much as well. "Even if someone is, naming the wrong person will be incredibly detrimental."

Her lips pressed into a thin line. "He's Norden, what do you care?"

"Because I did what you asked, I looked into him, and I know what you're saying to be untrue. Why would we still publish it?"

"Do you have another name?" she asked.

"No, but—"

"Then we print Darius Pierce."

"That will ruin his reputation with the new Norden Point."

She glanced up and met my gaze. Hers was hard.

"You already know that." I swallowed. "It's your goal? Why?"

"That's above your pay grade. All I need is for you to write the feature."

"I won't," I replied. "Not when I know it to be a lie."

"You'll write it, or you'll find other employment." She leaned back in her chair and folded her arms over her chest.

"Patricia." I leaned forward. She may not have always given me what I wanted, but she'd always been reasonable. This seemed entirely out of character. "What is going on?"

She ignored me and continued. "If you can't write this, don't bother submitting your next recommendation piece, either."

I stood, not believing what I was hearing. "'Benefits of Magic' is a staple. You can't go without it."

Her smile didn't meet her eyes as she replied. "It is, but I don't need you to write it."

I clenched my teeth. "Alright, then." My wind rustled inside me. It wanted to burst free and wreak havoc with the papers on this desk. At least this kind of reaction was one I could still control.

I wouldn't show Patricia my emotions. It was clear that wouldn't make a difference. I wouldn't tell her that this job was the one thing that kept me from my parents' leash. Writing "Benefits of Magic" funded my apartment and granted me distance from my parents' destructive opinions.

None of that would matter to Patricia. Something was forcing her hand.

I shook my head in frustration. Writing a piece about anyone—especially Luna's father—that I knew to be false was unacceptable, as was returning to Andiveron House. I'd figure something out.

"This is simply the way of things," she said, dismissing me.

The hair on the back of my neck prickled at the familiarity of the phrase. "Both drafts on my desk by the end of the day." She didn't glance up at me as she waved me away. Her focus returned to the notes before her.

I grabbed my things and left the office. Unfortunately, I knew what I had to do next.

32

Luna

We may have woken up in all the haze of a burgeoning relationship, but too quickly after Vincent left, I, too, had to return to my duties. I might have cleansed this room yesterday with my water magic, but it still needed a proper cleaning with a dust rag, mop, and bucket. I was scrubbing the floor when I heard the call from downstairs.

"Hello?"

I didn't recognize the voice. Standing, I wiped my hands on my skirt and descended the stairs. Two women stood by the check-in desk. Their clothes were slightly rumpled, and each had a large bag at their side. Both gave every appearance they had been traveling for days. My heart beat faster, though I couldn't quite put the why of it into a coherent thought.

"Can I help you?" I asked.

"I'm Nadia. This is Rachelle. We'd like to rent a room through Long Night if you have vacancy." They had the good grace not to glance around the empty inn.

Guests. They were *guests*.

"You want to stay here?" I asked, unable to stop the words falling from my lips. Vincent's article wouldn't come out for another few days. Besides unlocking the room, I'd done nothing differently.

Part of me hadn't wanted to believe the magic Mom used had caused all the inn's problems.

Nadia's brow furrowed, and she glanced at Rachelle as if double-checking that this was, in fact, what they wanted to do.

"Yes, we do," Rachelle said hesitantly.

Immediately, I realized I was not only driving away my first customers but also scaring them. I snapped into action. "Wonderful." I clapped my hands together and moved behind the desk. "You'll get our best room." I pulled out a check-in form and gave them the price before handing them a key. "I'm Luna, the manager. I'll be around if you need anything, and I live out in the cottage if you require assistance and can't find me."

They nodded, and I directed them to the room. I slumped into the chair behind the desk when they walked away. I pushed my hair back from my face in disbelief. "I have customers," I whispered to myself. The bright smile crossing my face was unstoppable.

"Luna?" a more familiar voice called. Darius was at the inn's entrance. I stood, making myself visible behind the desk, and he strode purposefully toward me. "I'm sorry to come. I know you said you needed time, but...I felt your magic last night, so I wanted to check on you." His blue-gray eyes searched mine with concern.

"You can do that?" I asked.

A blush touched his cheeks. "I think it's because we're family, but, yes, I've felt your magic multiple times on this property."

"The night the current swept me away?" I asked before I could think better of it.

He ran his hand through his hair and swallowed thickly. "Yes."

"Well, I'm fine," I said. He took a step back, and I realized that sounded a bit dismissive, which hadn't been my intention. Even these few words between us had opened up so much about my magic, my fae self, that had been lost to me the last twenty-five years.

"Let's have some tea," I said, gesturing to the library.

He nodded and followed me to the kitchen. I had been baking fresh bread while I cleaned.

"Did I see customers?" he asked as I boiled water.

I let the excitement slip into my voice as I replied. "Yes! My first ones."

"I knew you could figure it out, Luna." His smile was warm. I wondered if he knew what Mom had done. According to the memory, he'd left after their argument. Maybe he had no idea if the room was sealed the next day when we departed. I wasn't sure I wanted to be the one to tell him. Though, I guess he deserved to know.

"That smells great." He gestured to the oven.

"Thanks. I was planning to do breakfast for guests. Fresh bread and some muffins. You can help me test this batch for tomorrow."

He nodded, clearly wanting to say more, but maybe he wasn't sure how. "I'm sorry last night ended up being so eventful." He finished pouring the tea while I pulled the baked goods from the oven. "Whenever you're ready, we'd love to have you back for a quiet meal."

He carried the mugs as I pulled two muffins from the tray and gestured for him to lead us into the library. After setting the snacks aside on a table to cool, we took seats in the plush gold chairs, and when he offered me my mug, I held it in my hand for the comfort of its warmth. I searched his features as he performed a similar routine.

"Do you know what was wrong with the inn?" I asked. If I'd learned anything from my beginning with Vincent, it was that the truth helped, even when it hurt. My parents had both left so much out in everything I knew so far. I didn't want that to continue.

He set his mug aside and ran his hand through his hair. A nervous habit, I guessed. I assumed it meant he knew what I was asking and wasn't sure how to respond. "I suspect, Luna." He cleared his throat. "It's different than knowing, and I won't accuse someone so important to you without proof, which I know I'll never have."

I swallowed. That was honest, and I could respect the line he'd drawn. "I witnessed a memory when I opened the door with my magic last night. It was Mom's." I paused. "That same night, when you found me in the water. I was asleep in the room after, but you two argued. She had blood magic prepared already to use after you left. I don't know how she knew you'd offer to give me the inn, but she thought you couldn't give it to me if it didn't have customers."

There was no hint of surprise on his face. "I'd told her in a letter when we agreed on the date for your annual trip that I had a big surprise for you. Something I wanted to discuss giving you. She would have had plenty of time to prepare."

"Well, I cleansed it." I gestured toward the staircase. "And I have customers to prove it worked."

"It was moonlight, then?" he asked.

I blinked rapidly at his question, trying to determine if I heard him correctly.

He continued, "I always suspected, especially since that night when I found you in the sea. It was like the moon's glow fell directly on the safe space you'd created for yourself."

"Yes, and in the spirit of transparency, I think it's important to tell you I always thought it was you who saved me that day and then...disappeared as if saving me was a burden." I didn't know why it was so important to me to tell him. It felt like the more I could share about the picture of him I'd built in my mind, the more he'd understand as that picture changed. I didn't want to hurt him, but I thought it might help us wherever we went from here.

He coughed into his fist, and his eyes rimmed with water when he looked at me again. "I'm sorry, Luna. I'm so sorry for every time my actions made you feel unimportant or uncared for. You were never far from my thoughts." He swallowed. "I did what I thought was right, but I can see how bad it looked."

"There is nothing to be done about the past," I said, and I meant it. "I do hope we can move forward with more open communication."

"Of course. I would like that." He glanced out the window at the sea, watching the waves crash against the cliff side. "I guess, then, in the spirit of sharing, we should talk." He took a sip of the tea and met my gaze. "Do you have anything else you want to tell me about what you and Vincent were looking into at the house?"

I pursed my lips; Vincent had told him everything about the tip and the stairwell. Thinking of him brought a flush as memories from last night cascaded in. I coughed, shaking my head to clear it. "I don't think I have anything else to add."

His brow furrowed. "Luna." He set his mug down again and rested his hands on his knees. I knew whatever he would say, I really wouldn't like it. "The story is running." He held my gaze.

"The story is running," I repeated, unsure I understood. "That you are bribing the governor?"

His lips pressed into a thin line, and he nodded.

"It can't. Vincent said—" The look of pity in his gaze made sense to me now. He thought Vincent had gone ahead with the story anyway. He had accused Vincent of some terrible things last night. It didn't entirely surprise me that he would think this.

"Why do you dislike him so much?" I asked.

He shook his head in confusion. "I'm sorry, Luna. That family is bad news. Everything you were worried about me being—well, they are that." He tapped his fingers on the end table. "They've always appreciated the elevation of fae in society. They have no love for the changes at Compass Lake. And I think they'll do anything necessary to ensure things stay as they are."

"You think his parents are the ones bribing the governor?" I asked, realizing what he was saying. Still, he looked at me with concern. "You think Vincent is in on it with them?" My voice raised at the end.

"Luna, I know you care for him, but it doesn't make sense that he would act without them. He's an Andiveron."

I wondered how Darius could be so progressive in some areas and so...outdated in others. Of course, he didn't know what I did about Vincent's split from his family. It must be the best-kept secret in Sandrin.

"Parents and children can have differing views," I pointed out.

He pursed his lips. "Improbable."

"You don't know him."

"You're right. I don't, but I've known *them* for a long time. They wouldn't let their chosen heir out of their grasp."

I laughed, but Vincent's secret wasn't mine to share.

He pressed, unwilling to let me hold onto my view of Vincent Andiveron. "The paper is running the article. Someone came by this morning to ask if I had a comment. Vincent's parents don't work at the paper, Luna."

I tightened my grip around the mug. He did have me there, but I was sure there was a reasonable explanation, and I said as much.

"Luna—"

"Father," I said, and he stopped whatever he was about to

say, "we will work on our relationship no matter what you say here, but I must tell you. Just because you failed to protect Mom from the fae and it...imploded so badly across our lives doesn't mean that Vincent is the same. I can't expect you to understand how I know this about Vincent, but I do. And I need you to respect my decision. I will talk to him to see what can be done about the article, but I assure you he isn't the one running it."

Darius scratched his temple. "The article doesn't matter, Luna. I've been in communication with the Norden Point. She doesn't believe I'm working against her in such a fashion. I don't care about my reputation. All I care about is protecting you. I think Vincent Andiveron is bad news, but as you say, you're an adult, and I'll trust your judgment."

"Wonderful," I said with more confidence than I felt. "Now, I need to finish cleaning the last room and prepare for more customers." I stood, and Darius stood with me. "Thank you for coming by. I'd love to come for a meal again soon."

"Anytime," he said and smiled as he left the library.

I watched him go, but another familiar face walked in before I could hurry up the stairs.

"Eloise, you just missed Darius," I said. The names felt strange on my tongue. Maybe *Father* and *Grandmother* would work better eventually.

She gave me a wicked grin. "I waited for him to leave. I couldn't stop him from warning you about Vincent, but I did realize that as soon as he told you, you'd need to run off and see if everything was alright with the boy."

"You don't think I'm foolish for not assuming the worst?" I asked, tilting my head.

"Your father was blindsided by everything last night... Today"—she gestured around the inn—"he didn't really look at Vincent in the study yesterday. I admit I had doubts when I sat down, but before you left, it was clear that boy would do anything for you."

My heart warmed at her words. "Thank you."

"You can thank me by finishing whatever you were about to do and going after him. I assume you have guests checking in now that you have unleashed your magic on the place? I'll mind the inn while you're gone."

Tears pricked in my eyes, and I swallowed.

"No time for tears, dear." She shooed me along up the stairs.

I paused halfway up and turned. "What should I call you?"

"Eloise is fine." She swallowed, showing some emotion deep in the blue eyes that matched my own. "Maybe Gram, when you're comfortable."

I swallowed down a swell of emotion and took off up the stairs. I needed to clean up my mess in the recently opened room before I could chase after Vincent—especially if more guests might be arriving. I, like my gram, didn't believe for a second he was publishing that article, but I was sure something had gone terribly wrong to lead to this.

33

Vincent

Everything made sense in the worst possible way. Darius's distrust for me and my father's words that night at the restaurant that I'd been far too distracted to focus on. He'd said they'd stopped by the paper to talk to me about my feature piece—a piece they shouldn't have known about. They hadn't stopped by the paper before...ever. I couldn't believe it had taken so long for everything to come together in my mind. I'd been trying so hard to get Luna away from them that night that nothing else had sunk in. Patricia's phrase was the last clue: *this is simply the way of things.* My father said that phrase more often than talking about the benefits of magic. It had been a staple my entire childhood in Andiveron House.

"Why don't we see the fae from other courts?"

"That is simply the way of things."

Or my personal favorite. "Why don't we follow the human laws?"

"That is simply the way of things."

I was at Andiveron House before I realized where my feet were taking me. The picture hadn't fully formed yet, but I knew they were involved, and I'd get to the bottom of it.

I knocked. This was no longer my home, though I could count those aware of the fact on my fingers. It struck me how easily I'd given Luna that information. I'd wanted her to see me as separate from my parents. To know that, though we shared a family name, we shared no other beliefs.

Jeffrey, the butler, answered. "Vincent, I didn't know you had an appointment today." He smiled warmly.

"I don't."

His smile turned to a frown. Even though Jeffrey had always liked me, he was never one to allow the disruption of *the process*. "I'm not sure your parents have time today."

"They'll see me," I said.

He sighed and opened the door, granting me entry to the home that would presumably be mine someday—unless my parents finally disinherited me, favoring Skye. Eventually, I hoped they would do it, but whatever their part in the paper fiasco, I saw it for what it was: interference in my independent life. It must have angered them so much that I got away and could have made something of myself without Andiveron finances.

I wondered how true that was.

If my suspicions were correct, my parents pulled Patricia's strings. I could only imagine this being possible if they bought their way in, financing the paper or bribing Patricia directly. I wanted to believe they hadn't always controlled the paper. They would have never approved my hire if they had. How long had they been meddling, though?

My father was in his study when I stormed in, laid my hands on the wooden desk, and leaned toward him with as much authority as I could muster. "What have you done?"

He glanced up at me, unimpressed by my display. "Vincent, do sit down, you're being rude."

"Father, I want to know what you have done to force the paper to publish the story on Darius Pierce."

The corner of his lip curled into a smug smile, though he quickly tried to flatten it. "I don't know what you're talking about."

"Don't play coy, now. You were eager to ask me about the assignment a few weeks ago. Did you provide the tip?"

"Your sister said you wanted to write features. We're helping." He glanced at me before flipping through the papers on his desk.

I shook my head. "You are not helping. You are playing your own game and trying to use me to do it. It stops now."

His smirk was back in full force, not even attempting to hide his assurance. "And what are you going to do? Quit? You'd have to come home." He spread his hands. "We both know how... distasteful that would be to you."

"Is that what this is about?" I asked.

"This isn't about you, Vincent," he said. "It's merely a convenient way to stop Darius from causing further trouble."

My brow furrowed. My parents didn't like Darius. They didn't like any fae from other courts. They barely liked fae from their own court. But how was Darius in their way? "You're the one trying to block the school from being built?" I said, finally figuring it out.

"We're not blocking anything. We're reminding the governor that there is value in exclusivity."

His words made my skin crawl. Hadn't I said something similar to Luna when we first started talking about recommending the inn? I pushed my shoulders back. I was nothing like him. I'd chosen differently. I would continue to choose differently. "I'm not writing the piece."

"It doesn't matter." He wiped his hand through the air in

dismissal. "The piece will be published whether you write it or not. If you decide not to, we get the added bonus of you crawling back to Andiveron House."

My jaw clenched. I couldn't let him get away with this.

"It was inconvenient that you decided on a dalliance with the Pierce girl. A half-fae, Vincent? You should know better."

I should have known they had an agenda when they'd run into us at the restaurant. My parents were calculated in everything they did. Their words had been targeted to wound Luna; they'd known exactly who she was but had not acknowledged it.

"I don't ever want to hear you speak about Luna that way again," I said coldly. My wind rushed around the room, rattling the obnoxious trinkets on the bookshelves. "She has more character and more integrity than you ever will."

Father continued to look unimpressed. "She's not fae." He held down a few rustling papers as my wind whipped past him. "You really should be better able to control yourself."

"I won't spend any more time trying to convince you to change," I said, fuming. "I'll find a way out of this. I won't come back into this house while you still live in it. And I won't let you do this to Darius."

"We'll see," he said, not even bothering to look up at me this time. I turned and exited the room the same way I'd entered, letting my wind slam the door behind me. I frowned when I realized I wasn't heading out of the house, though. My wind swirled down the hall toward the front door, and I went in the opposite direction. The front door opened and closed with the power of my element. Before I considered what I was doing, the hall closet opened, and I slid inside.

I DON'T KNOW what came over me. One minute, I was heading toward the door, desperate to put this house and my parents behind me. The next minute, I was hiding in a closet per my wind's impulsive plan.

Footsteps echoed down the hall. "Did he leave?" Father asked.

"He must have. I heard the door close," Jeffrey replied.

"Headstrong boy," Father mumbled and then sighed. "It's not like he can do anything about it now." His footsteps echoed down the hall in the opposite direction.

I had to move quickly. Father was probably right. The article was going to get printed whether I participated or not, but there was a hopeful part of me that wanted to change the text of the article. Another part of me wanted to ensure my recommendation of Cliff House Inn made it into this issue. I knew Patricia would pull it if she didn't get the desired feature. A reckless hope had overtaken me—a hope that I could make this right. I had to believe it was Luna's voice in my head telling me not to leave a stone unturned when it came to something I wanted.

And I wanted to clear Darius's name, not only for Luna but for myself.

My father was right. I did love that job at the paper. Even if I only continued to write recommendations. I felt good about the new angle on how to feature Luna's inn, and it made me realize there was so much I could do, so much I could explore while still writing the recommendation column. I was a little ashamed it had taken me so long to realize, and even then, it had only been because of Luna's words.

But to keep writing, I had to have content for this article. I could see the headline: Old Fae Family Works Against Magic School. With the right proof, it didn't have to be Darius's name in the text.

I sent my wind through the keyhole of the door. It unfurled

and flew through the hall, searching for bodies as I had searched for whatever was in Luna's locked room.

The hallway was empty. Now was my chance. I slid from the closet and let myself back into Father's study. Quick steps led me across the room, behind the desk. I wasted no time finding the account books. Father was too meticulous not to keep a record of his payments. He was accurate to a fault. This was even easier than searching Darius's study because I knew what to look for. I opened the account book and skimmed the last few weeks of entries. Finding those I was looking for neatly labeled, I tore the page from Father's records and took it with me. I returned the book to its drawer, hoping Father wouldn't notice the missing page tonight. It wouldn't matter. I was going to the newspaper office now to draft this. He wouldn't have time to stop me. The issue was off to the printer tonight.

My wind checked the pathway to the exit. I was clear. Quiet feet in my favorite boots led me across the office. I opened the door to the hallway and was halfway through when I ran directly into Skye.

"Vincent, what are you doing here?" I held her arms to steady us both.

"Keep your voice down," I hissed.

She shook her head. "Father is in an uproar. He's yelling at someone now. He won't hear us."

"He's out of control. Trying to ruin Luna's father and my job at the paper."

Her face fell. "I'm so sorry, Vincent. What are you going to do?"

I held up my paper. "I'm going to fix it."

She ushered me down the hall toward the front door. "You need to get out of here."

"So do you," I said. My parents had never given Skye a hard time like they had me, but living here couldn't be good for her. I resolved to work harder to get her out of this house.

"I'm working on it, Vincent," she said. "Don't worry about me. Take care of this—of Luna." She winked. "I liked her."

My smile grew as something loosened in my chest. We were almost to the door when my wind alerted me to someone else in the hallway. Jeffrey cleared his throat behind us. "Vincent, Skye."

I glanced over my shoulder. "Jeffrey."

Skye held back a giggle. Jeffrey had always caught us getting into mischief. He had always been much more lenient on us than our parents, but this was different. He looked down at the paper in my hands. Though it was folded in half, it was still evident to anyone with knowledge of the household what it was. Father used red and black ink on the paper to track his ledgers.

"Do you know what you're doing?" Jeffrey asked, holding my gaze.

I dipped my chin. "I haven't been surer since the day I left this house."

"Very good, sir." He turned his back on us, freeing me to leave Andiveron House with my pilfered evidence.

Skye shoved me out. As the door slowly closed behind me, I let out a breath. I laughed, not believing my luck, not believing I'd gotten out of there with the document. I had no time to celebrate. The sun was setting, and I had to make it across town quickly. Tucking the paper in my jacket, I took off at a run.

34

Luna

My heart raced as I climbed the steps to the third floor of the newspaper office. I'd never had cause to go before. A receptionist pointed me toward Vincent's desk. It was empty. I looked around helplessly, unsure what to do. I couldn't believe he'd decided to publish a story he knew to be false. No matter what my father thought, I knew that wasn't him.

I didn't hold these beliefs simply because I was besotted, even though it was becoming increasingly apparent that I was. I shivered inadvertently as the memories from last night and this morning flooded my mind. I pulled my bright pink sweater tighter around my shoulders, fighting off the chill. I'd left in such a rush I hadn't changed into my fae-approved wardrobe. This time, I didn't care. Whatever was going on with Vincent was more important than the recommendation piece.

Something was wrong, and I needed to find him—needed to make sure he was alright.

"You look distressed, dear. Anything I can help with?" a familiar voice asked.

"Daisy!" I said, turning to see Earl's wife. "I'm so glad to see you. I'm looking for Vincent. Do you know where he is?"

She frowned and looked around sharply before stepping closer to me and whispering, "He had a meeting with the boss earlier today. He did not look happy when he left. Stormed out of here like he was going to his own funeral."

I worried my bottom lip. Where would he have— And just like that, I knew where he'd gone. "Andiveron House," I said quietly.

"Isn't that where he lives? Your face looks like his did. How can his home be that bad?"

That place wasn't his home. It hadn't been for years. Maybe it had never been, even if no one knew that but me.

"Thanks, Daisy, I appreciate the information," I said without answering her question, and left the way I'd come.

When I got outside, I stood on the sidewalk, watching people pass around me. Vincent would hate that I was standing frozen directly in everyone's way, but I couldn't be bothered to move. Indecision held me in place. I couldn't exactly interrupt whatever he was doing at his parents' house.

Part of me knew he was confronting them about the story. It was the only thing that made sense. My father said he didn't know Vincent but knew his parents and how he was raised. Darius believed, at a minimum, Vincent's parents were responsible for the story. Maybe even responsible for the bribes that he was attempting to counter.

Vincent, too, must have realized.

I dipped my chin as if answering my own internal question. He could handle this. It was his work and his promotion on the line.

What if he didn't get the promotion because he wouldn't print the article about my family? My stomach sank. They wouldn't force him to write a piece he could prove false, would they?

They would if his parents were bribing the paper like they might be bribing the governor. I sighed even as something tightened in my chest. This wasn't my fight; it was Vincent's. I'd be there the moment he asked for help. No matter Darius's suspicions, I trusted Vincent. He could handle it until he said otherwise.

Someone bumped my shoulder in the busy street. It was my fault for standing in the middle of foot traffic. The tap set my sights on Central Circle Park and a familiar warm glow therein. With that, I knew what I had to do. If Vincent was facing his parents, if he was standing up for what he believed in, then so could I.

I'd told Vincent this morning that I didn't need him to write the piece. That was true, but he'd been so determined to do it. I wanted to let him. Truth be told, with what I'd learned about Mom's actions and how much she'd kept a part of me hidden, I was second-guessing our plan to portray myself as fae. Initially, I hadn't minded that we were leading readers to that conclusion. My fae heritage was a part of me, and I accepted it as much as I accepted my humanity.

But that wasn't the whole truth.

Mom's actions had shown me that ignoring a part of myself was dangerous. And as much as the article was about saving the inn, it would also only tell half the truth. Yes, I was fae. I was old fae, even, but I was also human.

I didn't want people to like me or stay at the inn because they thought I was fae. I wanted the inn to be a place where everyone was welcome, a place where our individuality was celebrated, each of us essential in making up the whole of the community. If I wanted to build this business based on who I was and what I believed, I had to start with my roots. There was one place in Sandrin where I had been accepted since I'd shown up in town with no family, no money, and no idea what I would do.

The familiar bridge leading to Parkview Tavern was in my sights, and I was finally brave enough to do something about it.

~

A CRISP BREEZE followed me through the front door. I glanced over my shoulder, half hoping that Vincent was behind me and that his wind was already wrapping me in its familiar embrace. There was no sign of him, though. This was only the winter wind blowing. It reminded me that, while it was chilly and sometimes lonely in the city of Sandrin, I was with friends as soon as I stepped into Parkview Tavern and its warmth.

"Hey, Luna," Evelyn said as she dashed by with a drink tray in hand. "Seraphina is behind the bar."

I spied my friend in her usual place, mixing drinks. There were dozens of people between us. The tavern was packed, even more so than the last few times I'd been here. I couldn't believe more and more people continued to pour into Sandrin. We were only two weeks from Long Night. I was glad I'd left Eloise at the front desk.

As much as I didn't want to admit it, the proof of Mom's actions was evident in the guests' arrival this morning. Now that the blood magic was cleansed, I hoped more guests would naturally find their way to Cliff House, but that wouldn't be my only strategy.

As I pushed through the crowd, Seraphina caught my eye and smiled. "I could use some help if you've got a minute."

I nodded and slipped behind the counter like I belonged nowhere else. One of the hardest parts of accepting Cliff House Inn as my own was realizing I couldn't work here as often. If my wildest dreams came true and the inn became truly successful, I probably couldn't work here at all.

Seraphina bumped my hip as I tied an apron around my waist. "You'll always have this place, even if you don't work here."

"How did you—"

"Your face always says more than you do—which is impressive because you talk a lot." She smirked, and I snapped the dish towel in her direction. "I need two Solstice Sips. You can handle that, right?" she teased as we fell into a familiar rhythm.

I reached for the honey spirit bottle, one I could say had started this whole mess considering the drink's success was part of what had brought me to Vincent. Worry for him churned in my chest, but I knew I was doing what he would want. He'd find me when he was ready.

"What's up?" Seraphina asked as we both worked.

"I unlocked the room. Mom enacted blood magic to keep me from Darius." I tilted my head as Seraphina's mouth hung open in astonishment. "Oh, and I got my first customers today." I poured the ingredients into a shaker. "And I slept with Vincent." A smile curled my lips.

She stared at me. I put a finger under her chin and lifted her mouth to close it. She laughed. "We will have to chat about..." She waved her hands vaguely. "All of that at another time. At least you're in good spirits, and, of course, congratulations on the customers, Luna."

Evelyn approached at the last sentence. "Customers? We knew you could do it! Did you unlock the door? I need two more Sips while you're at it."

I nodded and increased the recipe I was already mixing.

"What triggered your magic?" she asked, though her cheeks flushed immediately at the question. "Sorry, maybe that's personal."

My hand cut through the air in a dismissive wave. "Not for you. You were the first to realize there was even magic at play. It's moonlight."

"Of course it is," Seraphina said. "We should have known."

"Maybe I should have, too," I said with a shrug. "But I figured it out. And learned a lot." My face grew somber as I shook the mix and poured it into four glasses. I glanced at Evelyn; she deserved to hear this, too. "My mom was the one who put it there. She wanted to keep me from my fae heritage and from the inn that Darius wanted to gift me."

Even though she'd already heard this, Seraphina's knuckles whitened as she gripped the shaker.

"I'm so sorry, Luna," Evelyn said, tucking a strand of her dark hair behind her ear. If anyone knew what it was to have family not approve of a part of her, it was Evelyn.

"There's nothing I can do about it now," I said, oddly at peace. "As much as I'd love to ask her about it, I can't. I'll never know if she hated my fae heritage, and me by extension, or if she was so lost she truly thought she was protecting me. I do know Darius didn't want to stay away. This whole thing got me thinking about how I'm as much fae as human, and I am oddly comfortable with that."

Seraphina nodded, and Evelyn seemed hesitant but said, "We're glad you figured it out."

"Thank you both for all your help." I took a deep breath. "If it's not too much trouble, I'd like to ask for a little more."

The sound of ice and liquid shaking stopped, and Seraphina turned me to face her. "You can always ask us for help. You know that. What do you need?" Her gaze held mine with a seriousness she hadn't expressed since she'd first hired me and told me not to spill on guests.

"I need your help filling the inn."

"Isn't Fae Charming helping with that?" Seraphina asked playfully. "Where is he, by the way?"

I bit the inside of my cheek. "He is helping, but we had decided on a plan that worked for all his past recommendations, and recently, I've been wondering if that will work for me. Or if that's the way I want to do things."

"What do you mean?" Evelyn asked.

"All his successful recommendations have been places that were fae establishments. They never said as much but presented the fae owners as purveyors of exclusive goods and services. Inviting the reader to seek out these uniquely qualified items."

"And you don't want to be that?" Evelyn asked.

"Well, I didn't have a problem with it before, but when I realized how much my mom had an issue with my fae heritage and how much she thought Darius would have an issue with my human side, I realized I needed to be true to who I am." My voice raised slightly as I gained confidence in my words. "I need to be both. I don't want to be seen as only fae or only human. I'm both and want to be accepted for that—and I'm sure there are those who would welcome me in the community, like this place has."

Seraphina smiled, and I swear she wiped a tear from the corner of her eye with her dish towel.

"So, what do we do?" Evelyn asked, but her mouth was already tilting into a smile.

It wasn't until then that I noticed how quiet the tavern had grown. Seraphina and I still had our backs to the bar. I turned slowly, to find wide-eyed patrons staring, their drinks raised half-way to their lips. More people might have heard my impassioned speech than anticipated.

"Tell us where to go to support a place like that," a voice called from the crowd.

My throat clenched, and I wasn't sure I could get out the words. I looked helplessly between Evelyn and Seraphina.

"Cliff House Inn," Seraphina said. "They have vacancies, especially if you're looking to stay through to Long Night. And it's the best view in the city of the sky for solstice."

The crowd cheered and clinked their glasses. More than one group started talking excitedly about the need for a change of accommodations. It seemed some had also arrived today and required somewhere to stay. My heart swelled and tears pricked my eyes. They wanted a place like I described—a place like my inn, where all were welcome.

I mixed a few more drinks with Seraphina behind the bar before she drew beside me, bumping my hip in her familiar greeting. "You should get out of here," she said. "Another group just left, heading to Cliff House. You should be there. Get some bread ready so you have your post-hike snacks for them in the morning." She winked.

"Thank you, Seraphina," I said, wrapping her in the tightest hug I could, not having the right words to express my gratitude.

"This was all you, Luna. The community here supports you, and, of course, so do we. Now go."

35

Vincent

A dull roar emanated from Cliff House Inn that was both unexpected and simultaneously utterly welcome. Sleep-deprived and a bit frazzled, I wondered if it was imagined. I ran a hand through my unkempt hair. This wasn't windswept perfection—I was a mess. Nothing could stop me from finding Luna, though. I was already much later than I'd promised.

I pulled open the door and stepped inside, and the sight brought an instant grin to my face. There were customers... everywhere. A couple chatted at the desk, each with a mug of tea in hand. It was mid-morning, and the smell of fresh-baked bread permeated the entire first floor as I searched for Luna.

Celebrating her accomplishments would be second on my list once I found her. First, groveling. I hadn't returned last night, and I couldn't imagine what she thought of that. All I needed was a chance to explain.

Two women sat in the high-back chairs in the library where

my and Luna's bargain had begun. I couldn't regret our beginnings when it was what had brought us together. I hoped the women chatting animatedly while sipping tea appreciated the history of the seats in which they sat. Another woman curled in the corner, happily reading, glancing up every few pages to look out the window, watching the waves crash.

Luna had done it. Not that I'd doubted her, but it was amazing to see. She had to be so excited. Immediately, my throat constricted. I wished I'd been here with her last night as the inn had filled.

She would understand. I hoped.

Turning the corner, I headed toward the kitchen. She had to be in there. My wind rushed forward to confirm that someone was, in fact, in the kitchen. I found myself uninterested in stopping it, uninterested in tamping it down. All my wind and I wanted was to be wrapped up in Luna, especially after the night we'd had.

I hadn't yet entered the small kitchen when I knew my wind had found her.

"Vincent," she whispered as the wind tangled in her hair.

My name on her lips was music to my ears. My shoulders fell in relief, releasing tension I hadn't known I carried. If she said my name like that, I think we'd be alright. I entered with hesitant steps. My mind and body were still at odds about her reaction. She was luxuriating in my wind's attention. I almost felt bad for it when she noticed I was there as well. She turned, throwing herself into my arms before I could speak.

"I was so worried," she said. Her gaze held mine, and every fear I'd had walking over here flew from my mind. She was worried about what I'd faced, not what I had done. Her unyielding faith in me was right there in her bright blue eyes. I wasn't sure what I'd done to deserve it, but I never wanted to let her down. Before I could explain, she raised on tiptoes and pressed her lips to mine.

"I'm sorry I went missing," I said when she broke the kiss. "I had a rather urgent deadline to meet and didn't have time to get you a message."

"Believe it or not, I figured that out," she said, placing a hand on her hip.

I tilted my head. "Ah, they must have warned Darius about the article?"

She nodded.

"Giving him another reason to tell you I'm not good enough for you?" I asked with a smile.

She gave me an appraising look as if she was indeed confirming I was joking. I let her see the delight on my face—the pure joy at being back here with her.

"What happened?" she asked.

"Well, I'm sure he had some of it right." I took off my jacket and rolled up my shirt sleeves, readying to help her with the baked goods she was preparing. I took a moment to appreciate her long perusal of my forearms as I did so. The smile on my face when her gaze finally met mine must have said it all.

She swatted me with her dishtowel. "Explain yourself."

"Only if you're done making eyes at my forearms." My ego was on full display. "Maybe it would be better if I kneaded the new batch of dough and you watched?"

Her cheeks pinked, but she bit her lip as if she was considering it. I chuckled as I took over the work at her instruction and proceeded to explain myself. I told her how they were going to print the article anyway. How there was nothing I could do to stop it. "I finally realized why your father mistrusted me so much."

"Vincent," she started.

I waved her off. "No, it's fine. He had every right to. My parents are the ones he's been fighting on the school development. It's my parents bribing the governor to stop the development, not yours." It was almost funny. Almost.

"What did you do?" she asked. It was the perfect response. My wind thrummed in my chest as I realized that no matter what her father said or others assumed, she knew I was capable of standing on my own. She'd expected I would confront my parents when I realized the truth.

I loved this about her.

The thought stopped me in my tracks. Everything about Luna made me strive to be the best version of myself. It was a privilege that she looked at me the way she did—not just her lustful gaze at my forearms but her certainty in my character. I smiled, my realization brimming inside. This wasn't the moment, but I wanted to tell her soon how she made me feel. Now, I needed to tell her everything about last night; about the feature piece, about her recommendation. I hoped she would be alright with my decision. I'd figure that out in a moment, but I knew she'd appreciate this next part of the story.

"Well, I hid in the closet after talking to my father," I started. Her lip tilted, and she worked to tamp it back down, clearly unsure where I was going with this. "It's alright," I said. "My wind shoved me into a closet before I could leave. While there, I realized the only way I could win was to change the story. Something was going to press that night, and I needed to find a way to ensure it was the right story, not the fabricated one."

She tilted her head. "You found proof that your parents were paying the governor?"

I nodded. "If there is one thing I can count on my father for, it's meticulous accounting records. I waited until he left his office, and I ran in, grabbed the pages I needed with proof, then took off to the newspaper office."

Her hand now covered her mouth like she wasn't sure if she was supposed to laugh. I had to admit, even I found the story amusing.

"I can't...picture it, Vincent. It sounds"—she giggled—"so undignified."

I grinned. She was teasing me. All of her focus was on holding her laugh in. Her shoulders shook, and she failed miserably. I adored every minute of it. She'd had no fear that I'd let the story run as it was about her father. I found myself basking in her faith. My hands were still a mess, sticky with dough, but I stooped to kiss her again. This time, my tongue swept into her mouth a little more thoroughly.

Though covered in flour, her arms wrapped around my waist, and she pulled me close. She groaned when she realized I couldn't reciprocate with dough on my fingers.

I bit her lip as we parted. "That's for laughing at the idea of me hiding in the closet."

She pulled her arms back, smiling, and wiped them together, flour coming off them in waves. "You're lucky you took your jacket off," she said. "Even so, there are remnants of flour on your shirt."

I glanced down and saw the white flour handprints on the crème-colored fabric. I tilted my head back, staring at the ceiling as if asking for patience I didn't need. She giggled again at my dramatics. My lips were on hers in a moment, greedy to capture the sound.

"That should be done," she said, pointing to the dough. "It will need to rise. You can wash your hands there while you tell me what happened next."

I moved to the sink and did as she instructed, thinking I could get used to our shared responsibility in the kitchen. I wasn't a baker like her, but I knew she liked to knead the dough as a form of stress release. Now that I'd tried it, I understood the appeal.

"I searched for you at the paper. It was probably while you were at your parents' house." Her hand grabbed my wet one as I reached for a towel. Before handing me the dry cloth, she squeezed my hand like she knew what that part of the adventure would have cost me.

"Well, once I had the evidence, I returned to the paper to change the column. It turned out that once I had proof, Patricia saw reason and ignored her orders." He shook his head. "She'd been told she had to print a story about the bribes to stop the school building. Not specifically who she had to name as the culprit."

"So, you did it? You got the story you wanted into the issue?" she asked.

"I did." Today's paper was once again clutched in my hand. My fingers felt clammy where I gripped it, not so much because of the article about my parents but because of the other change. "I know we didn't discuss this, but I made another change...to your recommendation." I glanced over my shoulder as more noise poured from the library. "Not that you need it, but I am sorry I didn't let you read this before it printed." I cleared my throat. "I didn't think our original plan...fit anymore."

I handed her the paper. "This one is much more you."

She took the paper from my hands and started reading.

36

Luna

I couldn't read the article fast enough. Every word written tugged at a piece of my heart. It was like he'd taken the words from my impromptu speech at the tavern yesterday and poured them onto the page. My heart swelled, and happy tears filled my vision, making it even harder to read. I'd barely finished when I threw myself at him again. This time, his wind anticipated my actions. My arms looped around his neck as I leaped from the floor into his hold.

He bore my weight effortlessly as my legs wrapped around his waist. His wind encircled us as I fused my lips to his. I wanted no space between us.

"It's perfect," I said between kisses. "I couldn't have said it better myself."

I struggled to catch my breath as my lips moved to his neck, and I ran my hands freely through his hair. His smile against my lips as I did so brought me warmth in a way that had nothing to do with my body pressed against his—though it did nothing to stop my thoughts from roaming to the closest place we could be alone.

He lifted his head and searched the room as if understanding my thoughts. The kitchen was not a great option. It had two doors and no locks.

"Do you have something in the oven?" he asked, his voice a little desperate with indecision.

"Yes, and it's almost done." I slipped from his arms, but not before pressing another lingering kiss to his lips. "As soon as it's done, you're mine," I said as I turned to check on the baking muffins.

His gaze tracked me as I crossed the room to the oven. Glancing over my shoulder, I couldn't help but sigh at the picture he made, arms folded across his chest as he leaned against the door frame. He looked thoughtful, even as his pose had me fanning myself.

"I'm sorry, I made this entirely about me when I walked in. I thought I'd need to do more groveling, having not returned when I said I would." His voice was a little gravelly as he spoke, attempting to suppress the emotion in the statement. Part of him must have expected me to assume the worst. "Please tell me about your day. How did you fill the inn?"

"It's not quite full," I said as I opened the oven. "But we do have guests. Lots of them. And they're all staying until Long Night."

He held my gaze, waiting for my explanation.

"I asked for help." I shrugged, not sure what else to say. "You inspired me."

This was how I would explain how much I admired what he'd done. Not just because it had saved Darius from unwarranted embarrassment but because it had been the right thing for him—for Vincent.

"When I couldn't find you and realized you had to be confronting your parents, I knew you were being true to yourself, standing up for the beliefs that drove you from Andiveron House in the first place. I went to Parkview Tavern to do the same. Mom's actions made me realize how much I wanted to embrace both parts of myself." I swallowed. "Once I knew the blood magic was gone, nothing was holding me back. The tavern was full, not only of friends and customers but of their guests and out-of-towners. I told them all about the inn and the kind of place I wanted it to be, very much like the article you wrote." I gestured to the paper. "And a lot of them came. Others came independently; the magic must have been working hard to drive people away."

He reached for me, unable to stay away after I closed the oven again and grabbed a towel to retrieve the muffins. "I'm so proud of you, Luna. This is amazing. You did it."

"We did it."

His lip tilted into a half smile. "I'm sure I didn't do anything."

I opened the oven a final time, pulling out the muffins and setting them on the rack to cool.

"You helped me realize I had magic," I started. "You stood by me while I figured out what to do about my father."

"Forced you to speak with the father you thought had abandoned you to get the promotion you requested for your inn," he said, giving me a winning smile. "Not my finest hour."

I pulled him to me, loving him for that. For how we'd met, the bargain we'd struck, and how our relationship had evolved. Turning to face him fully, I let the thought send butterflies through my stomach, and further words lodged in my throat.

"Luna?" he said, reading the change in my features.

I reached up to push a strand from his face. His wind wrapped around my hand as I did so, though it left me the actual work of running my fingers through his thick brown hair. When they slid to his neck, I pulled him down for another kiss.

"I love you, Vincent," I said.

He stared at me, mouth gaping like he was a fish. I wanted to laugh, but I was also feeling too much to stomach it. This male. He was everything I needed and hadn't known I was searching for. We might have been opposites—he might like fine things and proper etiquette, I might like to dance to the beat of my own drum—but his resistance to changing me, to trying to force me into the mold of his past successful recommendations, was part of what had made me realize the value of my uniqueness. I wanted to tell him that. I wanted to explain everything in detail, but when I tried to put the words together, they were a jumbled mess in my mind. The only clear words, the only words that expressed the sentiment I felt, were the ones I said.

"I love you, Vincent," I said again.

This time, he shook himself free from his stupor.

"I love you, too, Luna." He leaned into my space, pressing our foreheads together. "I never dreamed I'd find someone as right as you. Someone who challenges me while encouraging me to be the best version of myself, whatever that looks like."

His wind surrounded us, blowing my hair from my face as Vincent stooped to kiss me.

"I love you," he said again, quieter, as his lips found their way to my neck.

He paused his progress and glanced over my shoulder. He must have realized the muffins were out of the oven and I was free to leave the kitchen. At the same moment, his hands slid behind my thighs, and he hoisted me into his arms, wrapping my legs around his waist again. He carried me to the next room, the office. *It* had a lock on the door. My heartbeat raced in anticipation as he kicked the door closed behind us and slid the bolt into place.

Once it clicked, he had my back on the desk, and he leaned over me for another deep, scorching kiss.

"I love you." He tested the words again like he wasn't sure he could say them freely.

I smiled, running my fingers over any part of him I could reach as he shifted me to lift my skirt. I helped, and then a needy whine slipped free as his delicious weight lifted from me. He didn't leave me wanting, though, as he fell to his knees at the corner of the desk. My skirt was free to lift with the last shift. His hands ran over my skin, my calves, my thighs, my hips. Each movement had my body heating and squirming in anticipation of his next. He teased me mercilessly until his mouth finally pressed against my center, a layer of silk still separating him from where I needed him most.

My body trembled in anticipation as he slid the fabric out of the way and circled me with his tongue. Need overcame me, and I fell back against the desk. "Touch me, please," I said, my voice breathy.

He chuckled. "I am touching you." His voice was low and rumbly in a way my Vincent's usually wasn't.

"You know what I mean," I hissed, thrusting my hips toward him.

His laugh was decadent this time, a noise I wanted to hear a thousand more times. "So greedy," he said as his finger plunged inside.

My back bowed, and his mouth was on me all at once. I gasped and writhed as his lips, tongue, and fingers worked in tandem to stoke my pleasure. It was like he'd studied every hitch of my breath, every twitch of my body, each reaction to his every languid stroke our first night together. He was an artist, and I was his greatest work. The satisfied tilt of his lip grew along with my pleasure.

"Pleased with yourself?" I breathed between strokes of his tongue at my center.

"A little," he said when he came up for air. He swirled his tongue around my clit. "I love learning what winds you up." He paused, watching me. The intensity of his gaze had me as light-headed as the work of his fingers and tongue. His smirk grew, and before I could question it, he pounced, sucking hard precisely where I wanted him. I exploded. A moan escaped, and my back arched impossibly farther toward him. His fingers plunged into my heat as he coaxed me through my release.

I was a puddle against the desk, and I could only hope no one was around the office. My cheeks heated as I realized I had not been at all quiet.

His lip tilted into another smile as if reading my mind. "It's an inn. It could have been any of the guests."

"In the office?"

He shrugged. "You never know, with the scenery..."

I crooked a finger at him, and he brought his face to mine for another kiss. "Might as well keep going. Let everyone know all are satisfied at Cliff House Inn."

"Such service," he replied huskily as I grabbed his cock, exploring the silk and steel of him. I was thinking a girl could get used to this. Then I couldn't think of anything as our bodies joined, and all I knew was ecstasy.

37

Vincent

Every evening with Luna was bliss. The inn filled a little more each day, and Long Night was tomorrow. I knew it didn't matter anymore, that Darius wouldn't sell the inn if it wasn't at capacity, but I was so proud of her. She was so close. I had no doubt the last trickle of guests coming in for the festivities would fill the two remaining rooms.

I couldn't remember ever feeling…lighter.

"Vincent, are you listening to me?" Skye interrupted my thoughts, although maybe it was my fault for daydreaming during lunch.

"Sorry."

She waved me off. "I'm glad you're all moony over Luna, but I do need you to focus long enough to answer this question about the accounts."

I returned to the paper by day. Patricia had not told me how she'd handled my parents. Still, she must have done something, because she had not been removed from her position even though the paper had printed a story naming the Andiverons as the old fae family trying to keep the city divided.

The Osten Point, the leader of the wind fae, had not been pleased. My parents were packing while I was having lunch with Skye. The Osten Point had given them a mission: to live in a remote area on the continent's eastern edge and report should anyone try to enter the caverns there. No one entered those caves. They were rumored to be filled with deadly traps the Compass Points could barely get through. All of Sandrin saw the appointment for what it was—banishment.

The fae didn't usually resort to imprisonment when social ostracization did the trick. This punishment hit my parents where it hurt: their pride. The city and the whole continent knew what they had done, that they'd been caught, and that they were being sent away to a pointless task because of it.

I ran my finger down the list she had questions about. Skye was taking over the duties of managing the family estate and the Andiveron businesses. "Right. This one is for the farm on the other side of the bay. You should probably go check on it at some point. This one doesn't look familiar, but it's small. You have time to figure that out." I scratched my head. My time away from the house had been longer than I'd realized if I had forgotten payments and business lines.

"That's alright. I'll ask Jeffrey about that one." She swiped her hair over her shoulder. Her brow pinched with the question I knew she'd wanted to ask since we sat down to lunch. "Are you sure you don't want this?"

I sighed. "Skye. I was only afraid you didn't want it. I thought you might be more interested in clothing design now, but I'm more than happy for you to run the house if it's what you want. Don't do it out of some misguided guilt, though."

"I want it. Kristin's shop was fun. I liked the work, but not as much as I'd hoped."

"I still can't believe our parents let you work there." I laughed. "Though I'm glad they did."

"I also don't want you to think I'm throwing away the opportunity you gave me," Skye said. "You never acknowledge it, but I know what it cost you to get me the position with Kristin."

I tapped my finger on the list, seeing that we'd finished. "It all worked out. Truth be told, at the time, I wanted to make sure someone got something out of the situation. I'm glad it was you. And if you still like design, I'm sure you can start a new investment once you get your feet under you with all of this."

She beamed at that.

Part of me worried about what else she might unearth in our parents' records. I hoped she wouldn't bear the burden of anything she found alone. I knew she was more than capable of running everything. She was the elder; it always should have been her. Father had insisted on it being me when my power presented, though. While she hadn't had as much training as I had, she picked it up quickly and conquered every challenge she set her mind to. I was sure this would be no different.

We paid for the meal and left the restaurant. "I'll want to have meals regularly with you and Luna, if you'd like."

"We're happy to come to the house now that you're running it." I grabbed her arm, turning her to me. "I never meant to leave you there, so isolated."

"You didn't. I chose to stay. You always seem to forget that part."

I smirked as she headed back to the house while I returned to the paper. I hoped she changed everything about how Andiveron House was run—except Jeffrey.

My mood was like a ray of sunshine even though the sky darkened early. Arnold was writing a feature piece about my parents' punishment for next week's issue. I brought him a sandwich with extra jam when I returned to the paper to celebrate.

"Vincent, will you be at the tavern tonight?" Daisy asked me as I dropped into my seat next to hers.

"Not tonight. We have to get ready for the Long Night celebration at the inn," I replied.

"Oh, right. We'll be coming out to Cliff House for the star show viewing tomorrow night with the others."

"Tell Earl we bought the supplies to make Sweet Solstice Sips. Seraphina and Evelyn will run a makeshift bar on the beach."

I couldn't quite believe this was my reality. No matter how different from my others, the column celebrating Cliff House had been a resounding success. I'd received countless reader mailings saying they lived locally but wanted to come to the inn to watch the solstice sky and make their wishes. So, Luna had decided to host a Long Night celebration. Folk from the city came out to the cliffs for peace and darkness. The woods on her property made it hard to see the star show, but the beach had the perfect view.

We'd decided to turn it into a proper celebration.

I was trying to sneak out early to help her, and I was about ready to make my escape.

"Vincent, a word." Patricia stood leaning against the door frame of her office, arms folded over her chest.

"That doesn't look good," Daisy said quietly.

I swallowed, tending to agree with her, but reached for a little of Luna's eternal optimism instead. "We'll see." I stood and walked to Patricia's office.

"Take a seat." She gestured to the chair before her desk.

I did, but the whole thing felt too familiar. Wasn't this how the investigation into Darius had begun?

"You did well with the story I gave you."

I tended to disagree. I'd fulfilled the task, but I hadn't pressed forward once we found out it wasn't Darius. Clearing his name had been such a relief, I'd forgotten to ask the bigger question: if not Darius, who was bribing the governor? While I'd gotten there eventually, it had been a close call.

"You may not have had the answer when it would have been more convenient, but under normal circumstances, putting in the work and chasing down the lead, even to determine it was false, would have been enough. It wasn't your fault that powers beyond your control were working against you."

Powers beyond my control...I didn't care for her phrasing, especially when she was the one who had made the call, but this was a job for her as much as it was for me. I had no idea what kind of leverage my parents had had on her and how they had applied it. They were resourceful when they wanted to be. Too bad it was in the service of terrible initiatives.

"Thank you," I said. "I'm glad we found a solution that worked for everyone." I was not new to the world of power. I'd been raised to respect it and to wield it. It was disappointing to know that the paper wasn't beyond the influence of power in the city. The paper was supposed to be a tool that kept power in check. It was supposed to report truths, even when they weren't flattering. Though everything had worked out in the end, the paper had disappointed me regarding our position on the feature story. Only the outpouring of support for the change in "Benefits of Magic" kept me satisfied with my employment.

"I know you were interested in doing more here," she started. "To write feature stories, to have more of a platform to influence change in the city." She gave me a knowing look. "Is that still your goal?"

I folded my hands in my lap before responding. To have a platform to influence change in the city was still a desire I held close. Yet, now that I'd realized the ability to build community through "The Benefits of Magic," I wasn't sure things needed to change so drastically for me to do it. I hadn't responded when Patricia kept speaking.

"I didn't think it would be a quick response. So, while you're pondering, let me run an idea by you. You showed adeptness in accounting when you brought the data to clear Darius's name and the evidence to condemn your parents. I knew you were from an old fae family; I didn't realize that meant you were trained to run an estate." She tapped her finger on her chin as if she didn't quite comprehend this detail. "I understand you plan to stay on. You don't intend to run your family home in their absence."

"That's correct."

"Interesting." She didn't actually sound that interested. "As it happens, the new governor was...not pleased with your parents' ability to influence the paper on top of everything else."

That had been another quick change. My evidence had made it clear that Marion had accepted bribes from both sides of the school issue. She hadn't decided what to do with them, but the citizens weren't happy she'd accepted them. An emergency election had been held, and she'd been replaced.

"So, the new governor put a vote before the city council that provides funding for the paper from the people, since she believes it's them we should truly be working for. The vote passed, and now she needs someone to manage the reports between our office and the city council meetings. She asked if you would be interested."

My mouth hung open in a way my parents would have hated. The thought made me happy, so I let it hang open for a few moments longer than necessary. "The people are going to fund the paper?" I asked, not sure I'd heard her correctly.

She nodded. "No more private donors. It leaves too much room for...undue influence." She tapped her nails on the desk. "We're supposed to be the voice for the people, the ones investigating the Compass Points and the city leaders. We're supposed to keep power in check with the truth."

"And do you agree with this appointment?" I asked. I

couldn't quite tell where Patricia fell on this. Was this her once again caving to someone in power?

"I suggested your name to the new governor," she said matter-of-factly. "As long as you can keep writing 'The Benefits of Magic.' We've received excellent feedback on the new direction of the column."

I finally let a full smile break across my once-stoic face. "This sounds great. When do I start?"

"You'll have your first meeting with the governor after Long Night. You'll agree on format and reporting frequency, and we'll take it from there."

I stood, reaching to shake Patricia's outstretched hand. "Thank you."

"Thank you, Vincent. The article about Darius was not going to be my finest moment." She pursed her lips. "I didn't know what to do, but you didn't stop fighting. You gave me the solution I didn't know I needed, and I can't thank you enough for that." She coughed as if she'd said too much. Clearing her throat, she added, "Now, I think you must be going, right? I hear you have a Long Night celebration on the cliff to prepare for."

I dipped my chin and headed for the door.

38

Luna

Vincent kissed my neck as he zipped the back of my dress. After slipping my feet into shoes that I'd take off as soon as we got to the beach, we walked hand in hand to the inn. It was finally Long Night. There was one room vacant, but looking at the warm glow emanating from the inn's windows, I could happily say I was alright with that. We'd filled almost ten rooms in as many days. I couldn't be prouder. Plus, tonight, we were hosting *the* celebration to be at to make a solstice wish.

This was a great start. We'd have plenty more time to celebrate the inn's success.

In about an hour, when full dark fell, we would lead our guests and friends to the beach. Ambrose was already busy using his Vesten element to start the bonfires. Seraphina had closed the tavern for the night, and she and Evelyn had set up an impromptu bar on the beach, serving Solstice Sips to anyone in need of one.

"You should be proud," Vincent said, kissing the back of my hand still interlaced with his, as we walked up the steps to the inn's porch.

"I am," I replied. "Thank you for believing I could do it—as me."

He laughed. "You know you can do anything. You never needed me to tell you that."

"Sometimes I am over here just faking confidence until I believe it," I said quietly. "It's nice to know someone else bought the act."

He tugged gently on our intertwined fingers, pulling me to face him. "I bought the act the moment you *accidentally* threw your drink at me."

We'd kept testing my magic. I didn't need much moonlight to control my element. Darius was helping me understand its capabilities.

Vincent glanced up, probably thinking about the pull of my magic that had sent his drink flying at his face the night we met. The sky was dark. The solstice fell on a new moon this year; the moon was barely visible, but the power thrumming through my veins was now recognizable enough for me to realize it was there.

"So, it's my magic you're after," I said playfully.

"You are magic to me. It has nothing to do with your element." His wind swept in and wrapped around us even as he said it.

"*Your* element might have something to say about that."

He glanced over his shoulder like his magic was a physical thing perched there. "We're still in a heated debate about which of us brings you more pleasure." He winked.

"I'll never tell," I replied, dragging him to the front door.

The inn was packed. So many people from town had shown up to celebrate.

"Hi Daisy, hi Earl." I waved.

"Luna, this is Patricia and her partner, Sara," Vincent introduced me to his boss, who was standing to the left of the door. I noted that Vincent and Patricia seemed to be on better footing with the new funding structure announced for the paper.

"Wonderful to meet you both," I said, closing the door behind us.

Before it clicked shut, a large black bird flew in and landed atop the front desk. I stared at it as it tilted its head, examining the silver call bell. There was a sign that said *Ring me if no one is present* next to it. It allowed me to slip into the kitchen without guests waiting too long. My mouth hung open when the bird's long black beak closed around the handle and lifted. It was ringing the bell.

"Excuse me," I said as I left Vincent with Patricia and Sara and walked over to the desk. Vincent's gaze followed as I slipped behind it, but he stayed put. I felt more than a little ridiculous as I cleared my throat and looked at the bird. "Can I help you?"

The sentence wasn't out of my mouth before the bird transformed. My eyes widened as a man, fully clothed, appeared before me. He must be Vesten to shift from animal to fae like that. I'd never had someone do so right before me like this. He was tall, well over six feet, and had long blond hair messily tied back. His green eyes were bright with mischief at my surprise.

"I thought all were welcome here," he drawled. "Don't tell me it doesn't apply to Vesten...or gods."

My mouth remained open, trying to work through the order of his words and make them make sense. "Gods?"

Each of the fae courts was connected to one of the four gods. They were responsible for creating the fae, their courts, and granting the elemental magic. It was rumored that the gods had been seen on the continent again, some even working with the Compass Points to remove the recent mist plague.

"Of course you're welcome..." Admitting I'd never paid too

much attention to the gods didn't seem like a great idea, but I struggled to find the name for the Vesten god.

Evelyn walked up at that moment. Her mouth hung open farther than mine. "Lord Arctos?" she whispered, sliding into the space beside me.

I knew her big brain would continue to prove useful. I let out a sigh of relief as she glanced between me and the being... or god, Lord Arctos.

"Can we help you?" Evelyn asked, realizing I still hadn't said anything.

"Yes, I'd like one room, please." He peered at her like he was trying to place her. "You're not the proprietor here, are you?"

She shook her head and pointed to me while she went about the registration necessities.

"That would be me," I said, finally collecting myself. "Hi, I'm Luna. Welcome to Cliff House Inn. We're happy to have you. You're just in time for the solstice celebration."

"Very good." His gaze followed Evelyn, still watching her. "You, then, who are you? You look familiar."

At that moment, Ambrose walked up. "Evelyn, are you coming down to set up the bar? I started the fires." He, too, stopped in his tracks. I was pleased to say his reaction was much more like my own. "Lord Arctos," he said in a whisper.

The god nodded. "Miss?" he pressed Evelyn.

She handed him his key, obviously ignoring his question. What was going on? "How long will you be staying?" she asked, continuing with the check-in list.

Lord Arctos tilted his head in thought, the motion so bird-like I wanted to laugh. Instead, I was too focused on his interest in Evelyn. A light seemed to go off in his head, and a smile crept across his face. "Ahh, well, then, I think we met this afternoon. You would be Evelyn Knowles, if memory serves. And I'll stay as long as it takes you to complete my research."

Ambrose's mouth hung open. He shook himself free of his stupefied expression to say, "Excuse me?"

He immediately realized his mistake when Lord Arctos's penetrating green gaze snapped intriguingly to him. "Who are you? Do you have a problem with that?"

"No, my lord, of course not. I meant nothing— Evelyn... could I speak with you?" he asked through gritted teeth.

Whatever mutual respect they'd built for each other while we'd sorted out the blood magic used on the inn might be fracturing before my eyes.

"Welcome to Cliff House Inn," Evelyn said, handing Lord Arctos the key. "You are all set. Please enjoy the night's festivities." She slipped back out from behind the desk as quickly as she'd fallen behind it. As she turned the corner, I couldn't help but watch with my own stupefied expression.

She was doing research for him? We would be talking about that later.

"What she said," I echoed, noting that Ambrose followed her closely, hissing in her ear the entire way to the door.

"Well, then. I'll pretend she was excited to see me and work on my project." Lord Arctos's gaze roamed the room.

"I'm sure she is," I said with a forced smile. "It's a busy night. Will you be joining us on the beach?"

He glanced down the hallway toward the library. "No, I think I'll watch from up here. Seems as good a view as any." He sauntered into the library as the rest of the guests started to exit out the back door. Vincent waited for me there as the inn emptied and the guests traipsed through the woods toward the beach staircase.

"What was that?" he asked, his hand slipping around my shoulder and pulling me close. He pressed a kiss to my temple.

"I think we just had our first...godly guest," I said.

He turned his head, and his brow arched. "Which one? Oh, wait, I know." He snapped his fingers. "Don't tell me. It's Lord

Arctos, right? Ambrose told me he was coming to town for a special research project. Ambrose was hoping to be assigned to it at the Vesten Library."

I covered the laugh that slipped out from behind my hand. "I think Evelyn must have beat him to it."

His eyes widened. "So, they're rivals now? I thought they made a nice team working together to figure out the magic used on the inn."

I chuckled. "I'm sure they'll figure it out."

His hand slipped from my shoulder, and our fingers intertwined again as we descended to the beach. We were almost to the bottom when I realized what Lord Arctos's arrival meant.

I pulled Vincent to a stop at the bottom step, turning to face him. "We filled the inn," I said. "Lord Arctos took the last room."

I was so giddy with the accomplishment I hadn't taken a moment to appreciate all those already gathered on the beach. Darius tapped my shoulder, and I turned my beaming smile on him—and Gram standing beside him. They must have seen us descending the stairs, as Darius was prepared for our arrival, handing Solstice Sips to me and Vincent.

"You do realize I was never going to sell it, right?" he asked.

"I may have put that together, yes," I said, tucking my blond strands behind my ear. "A girl still likes achieving her goals."

He chuckled. Before he could say more, Eloise cut him off. "Don't let him fool you. The inn has been under your name for years. He couldn't have sold it even if he wanted to."

Darius's eyes narrowed. "Mother."

She shrugged. "She'll realize it when she looks at all the family paperwork."

I laughed. "Thank you both for being here. It means so much to me to celebrate with you."

Darius took a moment to respond. Eloise elbowed him in the ribs when she decided she was done waiting. I could tell he was working through his own swell of emotion, but I enjoyed the family dynamics at play. "Well, congratulations." He held up his drink for Vincent and me to cheers. "To many more solstice celebrations on the beach at a full Cliff House Inn."

I smiled, looking around. Seraphina worked the bar she'd set up. Evelyn rushed drinks to guests around the fire, clearly avoiding Ambrose after what had happened upstairs. I was sure that wouldn't be the last we heard of it.

"Let's go say hi to your sister." I dragged Vincent toward the water. "Hi, Skye!"

She stood alone. It hadn't occurred to me until that moment, the enormity of the responsibility she'd picked up with her parents' banishment.

"Hi, you guys." She kissed Vincent's cheek and hugged me warmly. "Thanks for inviting me."

"Didn't you have all manner of invitations as head of Andiveron House?"

She sighed. "Yes. Most of them wanted to gossip about Mother and Father. The others wanted to ensure their work or status wouldn't change with my tenure." She flipped her hair. "So, I'm quite happy to be here. No one seems to want anything from me. It's nice."

"We want you to have a good time," Vincent said. His brow furrowed at her response.

I knew Skye wanted the responsibility, and he'd been happy to give it to her; I hoped it wasn't worse than she expected.

"I'm so happy to see the inn full and so many here to celebrate," she said.

We continued chatting as the sky grew even darker.

There were dozens of guests and dozens more here for the party, everyone waiting for their chance to make their solstice wish. Vincent's arm slipped around my waist as we found spots near one of the fires and waited for the shooting stars. The first one elicited a cheer from the crowd. Then, a rapid-fire display of lights spread across the sky faster than the crowd could track. We stood in awe. Children pointed and shouted, "Look there!" while the rest enjoyed being here, together. As the lights continued to shoot across the sky, the group quieted, everyone whispering their wish for the coming year.

"This is perfect." I rested my head against Vincent's shoulder.

"What did you wish for?"

I smiled. "I have more than I ever needed."

"You deserve nothing less." His warm lips pressed against my cool skin, and I snuggled closer. I watched the Long Night star show with the male I loved, knowing that all I had to do was wish for thousands of nights like this one—where, together, Vincent and I had found our haven while creating a space where everyone could belong.

WANT to read more about this world? Check out Compass Points to learn about the changes in fae court leadership.

ABOUT THE AUTHOR

Jillian Witt reads more romantic fantasy than is strictly necessary and writes books she would love to read. Her stories unleash powerful women into fantasy worlds, usually turn enemies into lovers, and always offer an escape from reality.

When not reading or writing, she's enjoying all four seasons in Michigan with her partner and their dog, Loki.

instagram.com/author.jillianwitt
tiktok.com/@author.jillianwitt

ALSO BY JILLIAN WITT

For a full list of Jillian's books, please go to www.jillianwitt.com/books, or use the QR code below:

ACKNOWLEDGMENTS

First and foremost, I want to thank you for reading. I'm beyond thrilled that Luna and Vincent's story found its way to the top of your TBR.

I'd also like to thank everyone who helped get my book baby to this point: Kristen, Isla, Elle, Katie, Hillary, and Nicola.

To my mom, thanks for being my number one fan. Ian and Loki always find their way in this section. They may not know what plot point or magic system I'm rambling about, but they listen, and it's more helpful than they know.

www.ingramcontent.com/pod-product-compliance
Lightning Source LLC
Chambersburg PA
CBHW020912310726
48980CB00011B/844/J

* 9 7 9 8 9 9 2 3 3 6 1 3 9 *